I0762094

The Affected

James McNally

Copyright © 2018 James McNally

Front cover design: Horror scene of a scary woman @LarioTus

Back cover: Cracked face with sinister evil scary eyes @dundanim

ISBN: 978-1-7328277-1-4

All rights reserved. No part of this publication may be reproduced, stored in a retrieval system, or transmitted in any form or by any means, electronic, mechanical, recording or otherwise, without the prior written permission of the author.

Published by Stone Gargoyle Press

The characters and events in this book are fictitious. Any similarity to real persons, living or dead, is coincidental and not intended by the author.

Printed in the United States of America.

First Edition Hardcover

This book is dedicated to my dad, George. He was a hard worker and lived a short, hard life to provide for his family. I can only hope he knew how much he was appreciated. He is sorely missed by all who knew and loved him.

Table of Contents

Prologue: Jeffrey

Jeffrey Morris stood, lifting his head and squinting at the sun-streaked, blue sky. It was hot for early June, and sweat trickled down his temples. He wiped a work-gloved hand across his forehead, leaving a smear of black muck in its wake. He looked down at his feet, at the one-foot-wide row of black dirt. To his left and to his right were equally spaced columns of small, green sprouts. He had only been working at the onion farm for two weeks, and though it was hard, exhausting work; it was also the only work he could find. Besides, it was under the table, so he was able to take home the full $180 a week. And today was Friday. Payday.

He crouched back down and continued tugging at the weeds growing in among the sprouts. The weeds were placed in a barrel a few feet away. For the more stubborn weeds, there was a trowel for cutting into the roots. Jeffrey had shown a proficiency with the tool, causing little damage to the crop as he plucked the unwelcome plants from the ground. Mr. Dixon, Jeffrey's octogenarian mentor, had been impressed with his work.

What bothered Jeffrey about the job was the dirt. He brought way too much of it home on his clothes, on his body. His wife made him strip down to his underpants inside the little laundry room attached to the side door of their single-wide trailer. She dropped the mucked-up clothes into the washer on the spot, leaving Jeffrey to take the walk of shame all the way to the shower, in his skivvies, and in front of their cat, Bucky.

"That black dirt is going to gum up the works of our already overworked washer," his wife would announce, which only added to his growing disappointment. He was a failure at getting a decent job, with a respectable paycheck. And now there was this job, which was not ideal, causing his wife to carp and grumble over the less than savory working conditions.

It's work, though. It pays the rent and puts food on the table. There was that much to be proud of, he supposed.

He stepped farther down the row, and Mr. Dixon followed with the barrel. Although an old man, he hefted that heavy barrel without so much as a grunt.

"Nice day."

Jeffrey looked up when the old man spoke. His mentor wore a baseball cap, a dingy, white T-shirt, and khaki pants. Brown work boots were stained permanently black from years of walking in the muck.

"Yes." He returned to the task at hand, unsure why the old man was trying to engage him in conversation. *I'd rather just keep working if it's all the same.*

"Hot."

Jeffrey mumbled a reply without looking up.

"Only gonna get hotter. Can you handle this muck in the middle of July and August? When the humidity's at a hundred percent, and you swear the dirt under your shoes makes you think you're being cooked from your feet, on up to your head? Can you handle that?"

"I guess I'll see, won't I?"

When his knees started to hurt from crouching, Jeffrey stood and shook out, first one leg, and then the other. He glanced down the length of the row in which he stood, to the line of trees that marked the edge of the plantation, where the field met the wooded area beyond. The pattern of alternating rows of green sprouts, and black muck, caused his head to swim for a second, and he swayed on his legs.

"You alright there, young fella?" Dixon asked.

"Yeah. I'm good. Guess the heat, mixed with how fast I stood up, caused a bit of vertigo. I'm okay, though."

"Sure? Some people aren't cut out for this work."

Jeffrey glared at the old man. "I can handle it just fine."

Mr. Dixon shrugged, and leaned on the metal rim of the fiber barrel. Jeffrey watched the heat vapors rise up from the contents of the barrel, distorting Mr. Dixon's face. This reminded Jeffrey of the waves rising up off a hot road, causing what he had always thought of as wet spots. The spots would miraculously disappear as he grew closer to them.

Yeah, it was going to be a damn hot summer. Jeffrey couldn't fathom how Dixon could bear the smell wafting from the drum, a stench of rotting plants and shit.

Can't say bending over and yanking out these ragweed and dandelion scraps is any better than what he's doing, though.

"What d'ya think this is? Break time? We're not paying ya to stand around gawking. Get back to work."

He stared at Mr. Dixon. *Is he seriously reprimanding me? The old bastard's single job is to lug that damn barrel behind me.* Jeffrey frowned, and his brow furrowed.

The old man laughed, slapping his leg. "Just messing with you, son."

Jeffrey sighed, shaking his head. He glanced around at the multitude of other crop workers scattered across the hundred acres or so. They were all doing what he was doing. Some stood and stretched their legs, and some squatted down, pulling weeds. Other men, too old to get down on their knees, held their own barrel of odorous weeds.

A hundred yards behind Mr. Dixon, Jeffrey watched the foremen drinking coffee at the flatbeds that brought the migrants from the farm. Some stood, spitting tobacco into the dirt. Their hands were clean.

Jeffrey turned and looked east, toward the trees in the distance, where he had spotted movement from the corner of his eye. He thought it was another mirage caused by the sun—not so much different than the illusive water spots on the road—but the man coming out of the trees was no delusion. Jeffrey shielded his eyes with his hand and strained to see. The man was dressed in white. From the distance, Jeffrey thought he looked like Colonel Sanders. He rubbed his eyes and looked again. Still there.

I must be going crazy.

He turned to Mr. Dixon. The old man was looking in the direction of the stranger as well, scowling.

"Tell me I'm not crazy. You see him, too?" Jeffrey turned to study Mr. Dixon's face.

"You ain't crazy." The old man rubbed at the white scruff on his face. "Not unless I am, too. I see him plain as day."

They watched as the stranger approached the first of the farmhands in the distance. The stranger reached out toward the workers, as if playing the game of what's behind your ear. A game grandfathers had played on their grandchildren for years. Jeffrey recalled his own grandfather. The old man put his hand behind young Jeffrey's ear, saying, "What's this?" and would come out with the quarter he ostensibly found there between his fingers. This was what the stranger seemed to be doing to the field workers.

As if this interaction wasn't strange enough, the workers who had been approached by this stranger then turned and did the same thing to the workers next to them. A chain reaction. Jeffrey readied himself to sprint if any of them came near him.

By the time the thought had occurred to him to run, however, it was too late. The man in white approached him. He appeared from out of nowhere to stand next to Jeffrey, who stumbled back, but was stopped by the barrel behind him. The stranger reached out and touched him lightly on the ear.

Jeffrey relaxed. He hadn't hurt him, hadn't said anything to him. Everything was fine.

Then Jeffrey heard it. The sound was a high-pitched buzzing at first, like a mosquito flying in his ear. The buzzing grew louder, and then the answers were there. He knew why the man had touched his ear. He turned to Mr. Dixon.

The old man stared at him, confused and frightened.

No need to be scared, my old friend. Jeffrey touched Dixon on the ear.

The old man flinched away. "What are you doing?"

Jeffrey scowled. He turned to the stranger for answers.

"He cannot hear the siren call."

Jeffrey turned back to look at Mr. Dixon. Disappointment played across the younger man's face, and Mr. Dixon cried out, stumbled back.

The stranger in white continued. "His hearing is too weak to catch the frequency at which the siren call is issued. I'm afraid he cannot join us."

Jeffrey understood completely. He reached down at his feet and picked up the trowel. Mr. Dixon turned to run, but he was too old, too slow to escape. Jeffrey plunged the tip of the trowel into the old man's back, between the shoulder blades.

Mr. Dixon screamed. He turned to face Jeffrey, eyes wild and terrified.

Jeffrey drove the trowel into his throat.

As the dead man dropped to the ground, Jeffrey placed the trowel in the barrel. He picked up the corpse and crammed it into the barrel as well. Jeffrey then turned and followed the stranger in white back toward the woods. Not long after, others came and collected the barrel containing Mr. Dixon's corpse, and carried it into the woods.

All over the field, workers who heard the siren call collected the dead of those who could not, and carried them into the woods.

Chapter One: Demy

Demy Burnette woke that Saturday morning, the first day of summer vacation, as he always had, to dead silence. He opened his eyes and rubbed them. He sat up and looked toward his bedroom door, which was closed. This meant his mother and father were not up yet. If either of them awakened before him, they would have cracked his door. Demy scooted over to the edge of his bed and dropped his bare feet to the warm, carpeted floor. He stretched out one foot and snagged his slipper. Then did the same with the other foot. He dropped down off his bed and made his way to the window. He sat on his toy chest and peered out at the bird feeder near his bedroom window. There was no sound—none that he could hear, anyway—just happy birds eating and fluffing their feathers. Demy giggled as a cardinal plucked up a seed and flew to the nearby fence post, then laid the seed down at the feet of a female perched there. She accepted the offering, and the male flew away again.

Early bird may get the worm, but he will always give it to his true love. The thought made Demy laugh.

He pushed off the seat and walked over to the dresser. He looked down at his pajama bottoms. They were too small. His mom had said with disbelief that he had grown out of three pairs already that year. This made number four.

He pulled a pair of red shorts and a white T-shirt from the drawers, slipped out of the pajamas, and put on the play clothes. When he finished putting on his sneakers, he looked up. His door opened, and there stood his mother.

Smiling, she spoke to him with her hands. *Pancakes for breakfast.*

He nodded vigorously, and rubbed his belly. *Yum.*

He watched her walk away.

Demy entered the bathroom attached to his bedroom and brushed his teeth. He knew brushing them now would make his orange juice taste funny, but he planned to rush out the door after breakfast. He would gladly put up with the odd taste in his mouth.

When he finished in the bathroom, Demy stepped into the hall at the same time as his father. When they bought the house, the parents had opted to give Demy the larger room with the adjoining bathroom, which meant his mom and dad were delegated to the smaller room, and forced to use the hall bathroom. Seeing his father wearing only boxers was a typical sight, but it still made Demy giggle. His dad blew him a kiss and disappeared into the bathroom.

Demy headed to the kitchen. The smell of frying bacon filled the house. He took a seat at the table and sipped at the glass of orange juice in front of him. He winced at the acrid taste of toothpaste and orange juice. He set the glass back down and waited for his breakfast.

After breakfast, Demy wasted no time heading into the front yard to play.

There was not much of a back yard to speak of, only a few square yards of grass, and a pear tree that constantly dropped its rotting fruit. The few times Demy had gone back there, he had stepped on one of the nasty tree bombs, and hated it. The front yard was larger, with no rotting fruit, and it was surrounded by a white picket fence.

The house to the right of Demy belonged to sweet old Mrs. Kennedy. She had a huge, screened-in porch filled with plants and flowers. He often saw her there watering the plants, and—from her moving lips—talking to them as well. She said it helped them grow.

Mrs. Kennedy didn't know sign language, but as long as she had her teeth in, he could read her lips. She hated to be seen without her teeth, so she almost always had them in.

Demy glanced over and saw the woman in her usual place, watering the hanging plants. When she saw him looking at her, she waved. He waved back. She motioned for him to come to her.

Demy smiled and ran back into the house. His dad was dressed, and now sat at the table, eating. Demy asked his mother if he could go over to Mrs. Kennedy's place. She nodded. He turned and rushed toward the door, but stopped. He ran back and gave his father a hug. His dad kissed his cheek and ruffled his hair.

Demy continued out the front door, fixing his messy hair.

He opened the latch on the gate and stepped onto the sidewalk. He strode down the street to Mrs. Kennedy's house and stepped up to the screen door leading to the old woman's porch, waiting for her to open the door and let him in.

She rushed from inside the house carrying a plate. Setting it on a TV stand, she turned to the door and opened it for him. As he entered, he saw the plate of cookies, and a glass of milk, on the little folding table. He pointed to them and then to himself. *For me?*

She laughed. "Of course, they are for you."

Demy took a seat in the chair next to the table. He placed the fingers of his right hand to his mouth. *Thank you.*

He read her lips. "You're welcome, Sweetie."

He then proceeded to cram cookies greedily into his mouth.

She took a seat in the rocker nearby, but didn't rock. He had asked her not to, because it made reading her lips difficult. She obliged, and he appreciated her thoughtfulness.

Demy washed the cookies down with a glass of milk.

When Demy looked at her again, she asked him a question.

How are your mom and dad?

Demy offered another sign he knew she would understand, and repeated the sign for thank you, only this time the hand came down and rested in the palm of his left hand. *Good. They are good.* Had they not been good, he wasn't sure what he would say. But Mrs. Kennedy seemed to always know what to ask to get an answer she could understand.

She smiled and nodded.

He glanced around at the plants hanging from hooks, and sitting on stands all along the screens, soaking in the sunlight, and causing the inner area of the porch to be darker. Demy's heart expanded like a balloon filled with air as Mrs. Kennedy's sparkling eyes flitted from one plant to the next. He studied the lines of her face, feeling immense love for her, then turned his attention back to the cookies.

When the cookies and milk were gone, Mrs. Kennedy moved the tray aside. They sat and peered out at the sun-drenched world beyond the screened-in porch. Demy enjoyed the cool shade inside the porch, but there was also a strange heat coming off the plants. It made him feel as if he was an explorer in a tropical forest.

Mr. Gertz walked by on the sidewalk, and when he spotted Mrs. Kennedy, he waved. Demy saw his lips. "Good morning, Diane. Nice day, isn't it?" He spotted Demy sitting next to her and waved. "Hello, Demetrius." Demy waved back, but scowled. He hated when people called him that.

My name is Demy.

When Demy glanced up at Mrs. Kennedy, she was laughing. "You don't like that name, do you?"

Demy allowed his face to relax.

They sat in solitude awhile longer. Demy studied the plants around him. His favorites were the potted plants with leaves as big as his head.

As the day wore on, Mrs. Kennedy tapped his arm. He glanced up at her. "I picked some new leafy greens from my garden. How would you like a nice green smoothie?"

He nodded.

He followed her into the dry interior of her house. He wasn't a fan of green smoothies, but enjoyed watching her make them.

She removed a tray of ice from the freezer, and a large clump of leafy, green plants from the crisper in the fridge. She pulled the Ninja food processor from the cupboard and plugged it in. When all ingredients had been added to the pitcher-shaped container with the blades in it, Demy placed his hands on the counter near the machine. She placed the top on the processor and started it up. He felt the vibrations through the counter top as the machine pulverized the contents of the container. The vibrations moved up his arms to his chest, and he could even feel it in his teeth. When the appliance had done its job, Mrs. Kennedy turned it off and poured the thick green liquid into two glasses. She handed one to Demy, and they returned to the porch. Demy took his time drinking it.

They sat together for another half hour, waving to neighbors who walked by. Mrs. Kennedy carried on a conversation that she knew he couldn't hear, which didn't seem to matter to her. He caught a couple of words here and there, but most of the conversation went into the nether. He supposed she was used to carrying on one-sided conversations, as her most cherished thoughts were spoken to her plants.

When she caught his eye, she spoke. "I suppose you should run off and play. Lots of playing to be done out there, and an eight-year-old such as yourself shouldn't neglect it for too long."

Demy nodded and stood. She saw him to the door, and they hugged. He liked the soft feel of her warm flesh, like hugging warm bread dough. Hugging his mother was nice, too. That was like hugging a favorite stuffed toy. The giraffe, perhaps.

Demy walked down the porch steps, and down the walkway leading to the sidewalk. He returned to his own yard, unlatched the gate, and stepped through, latching the gate again behind him. He sat down on the swing and allowed it to rock him back and forth, but he didn't pump his feet to make it go high. He closed his eyes and let the sun warm his face.

When he opened his eyes again, his dad had come out of the house and stood halfway down the walkway leading to the gate. Demy gave him his full attention.

His dad spoke with his hands. *I'm heading to town. Want to go for a ride?*

Demy didn't bother to respond. He jumped off the swing and followed his dad out to the car sitting by the curb. Demy climbed into the passenger side of his dad's Chevy, fastened his seatbelt, and waited for his father to do the same. The car rumbled to life as his father turned the key in the ignition, and cool air soon blew from the vents. He hadn't been aware of how uncomfortably hot it was until the air from the vents cooled his sweat-soaked skin. He sat back and enjoyed the ride.

Demy's line of sight consisted of the tops of trees, the rooftops, and the sky. When he pulled himself up to the window, he could see the people on the streets—walking their dogs, or jogging—and people doing yard work. He liked to watch people, so he stayed propped up with his nose pressed against the window for the majority of the ride. He sat back when his father pulled up to the curb.

Once the car was turned off, Demy unhooked his seatbelt, and climbed out of the car. He waited for his dad on the curb.

Demy looked up and read the sign above the door: Deb's Hardware.

As Demy and his dad entered the store, the woman behind the counter waved.

Demy read her lips as she greeted them. *Good morning, Trevor.* She glanced down at Demy. He saw her enjoyment at the sight of him shining in her eyes. *Good morning, Demy.*

He waved to her, offering a shy smile.

As his father and Deb conversed, Demy glanced around. He let his eyes drift over the shelves of tools, and the upright displays with little baggies full of nuts, bolts, nails, and screws dangling from pegboards. The place was not a toy store, but he found its items fascinating all the same.

Demy glanced up, and snagged a portion of their conversation from Deb's lips.

. . . all thirty field workers just disappeared . . .

His dad was shaking his head as Deb continued to speak. He read his father's reply.

It's a bizarre thing, I know. So bizarre.

Demy didn't find their conversation interesting, so he wandered over to the door and glanced out at the people passing on the street. Demy knew many of the people in town. He waved to them as they passed by.

He laughed when Mr. Stockton removed his hat and bowed to him. *Good morning, Master Demy.*

Demy waved a reply.

Mr. Stockton replaced the hat on his head and continued down the street.

Demy turned and looked back at his dad. There was a strange-looking package inside a paper bag on the counter, and his dad was giving Deb money for the package. She provided his dad with the change, and his dad placed the bag in his sweatshirt pocket. They shook hands, and his dad turned to leave.

As he walked by, Demy followed his dad to the car.

After ensuring Demy was buckled in, Dad started the car. Before pulling out onto the street, Dad turned and placed the paper bag in the glove box, locked it. Dad turned to him with a stern expression on his face. *Don't you ever go in there, understand?* Dad used a mixture of hand gestures and his lips to convey this message. Demy nodded.

Dad's expression softened. *Are you thinking I forgot about you?*

Demy shrugged, unsure what he meant.

Dad laughed and pulled away from the curb. They drove down a couple of streets, stopping in front of another store, the Hobby Hotel.

Demy's heart beat faster. His eyes and smile grew wide. This was his favorite store in the whole world. There were train sets in there, books on shelves higher than him, and three flights of beautiful and colorful toys. Demy spent a long time playing with the train set, worked his way through a few picture books, and ended his tour on the third floor, mesmerized by Lego creations.

He left the store with three books, a new Lionel train set, and a Lego kit for a castle.

Demy sat in the car pawing through his bag of goodies, and barely registered when his dad pulled up to the drive-through at Burger King. When he glanced over, his dad handed him a bag of food, and a small drink. He opened the bag to find his usual cuisine: a six-piece order of chicken nuggets, small fries, and onion rings. The car pulled into the adjacent parking lot and stopped. Demy and his dad ate their lunch as a warm breeze blew through their open windows. When the meals were done, Dad tossed the trash away and started up the car once again.

The car turned onto Route 5, and they followed this road for a couple of minutes before stopping again. Demy peeked over the dashboard to see where they were. The sign on the building said Dad's Old-Fashioned Ice Cream.

Demy turned to his father, smiling.

Dad used his hands. *Don't tell Mom.*

Demy shook his head. Certainly, he wouldn't.

After all the ice-cream evidence was gone, Demy and his dad returned home. They entered the house, and Demy ran to his room to start working on building his Lego castle.

He was half finished when he discovered he had missed one of the steps, and he tore the creation apart and started over.

This second attempt left him even more frustrated. *I need Dad's help.*

He stood and exited his room. He started down the hall to the living room, but stopped when he saw his father leaning on the kitchen table, both palms flat against the surface. His mother stood at the sink, arms folded across her chest. They were both heaving, as if they had been running a marathon.

Demy's skin prickled with dread.

They're mad at something I've done. Or Mom found out about the ice cream.

His dad turned and spotted Demy. Dad's posture turned instantly soft, comforting.

What is it, Son?

Demy struggled to come up with a lie. He asked for a drink. *I can't ask him for help with the Legos now.* He struggled to not let the anxiety crippling him show on his face.

His mother poured him a glass of orange juice, and he carried it back to his room.

He set the juice on the bedside table without drinking it. He stared down at the mess of colored plastic bricks, ashamed of himself for having them.

I don't deserve them. He scooped them up and dumped them back into the box. He shoved the box of Legos and the unopened train set under the bed. He sat on his bed with his hands in his lap. His lips quivered, and his breath came in raspy gasps. He got the hiccups. From the corner of his eye, he saw his door open and turned to see his dad standing there.

Demy used his hands in quick, frantic motions. *Mommy's mad at us.*

That was all it took. Tears streamed down Demy's cheeks. He tried to speak. "I horry daa . . ." Sobs overtook him, and he couldn't go on.

His dad scooped him up, and pulled him into an embrace. Dad pulled back, and Demy wiped his eyes. He read his dad's lips.

Why are you sorry?

Demy sniffled as his father placed him back on the bed. His nose was running, so he used the back of his hand to clear it. He swallowed hard and used his hands.

I made you and Mommy fight.

Dad wiped away his tears. He took Demy's head in his hands. He spoke to Demy directly. "You did no such thing. What's happening between your mother and me has nothing to do with you."

When his dad released his face, Demy turned toward the bedroom door. His mother was there, crying. She came forward. *We tried to keep this from you. It was a mistake. We never should have tried to do this behind your back like this.* Mom used her hands with her words. It was easier for him to understand complex sentences this way.

Why are you fighting? Demy's hands flapped wildly, and a scowl furrowed his brow.

His mom and dad shared a look.

Demy turned to his dad.

Dad looked down, and Demy knew his dad was ashamed of something. When his dad looked back up, he spoke.

"I did a bad thing. I made your mother very mad at me. As a result, I'm going to have to move out. I have to—"

"Doh, ooo cand." *No, you can't.*

"Yes, I have to. But it's okay. We'll still spend time together, okay? I'll still be here for you, Buddy. I love you."

Mom ran a hand through Demy's hair, maybe trying to smooth out his unruly, curly blond locks. When he looked at her, she spoke. "Trust us. This has absolutely nothing to do with you."

Demy hugged her. He wanted to know more, understand why his dad said he was leaving, but didn't know how to ask.

Wash your hands and get ready for dinner. Mom stood and walked out of the room.

Demy and his dad watched her go. When she was gone, and down the hall, Dad used his hands to say, *better do as she says. She means business.*

Demy smirked, blinking away the last of his tears.

Dad kissed his cheek and stood. He lingered for a few seconds and walked out of the room.

Demy headed to the bathroom to wash up.

-:-:-:-:-

After dinner, Demy returned to his room. He pulled the train set from under his bed, and began to set up the track. His father came into the room. As Demy lay across the floor on his stomach, his dad sat next to him, legs crossed. They set up the little houses and street signs. They connected the train's engine to the boxcar pieces, and that to the caboose, then placed them on the track. After a few minutes of watching the train move around the track on its own, Demy stopped it and turned it off.

He looked out the window. The sun was still out. He turned to his dad. *Can I go outside and play?*

Dad looked toward the window. He looked at his watch. *Sure, for a little while.*

Demy scrambled off the floor and headed out of his room. He raced down the hall and out the front door. He jumped onto the swing, pumping as hard as he could. He didn't stop until he was swinging so high he could feel his butt rising off the seat in the upward momentum, just as he started to come back down. He kicked his feet with an aggression that caused the poles to rise off the ground. He wanted to jump off the swing and land on the other side of the gate. He would run until his legs gave out. He would run away. Maybe if he was gone, his parents would stop fighting. Maybe if he was gone, his father would stay.

Demy slowed his swinging. He glanced toward Mrs. Kennedy's screened-in porch, and the plants hanging there. She was not there. It didn't matter. He needed someone to talk to, and she couldn't understand him. He dragged his feet in the dirt under the swing, kicking up dust.

He could not talk to Mrs. Kennedy, and he couldn't talk to his parents, either.

He was alone.

He stepped off the swing, walked over to the sandbox, and sat on the wooden edge. He reached in and scooped up a handful of sand. As the fine grains passed through his fingers, he looked back toward the house. It seemed oddly dark inside. The light of the sun was hidden behind the house, and no lamps had been turned on yet. Orange rays of the setting sun shot out around the edges of the house, elongating the shadows, making it seem as though the walls were reaching out toward him. A shiver passed through him then, as if an unseen danger hid within his home. He was suddenly afraid for his future. He was afraid for his parents.

Demy stood and walked around the yard. He didn't want to leave his home, and he didn't want his parents to part; but his dad had said it was going to happen. His dad was going to leave. If his dad was leaving, then so was he.

I'm not living here without him. He wiped his eyes again.

A car came up the street. Its headlights were on, and the light bled through the slats in the fence, giving the illusion that the light was dancing. He watched as the car pulled into the driveway of the house across the street. A sign driven into the yard of that house read For Sale. And a smaller sign dangled below, which read Sold.

A man stepped out of the car and glanced around him. When the man spotted Demy peering over the picket fence, he waved. Demy waved back. The man turned away and walked toward the house.

We have a new neighbor.

Demy stepped away from the fence and walked back toward his home. The man was a stranger, and he knew to stay away from strangers.

He entered the house and stood just inside the door. From the foyer, he could see his mother finishing up the dinner dishes. She turned to face him.

"Go wash up for bed. Your bath is waiting for you. Get started, and I'll come in to wash your hair." She turned back to the sink.

Demy trudged toward the back of the house to his room. The light was on in his bathroom as he entered. A warm bath waited for him, bubbles covering the surface. Demy stripped out of his play clothes and stepped into the tub. He sank down.

He found his plastic boat floating in the suds, and moved it through the water. He pushed it under water and released it. The boat popped up and skidded across the soapy surface. He reached out and caught it, pushed it down even deeper. The boat popped back up again, going even higher in the air, before it came back down and skidded across the water again. He moved it over the water, making lines in the bubbles.

His mother came in, and the boat was lost as she dumped shampoo on his head. She scrubbed hard at his scalp, then dumped water from the tap over his head. He used a washcloth to wipe the water and soap out of his eyes. She took the cloth from him and lathered it up with the bar of Ivory soap on the tub's ledge. She scrubbed his armpits and then his feet. She handed him the cloth and commanded he wash behind his ears.

When the bath was over, the water draining, Demy dried off and dressed in the clean pair of pajamas his mother left out for him on the bed.

It was still early, so he returned his attention to the train set.

As the electric train circled the track, his dad stepped into the room. Demy looked up.

Ready to call it a night, sport?

Demy nodded. He stopped the train and turned it off. He climbed into bed, and his dad covered him with the sheet.

Do you want me to read you a story?

Demy shook his head. *No.* He yawned. He used his hands to talk. *A man moved into the house across the street.*

His dad nodded. *Yes. His name is Mr. Edwards.* Dad spelled out the name to ensure Demy understood. *Your mom and I met him last week. He's excited to meet you.*

Demy sat up, curious.

Dad's eyes danced, amused. *He knows sign language. His sister was deaf.*

Demy used his hands. *Was? Is she not deaf anymore?*

Dad's face lost some of its jubilation. His eyes lowered. It was what his dad did when he had bad news. It was the look he used when he told Demy he was moving out. *She passed away.*

Demy mulled this over. It was sad news, but he was excited to meet his new neighbor, Mr. Edwards. Someone he could talk to besides his parents, maybe. He hoped Mr. Edwards and he would be friends. He yawned again.

Good night, Dad.

Good night, Son. I love you.

Demy closed his eyes, and was asleep in minutes.

Chapter Two: Trevor

Trevor Burnette stepped out of his son's room, closing the door softly behind him. Demy was deaf—had been since birth—but the boy was hypersensitive to vibrations and would react to a hard slam. He waited for any sound of alarm from inside the room, and when he heard nothing, he walked to the living room. He turned the television on, sound down low. He hadn't seen Krista since tucking Demy in, and if she had retired early, he didn't want to disturb her.

Trevor had been sleeping in the guest bedroom, taking care not to let Demy see him going in, or coming out of, that room. He had taken up sleeping in the guest room at Krista's request.

The word *request* was too mild. She commanded it. It was his fault.

He had been working late with a coworker, Luanne. They were tired, and the office had been empty. He hadn't been happy in his marriage for a long time, and the chemistry between him and Luanne had been strong. Trevor convinced himself Krista had been cheating on him.

Luanne placed a hand on Trevor's knee, and that was all it took.

He crawled to his car in his underwear, clothes balled up under his arm, and sat behind the wheel, crying.

Wracked with guilt, Trevor told Krista of the affair right away. She was adamant that he was to leave the house. After a few hours, though, she calmed down and agreed he could stay in the guest room until he had someplace to go.

He found an apartment in town, and would be moving out in the next few days. He hadn't wanted Demy to find out the way he did, but he supposed it was all over now. Demy knew, and the truth was out. Nothing more to do but get the hell out of Dodge.

Trevor laughed. It wasn't a happy sound. He shook his head, disgusted at the way his life was headed. He had it all, and he blew it.

He watched the black-and-white Western on the TV, without really seeing it. He was replaying the argument in his head from earlier that day, the one Demy had walked in on. Krista had been angry that he had spent so much money on Demy.

"You treat him like he's special," she had said.

"He *is* special." Trevor had been livid at her choice of words. "He's special to me."

She had recoiled. "You know what I mean."

"I'm not going to let you make me feel guilty about spoiling my son. I had some very bad news to tell him, and I thought maybe the toys would help soften the blow."

But the truth was, he hadn't even told Demy what he meant to tell him over lunch. He just couldn't. Demy had looked so happy; Trevor couldn't take that happiness away from his son.

So, he took Demy for ice cream instead, deciding there would be another chance, another time to bring his son's world down around him.

"Demy's strong. He can handle whatever we throw at him."

She was right. The boy had an uncanny ability to bounce back from any unfortunate event. Demy had proven this time and again.

Trevor stood and worked his way to the kitchen. He hoped there was still a beer left in the fridge. When he opened the door, and saw a fresh six-pack of Sam Adams Rebel IPA in there, he gaped.

She bought him a six-pack of his favorite beer when she went shopping. He was the only one in the house who drank the stuff, so it had to be for him. He pondered the implications.

He pulled a beer out of the carton and popped the top with an opener, taking a swig.

As he leaned against the counter, lowering his beer, he watched as Krista entered the kitchen. She was dressed in a skimpy nightie, and he learned that he still felt an attraction for her. That hadn't changed, at least. He studied her shapely legs as she made her way to the sink.

She could at least wear an old grannie nightie so I don't have to see how beautiful she is. He lifted the beer to his lips.

"Don't worry," she said. "I'm just here for a glass of water. I'm not in the mood to fight."

Trevor held the bottle out at her. "Thanks for the beer."

She nodded without looking at him, then took a glass from the cupboard, filled it with water from the tap, and took a drink.

He watched her, liking how the curve of her butt showed through the lacy nightie. Her nipples were visible through the fabric.

She's purposely dressing provocatively to inflame me. He held the bottle to his lips without drinking so he could watch her a little longer without being overt about it.

But she gave him a sideways glance, and he turned away.

"I can see your breasts through your nightclothes. You should have worn a robe."

She turned and leaned against the sink. "It's nothing you haven't seen before." She took another sip of the water.

"I have, but Demy hasn't. What if he woke up and came out?"

"He won't."

Her logic was infuriating. *Is she purposely trying to entice me – to what? . . . to make a move on her? What is her game? If we have sex, will she claim I raped her?*

No, he had to stop vilifying her. She didn't do anything wrong. *It's me. I'm the bad guy here, not her.*

Trevor downed his beer, rinsed the bottle, and tossed it into the recycling bin. He pulled out another, and popped the top. He carried it to the living room, and continued not watching the Western.

He finished the last beer in the six-pack by midnight (*another soldier, fallen to the wayside),* and placed the empty bottle on the coffee table.

He wasn't sure when he passed out, but when he woke, Demy was curled up beside him, the boy's head on his leg. He placed his hand on his son's chest and felt the rise and fall of his heavy breathing.

He held Demy's head gently as he squirmed his way out from under the boy, careful not to wake him. He replaced his leg with a throw pillow. The boy fidgeted but did not wake. Once free, Trevor collected his empties and sent them to recycling heaven.

Trevor's head throbbed like an open wound. He stumbled to the bathroom and threw open the cabinet. He downed four Tylenol, scooping water in his hand from the tap to wash them down. He leaned on the sink until the room stopped spinning.

Today was Sunday. Back to work tomorrow. He also had to find time to move out. His head hurt even more.

He closed the door and urinated, swaying on his feet. After washing his hands, he returned to the living room. Demy was still asleep, and there was no sign of Krista. He glanced at the DVR screen for the time. 6:41 a.m.

Trevor walked out to the front yard to collect the Sunday paper. The paper boy—or whoever delivered the papers—insisted on leaving it outside the gate. Trevor leaned over the gate and scooped it off the sidewalk.

Would it kill him to toss it into the yard? Anyone could steal it out there.

Though this might be true, in the three years they had lived at that address, no one had ever actually stolen it.

As Trevor stood, he glanced across the street and saw that his new neighbor was outside as well. Mr. Edwards—Ethan—waved to him. Trevor used the paper to wave back.

Ethan walked to the end of the driveway to meet Trevor. "Are you an early riser, too?"

Trevor laughed. "Not normally, but I guess I am today."

"Rough night?"

Trevor looked down at his appearance. He must have been a sight, with wrinkled slacks, and a beer-stained T-shirt. And he could only imagine how his hair was laying on his head. He used his free hand to pat down his tousled hair.

Rough several nights. "You could say that."

Trevor looked down as Demy came up on his right and stood next to him, barefoot and wearing Power Ranger PJs. The boy rubbed his sleep-laden eyes.

Ethan waved and used sign language when Demy glanced across the street. *Hi, Demy. Nice to meet you.*

Demy waved.

Trevor placed an arm around the boy's shoulder. Demy leaned closer to his leg.

Ethan spoke to Demy, allowing the boy to read his lips. "I'm looking forward to spending time with you."

Demy simply stared at the man.

Ethan turned to Trevor. "Hey, if you guys aren't doing anything later, I'd love to have you over for brunch."

Trevor looked down. The boy didn't seem to object. He looked back at his neighbor. "Sounds good. What time?"

"Eleven?"

"Okay, we'll see you then."

"Feel free to invite the missus."

I'll invite her, just don't expect her to come.

Trevor guided Demy into the house to get dressed.

When Krista woke, Trevor told her about the invitation.

"Send my regrets, but I'll have to decline," she said. "I'm thrilled that I don't have to cook breakfast, though."

As eleven o'clock neared, Trevor entered his son's room where the boy played with his toys. He tapped Demy on the shoulder, then used his hands to speak. *Are you still interested in going to brunch with Mr. Edwards?*

Demy nodded vigorously.

You should get dressed then, don't you think? It's almost time to go.

The father and son duo headed across the street and knocked on Mr. Edwards' door.

The door opened. "Welcome." Ethan led them through the house to the breakfast nook. The small table near the line of windows overlooking the property's backyard was covered with food. Demy rushed up and chose a jelly-filled doughnut from a plate covered in a variety of pastries. Another plate held bacon and sausage, and still another plate held an assortment of bagels. Demy seemed unable to make up his mind what else to take. Eventually, he chose the bacon.

Trevor took a seat, and Demy sat on his lap.

"Would you like coffee?" Ethan asked.

"Sure."

"How do you take it?"

"A little cream, no sugar."

"Coming right up."

Ethan poured Demy a glass of fresh-squeezed orange juice.

Demy placed his fingers to his mouth. *Thank you.*

Demy shoved the jelly doughnut into his mouth. Trevor helped himself to a plate of bacon and southwestern scrambled eggs, and a bagel smeared with cream cheese. Ethan pulled a bagel apart and ate it, chewing each bite slowly.

"Very nice of you to invite us over," Trevor said. "Thank you."

Demy stole a piece of bacon from his father's plate.

"The food is amazing. You cooked all this?"

Ethan looked down at his spread, clearly proud of his work. "It's a hobby of mine, cooking. In fact, I just bought an old farmhouse, the Garlock place."

"I know the place. On Quarry Road."

Ethan nodded. "My plan is to renovate it and start an old-fashioned, country bed and breakfast."

Trevor sensed a "but" coming on.

"It was a silly pipe dream." Ethan's eyes dropped to his lap.

"What's wrong?"

Ethan took a deep breath and looked up. "Turns out, the house is laced with asbestos, and it will cost a fortune to renovate." He shrugged.

"Oh, that's rough. Shouldn't they have told you about the asbestos problem before you bought it?"

"I asked that same question. I was told some spiel about how they didn't have to disclose anything unless I asked. How was I supposed to know to ask if the place was full of cancer-causing poison? I guess I was thinking they would have told me if there was something wrong with the place. I was naïve."

"Have you thought about getting a lawyer? Try to get out of the deal?"

Ethan shrugged. "Truth is, I really love this house. I still want to find a way to make it work."

Trevor glanced out the window at the backyard. It was huge, a nice yard. He then looked in at the living room. The furniture seemed haphazardly placed, and the 55" flat screen TV sat on the floor. There were boxes still stacked up all over the house. In fact, it appeared the only boxes Ethan had unpacked were the kitchen utensils he used to cook brunch.

"You've got your work cut out for you."

Ethan nodded in agreement. "I've considered clearing the asbestos myself, but—"

Ethan noticed Trevor looking at the clutter. "Oh, the unpacking?" Ethan laughed. "That's the least of my problems."

I hear that. Trevor ran a hand through Demy's blond curls. Demy leaned against his chest. Red strawberry jelly stained the boy's lips. Trevor picked up a napkin and wiped his son's mouth. Demy smiled, took the napkin from his father, and finished the job himself.

Trevor turned back to Ethan. "You have a nice place here."

Ethan glanced around. "Yeah, I got lucky." He focused on Trevor. "And I'm glad to have you as a neighbor."

Trevor looked away. His shoulders sagged, ashamed.

Ethan continued. "I was afraid I'd be in a neighborhood where everyone kept to themselves, you know. One of those places where you could live there ten years, and never know any of your neighbors by name."

Trevor laughed. "You don't have to worry about that here. In this town, everyone knows everyone else. And they don't mind getting into your business, either." Trevor exhaled sharply. *And I'm sure my business is already making the rounds.*

"That's fine with me. I have nothing to hide. But I truly appreciate you and Krista reaching out and offering your friendship."

Trevor smiled. "You got it."

Ethan reached across the table and touched Demy on the nose. When he spoke, he used his hands. *And I'm really looking forward to getting to know you.*

Demy rubbed his nose, giggling. He hopped off his father's lap and went to investigate his surroundings.

The men continued to talk for another half hour or so, until Trevor decided it was time to go. He collected Demy, and Ethan walked them to the door. As they stood in the open doorway, Demy raced across the street as his father watched him. Once the boy was safely behind the gate, Trevor turned to Ethan.

"I've enjoyed our visit. I think it's only fair I warn you that I won't be living across the street for much longer."

Ethan's face went blank as confusion set in. "You're all moving? I just got—"

"No, not all of us. Just me."

"Oh." Ethan's look of shock made his eyes widen. "I'm sorry to hear that."

"I . . . I'm working on getting a place in town. Should be out by the end of the week. I'll be around, though. Hope we can still be friends and—"

"Of course, of course." Ethan took Trevor's hand and shook it. "If you ever need anything, let me know.

I'll do whatever I can to help." Ethan ripped off a scrap of notepaper, and grabbed a pen. He scribbled something on the paper and handed it to Trevor. "This is my number. If you need me, call me. Okay?"

"Thank you." Trevor tucked the paper into his pocket and headed out to the road. He crossed the street and entered his yard through the gate to the front door. He spotted Krista in the kitchen, and decided to go the other way. He entered the living room and turned on the television. He flipped through the channels, but there was nothing on. Seven thousand channels, and nothing but infomercials.

"How would you like to increase your libido, as well as your pecs and gluts. She'll think she's married to a new man! Just 4 easy payments of 29.99 for the Flex-o-mizer..."

Trevor dropped the remote.

Krista came into the room drying her hands on a towel, and sat down next to Trevor. He glanced at her, and she nodded politely. He watched her fold the towel and set it down next to her. She turned back to face him.

"How did your brunch go with Mr. Edwards?"

"Very well. He's an interesting person. Did you know he bought the old Garlock place, and plans to turn it into a country B&B?"

"No, I didn't even know it was for sale. That sounds interesting."

"He's a good cook, too. From the sounds of it, he plans to do all the cooking for the business. He's very ambitious."

"I'm glad you finally found a friend."

Trevor turned to her. "What are you talking about? I have lots of friends. There's Bill, and Terry, and Rob. Just to name a few."

She shook her head. "You misunderstood me. I mean a friend who's not mutual. Bill and Wendy used to play cards with us. You really can't turn to Bill if you need a friend's ear. He'll tell Wendy, and she'll tell me. Terry and Connie . . . same problem. It will be awkward with our mutual friends when we're separated. Mr. Edwards could be someone you can confide in, and spend time with—"

"Wait a minute. Doesn't that work both ways? Won't Wendy and Connie tell their husbands, who will then tell me?" He sat with one leg pulled up onto the couch so he could turn his entire body to face her. His breathing came in shallow, panting rasps. His face heated, and he struggled to control a sudden burst of anger.

"Well, I've been going to them all along. Have any of their husbands come to you?"

"No." His anger deflated.

"That's because their wives have them on a tight leash. They probably aren't even allowed to talk to you. At least, not until this mess works itself out. So, yeah. You need new friends."

She's loving this. She's reveling in it, like some kind of a woman-scorned thing. The realization made him angrier than ever. He couldn't stand to be near her. He stood and headed toward the front door.

"Where are you going?"

"Out." He reached for the knob, hesitated.

"Don't go without telling your son. He'll be upset if he sees you're not here."

Trevor released a long-held breath. "He'll get over it."

He opened the door and stepped into the yard. The door closed behind him. He paced, clenching his fists. When he thought he could drive without steering the car into a tree, he climbed in and started the engine. He pulled away from the curb and drove away. He didn't think about where he was headed, he just drove. When Krista entered his mind, he forced her out again.

I'm not going to make it to the end of the week.

He glanced out the side window. The streets and houses were replaced with fields, and wooded areas. He was in the country. He drove down Lakeport Road, past Dad's Old-Fashioned Ice Cream, turned left onto Chestnut Ridge Road, and drove to the potato farm, then pulled into the driveway. He climbed out of his car and walked up to the wooden vegetable stand. The woman working the stand, Melonie Moroney, smiled as he approached.

"Hi there, Trevor. You look intense. You're serious about your fresh meats and vegetables." She laughed.

Trevor smiled, trying to soften his rough edges. "Got any of that terrific venison jerky? It's good stuff."

"I sure do." She grabbed a small wax paper pouch and opened a wooden barrel with a clear, plastic lid. She used tongs to remove three long, gnarled strips of dried meat and placed them in the wax paper. She handed the package to Trevor. "Three for a dollar."

He paid her and took the jerky. He pulled one strip out and tore a chunk off with his teeth. He chewed the dried meat, relishing the taste as it turned to mush in his mouth.

"How is that sweet boy of yours doing?" She clasped her hands in front of her and rested them on the counter.

"He's great. He's really excited about summer vacation." Trevor chewed.

"That's right . . . school let out, didn't it?"

Trevor nodded. He swallowed his first bite and bit off another piece.

"You hear about the strange goings-on at the Rhapsody's onion farm? Everyone is gone. And not just gone . . . missing. More than thirty of 'em. All with missing person's reports filed. They're talking about bringing in the FBI to investigate."

"I have heard some reports. Everyone in town's talking about it. But I don't understand the big deal. Weren't they all migrant workers? Maybe they just moved on to other work?"

"Before any of them even got paid? Why would they work all week, and then just pick up and go on the morning of payday, before any of 'em even got their week's wages? Besides, it wasn't just the migrant workers. Some of the missing have been working there for years. Even the foremen and stakeholders who were on site are gone."

"It's something to ponder, I guess."

She hooked a thumb behind her, gesturing at the farm. "Potato farming isn't much different than onion farming. I'd hate for something like that to happen here."

Trevor finished off his first strip of jerky. "Okay, well, thank you for the jerky."

"Here, before you go." Melonie opened the lid to her stash of jerky. She once again used the tongs to fish out three more strips of jerky and packaged them up in a wax paper bag. She handed this to Trevor. "For the boy. No charge."

"Thank you so much, Mel. He'll appreciate that."

Melonie's husband Glen ambled out from one of the storage barns, holding a sack of potatoes on his shoulder.

"Good day to ya, Trev," he said as he passed by.

Trevor turned, watching as Glen opened the back door of Trevor's car and dumped the sack of potatoes onto the floor of the backseat. He closed the door and sauntered toward their farmhouse.

Trevor turned and gave Melonie a questioning glance.

She shrugged, giggling. "No charge."

Generous people. He smiled. "Thank you."

He waved goodbye to Melonie and headed to his car. He climbed in and drove out of the yard. He drove back to town, but wasn't ready to go home just yet. Instead, he drove down Russell Street, pulling up to the gray house on the corner. He climbed out of his car and approached the man leaning over a row of plants running along the length of the house. The man stood and turned, smiling.

The smile faded.

"Trevor." It wasn't a friendly greeting. This was someone confused and shocked.

"Hi, Bill. How are you and Wendy doing these days? Haven't seen you in a few weeks."

Trevor wanted to laugh at the way Bill seemed to be searching for an escape route. He stopped and looked at Trevor. He sighed. "Yea, we've been, ah, busy. You know how it is." His wandering right eye irritated Trevor, like the man was trying to look away, even as he glanced directly at him.

Trevor's smile morphed into a frown. His brows furrowed. "Yeah, I know."

"Okay, well, I've got a ton of stuff to get to inside. I'll catch you later, right? We'll have to get together sometime."

"Yeah, that sounds good."

"Okay. See ya." Bill slipped into the darkness of his house and closed the door.

Trevor didn't move off right away. He stayed and watched the door. The curtain covering the small window in the door moved back, and then fell in place again. After another moment, the curtain in the window of the living room did the same thing.

Trevor stepped backward until he touched the hood of his car. He slid around to the driver's side and climbed in. He drove away, unsure of what he might have done if he had stayed any longer.

He shouldn't have been shocked. Everything he knew told him it was exactly how that scenario would play out. Still, there was a small part of him that hoped Bill would show a little backbone, maybe even invite him in for a beer.

I've shared a lot of good times with that guy – we bonded over beers – and none of it means a thing to him?

Trevor drove right on Genesee Street and stopped at the business office of the realty company where he had found his apartment. He climbed out of the car and headed inside. Mrs. Milton was at her desk. He knocked on her open door to draw her attention.

"Trevor, hello." She stood and shook his hand. She offered him a seat at her desk.

Sinking down, he said, "I'm shocked you're working on a Sunday."

"Normally, I wouldn't be. But I came in to finish up some paperwork from last week. I just forgot to lock the door behind me. What can I do for you?"

"I'm sorry. I don't mean to intrude. I can come back tomorrow after work." He placed his hands on the arms of his chair, intending to stand.

"Stay. The truth is, I left the door open on purpose. I don't mind if someone comes in, just like you did. Tell me what you need."

"I was just wondering if there was any way I could move into the house sooner than July first." He relaxed back in the chair.

Mrs. Milton placed a pair of reading glasses on her face, reached into a lowboy filing cabinet for the file on Trevor, and pulled it out. She glanced at Trevor over the top of her glasses. "Let's see what we can do." Her eyes dropped back to the page.

Trevor watched her, rubbing his sweaty hands on his pant leg. He bounced one knee nervously, but stopped when he realized he was doing it. He glanced around the room, looking for something—anything—to ease his nervousness. His eye was drawn to a poster of Garfield the cat hanging on the wall behind the Realtor's head. The orange cat's face epitomized a grumpy mood, as a steaming cup of coffee sat on the table in front of him. The caption read: Feel free to waste my valuable time.

Trevor sniggered at this, and then realized it was exactly what he was doing.

He shouldn't have come.

Mrs. Milton took her reading glasses and placed them on the file. She looked up at Trevor, her eyes downcast. "Mr. Burnette, I'm sorry but the owner of the complex called late Friday afternoon and left a note in your file. The apartment may not be ready in time. He says it may be July fifteenth before an apartment is ready."

Trevor sat up. "What? Why are you only just now telling me this?"

The woman leaned back in her chair and crossed her arms over her chest.

She's getting defensive. Is she afraid of me? Trevor took a deep breath to calm himself. "I'm sorry. As you said, it was late Friday. I don't mean to get so riled up, but you don't understand my situation. I'm separating from my wife. The longer I spend in the same house with her, the more volatile things become. If I'm ever going to get my life back to some sense of normalcy, I need my own place."

Mrs. Milton unfolded her arms, and the sympathy in her eyes returned. She leaned forward and clasped her hands together on the desk. "I do understand your situation, Mr. Burnette. And I'm sorry about this. I don't know why the Realtor who took the message didn't call you when this news came in, but I assure you, I will be in very early in the morning to work on this. If we can't get him to agree to the original terms, I'll find you another apartment."

Trevor felt anger brewing in him again, but he knew this woman had nothing to do with the delay, so he didn't allow it to show on his face, or in his posture. He smiled. "Thank you, Mrs. Milton. I appreciate your help."

Trevor stood, and Mrs. Milton followed him to the door. They shook hands.

"Again, I'm very sorry."

Trevor nodded and stepped out the door. She closed the door behind him, and he was sure he heard the click of the lock. He walked out to the street and climbed into his car. He still didn't want to go home, but there was nowhere else to go.

No, that wasn't true. He climbed back out of his car and used the fob to lock the doors. He walked down the street to the bar known as Delphia's Lounge. He entered the dark interior and sat down at the bar. He smelled a mixture of frying fish and steak. Though there were several patrons sitting at the tables, eating and talking in hushed tones, the interior of the lounge was strangely quiet.

The bartender, a tall, thin man wiping his hands on an apron, approached him. "What can I get you?"

"I'll have whatever IPA you have on tap, please."

The bartender nodded, grabbed an ice-cold glass mug from a freezer under the counter, and deftly filled it from the tap. He placed the beer on the counter. Trevor pulled a ten out of his wallet and handed it to the man. He received six dollars in change. As the man walked away, Trevor lifted the mug and took a long, deep swallow.

Trevor looked around the room. He recognized some faces, acquaintances he'd seen at the supermarket, or in the park, but there was no one here he knew on a personal level. The lounge wasn't someplace he'd visited often; in fact, he'd never actually been here before, but it had been someplace he'd always been curious about. He didn't mind being surrounded by strangers. Krista was right; he no longer had any friends.

His intention had been to drown his sorrows in a beer or two, and then head out; but after his seventh beer, he was still sitting at the same spot as people came and went around him. The bartender, whose name, Trevor learned, was Joe, was the only constant companion.

"Joe." Trevor tapped the bar with his knuckles. He concentrated on the spot where he was tapping. "Joe. Can I ask you something? Can I ask you some...?" He lost his train of thought, found it again. "Ask you something?"

"Of course, Trev. What is it?" Joe rinsed two glasses, first in a bin of soapy water, and then in a bin of clear water. He placed the glasses in a strainer to dry. Trevor watched him intently.

"I need a place . . . a place to live. What do you think . . . of . . . me? Being homeless?"

"I wouldn't like that at all. I hope you find a place to live."

"Thank you, Joe. Thank you. You're a good man. You are."

"How did you get here, Trevor? If you don't mind my asking?"

"I drove." This came out as *I jrove.*

"Do you have someone who could come and get you? You're not homeless yet, are you? Or if you want, I can call you a cab."

"No, it's good. I got this. What do I owe you, Joe?"

Trevor reached into his pocket and pulled out a wad of money. Along with the bills came a white piece of paper. The bartender spotted the name and number written on it. He picked up his phone and dialed the number.

Five minutes later, Ethan walked into the bar.

Trevor looked up at Ethan with watery, bloodshot eyes. "Hey, Buddy. What are you doing here?"

Ethan glanced at the bartender, then back at Trevor. "I was in the neighborhood. Thought I'd stop in. How are you doing? Need anything?"

"Just a place to live."

"How about a ride for now? Come on, I'll take you home."

"Got to pay Joe first."

Ethan reached into his pocket, but the bartender stopped him.

"He's all paid up."

Ethan nodded and wrapped an arm around Trevor's waist. He helped Trevor out to the street. They staggered once or twice, but were able to get to the car without falling down. He drove Trevor back to his house.

"I'm thinking it might be better if you stayed with me tonight. You don't want Demy seeing you like this, do you?"

Trevor didn't reply, but let Ethan lead him to the front door.

"I didn't think so."

Trevor staggered in and dropped heavily onto the sofa. Within minutes, he was snoring.

-:-:-:-:-

Trevor opened his eyes. His first thought filled him with alarm. *I'm not in my house.* He remembered entering a bar, but everything was foggy after that. Now he was laying on an unfamiliar sofa. He sat up, as confused and startled as he would have been if he found himself on an alien planet. He looked around.

"Hi there."

Ethan. He was in Ethan's house.

"How did I get here?"

"I picked you up."

Trevor placed his palm to his forehead, trying to stop the pounding. His temples throbbed. After a moment, he looked again at Ethan. "Thank you so much. Did I call you? I don't remember."

"The bartender called, I believe. He found my number in a wad of bills you tried to use when paying him."

"I'm sorry I put you out. I don't usually do this. I don't know what got into me."

"I wasn't put out. I was happy to help."

Trevor's eyes went wide. His heart beat faster. "What time is it?"

"Nine at night, Sunday."

He hadn't slept through the night. That was good. He thought he had missed work. But still, he needed his car. He glanced at Ethan with baleful eyes. "I'd hate to put you out again, but would you mind taking me back to my car?"

"Not at all. I expected you'd ask. But first, I want you to drink something." Ethan stood and walked into his kitchen. Trevor heard him pouring liquid. Ethan returned with a cup of hot coffee. "I remember how you like it."

Trevor took it without complaint. He wanted it. He sipped at the steaming cup, holding it with both hands.

He stared into the milky black void of the cup as he drank. He thought about his life, his failing marriage, and his shaky future. He closed his eyes and fought back the demons threatening to crush his spirit.

"You sure you're okay to drive?"

"I'm good. About that, anyway." He offered a tired little laugh.

"I think we should wait a little longer. You still look a little 'out there,' if you know what I mean." Ethan sat in the recliner facing him.

Trevor drank from his coffee cup.

An hour later, Trevor finished a second coffee, and placed the cup on the table. He might have dozed off again—he couldn't be sure—but now he was wide awake and felt fine. He stood and turned to Ethan. "I'm good now. Let's do this."

Ethan sighed. "If you're sure—"

Trevor placed a hand on Ethan's shoulder. "I'm sure."

Ethan paused, then nodded.

Trevor climbed into the passenger side of Ethan's BMW. He marveled at the plush, comfortable interior, and the state-of-the-art dashboard. He whistled. "Nice ride."

"Thanks."

Ethan drove to town and pulled up behind Trevor's Ford Taurus. Trevor hopped out and climbed into his own car. They drove back to their homes on Kinderhook Road. They pulled into their respective driveways.

As Trevor climbed out of his car, he saw Ethan waiting near his mailbox. As Trevor walked around his car, heading toward the gate to his yard, Ethan waved him over. Trevor crossed the street.

"If you're not in a big hurry, I have something else I'd like to talk to you about."

"I have time. What's up?"

"Come on inside. I have something I'd like to run by you."

Trevor followed Ethan into the house. Ethan offered Trevor another cup of coffee, but it was declined. Trevor sat down on the couch and waited as Ethan took a seat in the recliner. He sat on the edge of it, leaning toward Trevor, as if in confidence.

Ethan looked down at his hands, then quickly snapped his head up to look at Trevor. He spoke in a hushed tone. "Have you signed any paperwork with the rental agency? For your apartment, I mean."

"No, I haven't signed the rental agreement, if that's what you mean. I filled out a request for a rental, and authorized a credit check."

"But you're not locked into a yearly lease, or anything like that?"

"No." Trevor dragged out the word. "In fact, I just received word that the apartment is being held up. Let's just say that nice piece of news drove me into the bar tonight."

"Well, that might be a good thing, because I think you should move in here. With me."

Trevor sat back. "Here?" He wasn't sure he heard him correctly.

"Yeah, why not?" When Trevor said nothing, Ethan continued. "If you don't mind my asking, what were they going to charge you for the rental?"

"Eight hundred dollars."

"I'll only charge you four hundred. You'll get your own room, and I'll be able to refine my skills as a hotelier. I'll have breakfast ready when you get up, and I'll even cook dinner. Or you can fend for yourself if you prefer. It would totally be up to you. You would be my first B&B houseguest."

Trevor stared at him for a moment, thinking the man was messing with him, or crazy. But Ethan was serious.

Move in here? Trevor glanced around. The place was nice, roomy, and comfortable. It wouldn't be a bad place to live. But could he impose on his new friend in such a way?

Ethan stood. "I'll show you the bedroom where you'd stay."

Trevor stood, slowly. He waited for Ethan to show the way.

They walked down the hall to a door on the left. The doorway leading to the bathroom was directly across the hall from the room.

"You'll have this bathroom all to yourself. I have a master bath."

Trevor peeked in at the bathroom. It was blue, with a lighthouse motif. Ethan then turned and opened the door to the bedroom.

Trevor entered the room. He sat on the queen-sized bed and felt the springs. The pillow-top mattress hugged his body. He glanced at the dresser, and then stood and inspected the closet. It was a partial walk-in. He could enter the closet, but it wasn't deep. There were plastic hangers on a metal rod, but other than that the closet was empty.

The window looked out at the backyard.

"You have a pool here?" He hadn't noticed that before.

"I do. It's clean and ready to go. Use it whenever you wish. Even if you decide not to stay here, you should feel free to use the pool."

Trevor didn't respond. He stared at the shimmering water, stained gold and copper in the dim glow of the fog lights. He did want to teach Demy how to swim. The place was perfect. The thought of moving into that rundown apartment was quickly becoming depressing.

Still, could he just move in? Would it be like taking advantage of his new friendship with Ethan? What if Ethan decided it was a bad idea? Where would that leave their friendship then?

"You don't have to decide right now. Go home. Sleep on it. Let me know what you decide after a few days."

"I have to be honest and tell you the offer is tempting, but I'm afraid that if I moved in, you'd quickly decide it was not such a good idea. I'm concerned about you regretting your offer."

Ethan shook his head. "I have the patience of a saint. You couldn't possibly bother me. Besides, I'm planning to run a B&B. What kind of host would I be if I let the slightest little thing get on my nerves? I'd run myself out of business."

Trevor let out a long, slow breath. "I hope I don't make you sorry for offering."

"Truly, don't worry about me. I'll be happy to have someone else besides myself running around here."

"If you're really sure, I'll seriously think it over."

"Do that. The offer isn't going anywhere."

Ethan walked with Trevor back through the house. Trevor headed for the door and stepped out onto the porch. He sniffed the warm, fragrant night air. There was a slight touch of humidity, and the hair on his forehead stuck to his skin.

Trevor shook Ethan's hand. After crossing the road, he turned and waved. Ethan waved back then stepped into the house and closed the door.

Trevor entered his house, or his soon-to-be ex-house, and checked on his son. The boy was asleep. Apparently, so was Krista.

He thought to check in on her—hating the idea that she might not be there—but was worried she would get the wrong impression of him.

He did it anyway; she knew he had an aversion to being alone.

Chapter Three: Ethan

Though his offer to allow Trevor to stay with him was genuine, his motives were not altogether noble. He truly hoped Trevor would take him up on his offer, but that was for the rent money Trevor's stay would generate. He was broke. He had dropped every last cent he had to his name into buying that money pit. And although he didn't think the rent would get him to his goal, it would be enough to keep food in the house. Without Trevor, Ethan would be eating Ramen noodles like they were going out of style. He was still about a hundred thousand short to fulfill his dream, and barring a miracle, he didn't know where he would come up with that bit of cash. But all that would be moot, anyway, if his meeting tomorrow did not go his way.

Tomorrow he had an appointment with the zoning commission to find out if the place could serve as a business. He felt confident the location was far enough from the main part of town to be acceptable. Once he got the go-ahead, his next step would be to begin the renovations. He wanted to keep the authenticity of the place. The goal was to restore it to its former glory. Anyone could build a new place, start over. He wanted something straight from the past.

He stripped out of his clothes and climbed into bed. Ethan rolled to the left, but wasn't comfortable, so he rolled the other way. He punched his pillow to make it softer. He tried to move lower in the bed. That wasn't working either, so he moved up, so far up, in fact, he was practically sitting up against the headboard. He lay diagonally across the big bed, but still he couldn't sleep. He kicked the sheet off and turned again.

His mind kept rolling back to the asbestos. He couldn't afford to hire a company to handle the asbestos removal. And yet, doing it himself was no better. Without the proper equipment, he was looking at an early death from mesothelioma. In the early eighties, when asbestos was first found to be the cause of the cancer, people were removing it wearing a cloth surgical mask over their nose and mouth. Now, it was a respirator mask, as well as full body suits. No killer dust could be allowed to get through the barriers.

He had priced the equipment he would need to do the project on his own: A Micro-Vac, a moveable dumpster, the stripping equipment and gear—it would cost him a couple thousand. That would mean maxing out credit cards.

Ethan tried to clear his mind. He was afraid to look at the digital clock next to his bed; he didn't want to know just how much time had gotten away from him. He rolled over once again and squeezed his eyes shut, willing himself to sleep.

He eventually did fall asleep, and two hours later his alarm went off. He groaned, slapped the snooze button, and fell back to sleep. When the snooze went off again, he bolted up in bed. His heart pounded in his chest, thinking he had overslept.

A glance at the clock said it was only six-fifteen in the morning. He relaxed.

He yawned and climbed out of bed.

After a shower, and dressing in the suit he had laid out for his meeting, Ethan didn't feel stretched quite as thin as he had when he first awoke. He examined himself in the mirror. There were bags under his eyes, but not so bad that he looked undependable. He performed a few touch-ups, finding a few loose black hairs out of place on his head. He stuck out his tongue. It was pale, but he didn't think it made him look sickly or malnourished.

His stomach was in knots, so eating was out of the question. He thought maybe a slice of toast, so his stomach didn't growl while he was negotiating for his life, but he didn't want to take the chance of messing up his suit.

When he slipped into his shoes and stepped out the door, it was seven-twenty. The meeting was at eight o'clock, and since the place where he was going was only five minutes away, he was doing well on time.

He climbed into his car and started the engine. He turned right from his driveway, drove to the end of Kinderhook Road, and turned right onto Bolivar Road. He drove into town and parked on the street. The office where he would have his meeting was in a white, three-story house that had been converted into office space. Mr. Wallace, his surveyor, had an office on the first floor.

Ethan exited the car and walked up the steps to the front door. He knew he was a half hour early, but he hoped the surveyor would bump his meeting up if possible. When he tried the knob, he found that the door was still locked. He sighed and returned to his car to wait.

He didn't have to wait long. Within a few minutes, a man with a briefcase approached and trundled up the porch steps to the door. The man gingerly put the case down, fumbled in the pocket of his slacks, and pulled out a set of keys. Ethan stepped out of the car and approached. The man did not notice him until Ethan spoke.

"Hello, are you Mr. Wallace?"

The man squealed and dropped the keys. "Oh, for Christ's sake. Who are you and why are you trying to give me a heart attack?"

Ethan stopped in his tracks. He gulped. "I am so sorry, really sorry. I didn't mean to startle you." He repeated his question. "Are you Mr. Wallace?"

The man reached down and picked up his keys and finished opening the door. "Yes, I'm Mr. Wallace. Call me Lou."

"Thank you, Lou. I'm Ethan Edwards. I have a meeting with you at eight o'clock."

Lou looked at his watch. He grunted. "You're early." He held the door open. "Come on in. We can get started."

Ethan rushed up the stairs and through the door, following Lou into his office. He didn't want the man to change his mind.

Lou tossed his briefcase onto a cabinet near his desk. The short, fat man huffed and puffed as he situated himself in his chair. The man had a mustache, though the rest of his face was clean-shaven, and he rubbed his chin as he studied the papers on his desk. With stubby little fingers, he rummaged through a stack of files. "I have your information here somewhere, just give me a second."

"Take your time." Ethan sat on the edge of his seat, looking like a rabbit ready to bolt at the first sign of danger.

"Ah, here it is." He pulled the folder out from the others and held it up. He opened it up and laid it out in front of him. He flipped through a few of the pages and folded his hands together on top of the folder. He looked up at Ethan. "You've purchased the Garlock place, it says here. Is that correct?"

"Yes," Ethan said quickly.

"The estimates provided to us by the company we chose to inspect the house indicated that there were no less than fifty instances of asbestos contamination." Lou lifted his hands as if in sublimation. "I know, I know; this sounds bad, but it's really not. Don't let this upset you. There are several choices you have to take care of the situation. Asbestos isn't like radiation. It can't be detected with a gadget like a Geiger counter. Samples have to be collected and sent to a lab. The real problem with asbestos is the dust. The dust in the lungs causes damage that, over time, causes cancers like mesothelioma. The trick is to remove the asbestos without getting sick. There are several different ways we can do this. One is to hire a company trained in asbestos removal. This could get expensive, but there's another alternative. Remove it yourself."

Ethan knew all this already. He concentrated on keeping his foot from tapping. "I'm aware of this. I need to know the cost, in time and money. I'm afraid this project will become a lifetime commitment, never to be completed. What do I need to know to do this project myself?"

Lou pulled something from the folder that looked like a newspaper clipping. "The front of the house suffered extensive damage when a backhoe tore through it."

"A what? A back . . . hoe?"

"It's a tractor with a shovel on the front and a crane on the back. Anyway, the thing plowed through the front of the house back in the seventies and was rebuilt. That section of the house is free of asbestos." He handed the clipping to Ethan.

The grainy photo in the old news clipping showed a gaping hole in the front of the house. The caption under the photo stated, "Young boy, alone in house, survives when tractor crashed into it." Ethan handed the clipping back to Mr. Wallace.

"Okay, so that part of the house is uncontaminated. I'm more concerned with the part of the house that is contaminated."

"This is a list of everything they found in the house with asbestos. If you're going to do this yourself, I highly recommend you find someone knowledgeable to guide you on how to do it." Lou handed him another paper from the folder.

Ethan took the paper, glanced over it briefly.

"All the required permits for the renovation are in place. All that's left for us to do is to begin the work." Lou's voice was filled with friendly commiseration.

What's this "us"? When will I expect you there to help, Lou?

Ethan remained quiet and stood. Lou stood as well, and they shook hands. Ethan excused himself and exited the building. As he got into his car and drove away, his mind kept turning over Lou's comment to find a knowledgeable guide. The best he could do, the most he could afford, was the pimple-faced teenager at Home Depot.

Ethan drove to the farmhouse and parked on the road. He stared at the dilapidated building, weeds overgrowing the yard, and bushes rising up the side of the structure. His heart sank with the realization that this project was more than he could handle. He closed his eyes, and an exhausted, distraught breath escaped him.

The front of the house, which Ethan now understood had been rebuilt in the seventies, featured a wraparound porch surrounded by fluted pillars.

The older portion of the house was a long, rectangular section that stretched to a gravel driveway, which wound around a garage large enough to store farm equipment, and a shed behind that. Behind these structures was the barn that had fallen into worse disrepair than the house. *I'll have to have all the barnyard buildings demolished. No real need for them in a bed-and-breakfast, and they pose a health hazard.*

There were fields behind the house that had once been where cows ran free, but without the cattle in them to tamp down the plants, the weeds had grown to the size of cornstalks. He still wasn't sure what to do with the fields. Maybe he could rent them out to other farmers in the area. After all, what good was an old-style country B&B without the country? And nothing said country like a field full of grazing cattle chewing their cud.

He glanced over the paper that Lou had given him and scanned the list of problem areas that had been detected. He read off a few of the areas of concern: roof tiles, floor tiles in the kitchen, floor tiles in the bathrooms, of which there were three, insulation in the attic, insulation in the basement, insulation over the piping. He stopped reading. He sat back and placed his hands over his face. After letting out a low moan, he lowered his hands and looked around.

I'll just have to start with the easiest things to do and go from there. And right now, that would be the yard. Ethan climbed out of the car and walked across the yard to the nearby shed. He pulled the shed door open, and it almost broke off its hinges. He peered into the dark, gloomy interior for anything he could use to begin his chore. He spotted a string hanging from the ceiling and pulled it. Of all the glorious luck, a light illuminated the interior. *At least there is power.* The shed was full of ancient-looking gardening equipment. A dusty and cobweb-choked push lawnmower sat against one wall. *Why the hell not?* He fought through the gossamer curtains of cobwebs and pushed the lawnmower into the sunlight. He unscrewed the gas cap and peered into the hole. Just as he suspected—dry as a bone.

Okay, so that was going to have to wait. He looked into the shed again and spotted an electric hedge trimmer. He grabbed it, grabbed the cord, and also grabbed a sturdy-looking extension cord. *Please, oh please, let this work.*

He found an exterior outlet and plugged in the extension cord, then plugged the hedge trimmer into that. He held it out away from him and flicked the switch. The thing buzzed to life. He was so excited, he started trimming hedges on the spot. He wondered what people would think as they drove by and saw this lunatic dressed in a three-piece suit cutting hedges around a house that looked about to fall down. He turned off the hedge trimmer and returned it to the shed, laughing. He hadn't felt this exuberant in a very long time. It was amazing what a feeling of accomplishment could do for one's self-esteem.

He pulled the lawnmower back into the shed, forced the door closed again, and went back to his car. He drove home to change into something a little less formal. His next stop was the lawn and garden store in Canastota where he bought a rake, some gloves, and a plastic gas can. Driving to the gas station, he filled his can partly with gas and then added oil.

Now he felt ready to get down to business. He returned to the farmhouse and parked in front of the garage. He entered the shed, pulled out the lawnmower again, and added the gas/oil mixture. He pressed a little primer button until he saw the gas splashing back into the button, and then engaged the choke. He gripped the ripcord, closed his eyes, and prayed.

He yanked hard on the cord.

Nothing happened. He tried again. And again.

Nothing.

He didn't know what he expected from such a neglected piece of equipment. He primed the pump again, readjusted the choke, and pulled the cord again. The engine sputtered, and black smoke puffed out of the exhaust pipe.

His heart skipped a beat. Could he possibly get the thing running? He tried again, harder. This time the engine caught, and the mower ran for thirty seconds, but then died.

"Come on, you filthy bitch, start."

He pulled the ripcord again, and the mower started. This time it didn't shut off. He pushed the mower to the edge of the yard and lowered the blades. The machine cut a path through the tall grass and spit the trimmings out through the plastic chute.

He had to stop and start several times because of how thick the grass was, but he managed to get the front yard mowed by noon. He shut the mower down and pulled a cold Pepsi from the cooler he had packed, but before he opened it he placed its cold, wet, and refreshing glass against his face and neck. He drank half the bottle in one gulp. Setting the bottle of Pepsi aside, he pulled the sandwich from the cooler, removed the plastic wrap, and chomped down on it. As he chewed the lettuce, tomato, and ham with Swiss on rye bread, he surveyed his work.

Not half bad, if I must say so myself. He finished off the sandwich and relaxed in the shade of a maple tree on the side of the house. He set the alarm on his watch for one thirty and promptly fell asleep.

The alarm chimed, and he woke with a start. He glanced around, not sure where he was. As a breeze rustled his fine dark hair, he spotted the lawnmower still parked in the front yard.

Ah, yes. He knew where he was.

He walked up to the lawnmower and removed the gas cap again, checking the gas level. He still had over half a tank, so he pushed the mower to the side yard, and started it up. It thrummed to life without a hitch.

When he finished the side and back yards, it was nearly four o'clock, but still he had so much more to do. He was finished with the lawnmower, however, so he packed it away in the shed. Next, he picked up the hedge trimmer, and commenced giving the yard a haircut. He moved from hedge to hedge, trimming them down so the tops were beneath the windows. Though he was no expert, he thought he did a pretty damn good job. With the hedges trimmed, he used the rake to remove the unwanted clippings. That was bagged up and placed at the curb. He believed lawn debris was picked up on the second Tuesday of every month. This would mean the trash would be waiting there for at least another two weeks before it was removed.

Though there was still plenty of daylight, he figured he was finished for the day. Now that the yard work was complete, the next step of his new property's evolution would be the actual removal of the asbestos-tainted things outside and inside the house. He figured he would start from the top and move his way down, which meant the roofing shingles would be his next project.

He opened his BMW, retrieved the house key from the center console, and turned to the front porch. The floorboards creaked under his feet, but they felt sturdy enough. He turned the key and opened the door. He stepped into the foyer and glanced around. Stairs leading to the second floor were on his left.

But Ethan didn't use the stairs just now.

To his right was a front room parlor with bay windows on two walls, one overlooking the front yard, and the other to the side. The wraparound porch lay just beyond the windows.

The next room, deeper into the house, was the kitchen. The windows in this room looked out at more of the side yard, and the western wall looked out at the backyard. He tried the faucet, and water ran clear from it.

The house seemed to have all its utilities in working order.

Ethan returned to the foyer and studied a wall, made completely of glass. Two French doors, closed now, led deeper into the house. Large, heavy drapes covered the windows from one end to the other, including the glass French doors, but on the other side. Ethan opened the French doors and peered in.

This room was expansive. There was a fireplace on the farthest wall from the door. *This room will make an impressive reception area. In the winter, that fireplace is going to be a real tourist attraction.*

He entered a door to the left, which led to a smaller living room area. To the west was another kitchen, and beyond that was a back door, a bathroom, and a bedroom. He returned to the small living room and entered the east wing of the house. A small landing beyond led to more stairs leading up, and that long, screened-in porch in the front of the house.

He took these stairs up to the second floor. Along the upper banister, he counted three rooms. Following the hall around, he entered a large room that had windows looking out at the front and back yards. Another door on the north wall led to that larger, reconstructed front portion of the house. This part of the house held another four rooms. That made seven rooms to rent out.

He exited the house through the back door, which led out to the driveway. After making sure the house was locked up tight again, Ethan climbed behind the wheel of his BMW.

He returned home, started up his computer, and jumped in the shower, cleaning off not only the sweat of the yard work, but also any possible asbestos dust he might have come into contact with during his inspection inside the house.

After redressing in a pair of shorts and a T-shirt, he sat down in front of his computer and did a google search for dumpster rentals. He slipped on a headset and dialed directly from his computer.

After a single ring, an automated voice came on the line.

"Thank you for calling Mann Rubbish Removal Incorporated. Please listen carefully to the following choices, as our menu options have changed. If you're calling for—"

Ethan pressed the "0" button repeatedly.

"Our normal business hours are nine a.m. to nine p.m. Monday through Friday, and ten a.m. to eight p.m. on Saturday and Sunday."

Ethan hit the "0" button again.

The phone began to ring. A real person answered this time. "Mann Rubbish Removal."

"Hello, my name is Ethan Edwards, and I'm calling about renting a dumpster for the removal of asbestos. Can you help me?" He gave the woman the address.

"Yes, we can do that for you. When would you need the dumpster?"

"Tomorrow morning?" He said this as a question, and then thought he should have been more forceful. "Tomorrow morning."

Silence hung on the other end of the line for several seconds. Then the woman who was talking to him came back on the line. "I'm sorry, but the soonest we could have it to you is Tuesday morning."

Then why did you ask when I wanted it? Ethan let out an exhausted breath. "That'll be fine." *It would have to do, anyway.* "I'll need it along the north-facing wall. Is that okay?"

"I'm sure it is. I'll make a note in the file. Will you be there when it's delivered?"

"Yes. What time can I expect it?"

"We can have it to you by nine a.m."

"Thank you." Ethan ended the call. *I suppose I'll be doing more lawn work tomorrow.*

He slipped into a pair of sandals and headed out to the local Home Depot. There, he sought out another bit of hardware he would need for his project, and found what he was looking for in the paint supply aisle. There were four different types of respirators to choose from. He chose a full-face respirator mask and the plastic bodysuit that went with it. The ensemble wasn't that dissimilar from the respirator suits used in the show *Breaking Bad*. He bought two full suits, in case he needed a backup. While he was there, he picked up a few more items he thought he might need, and even opened up a credit account. Something told him he was going to need it.

As Ethan pulled onto Kinderhook, his eye landed on the yellow, diamond sign reading DEAF CHILD AREA, and it made him think of Demy. Thinking of Demy led to thoughts of Ellen, his sister. He smiled.

It was eight thirty by the time he returned home, and his stomach was growling. He didn't have the time or energy to cook anything new, so he warmed up the angel hair pasta and garlic butter with roasted chicken, left over from the night before. He decided it was even better the second night. Once finished with his dinner, he put the dirty dishes in the dishwasher but didn't turn it on, not wanting to waste water on the few dishes he had in there.

Ethan kicked off his sandals and relaxed on the sofa. He turned on the television, found a quiet, relaxing show about baby animals being born in the zoo, and fell asleep with a soft flicker of light from the TV splashing across his face.

When he woke up, it was after ten o'clock, so he turned off the television and went to the bedroom. He changed into a pair of pajama bottoms, climbed into bed, and fell asleep as soon as his head hit the pillow.

He was awakened again when his phone chimed on the bedside table. He reached out with groping, numb fingers and pulled the phone closer to him. He struggled with half open eyes to see the display on the phone. He didn't recognize the number, but answered anyway. "Who is this?" He couldn't wait to tell the jerk on the other end how rude he was for calling at such an ungodly hour.

"Hi, Ethan, I was calling to tell you that I will take you up on your offer."

Now his tired mind scrambled to come up with what offer he had made recently. He said again, "Who is this?"

"It's Trevor." The voice was not as excited as it had been originally. "I, uh, I want to move in with you."

Ethan sat up quickly in bed. He rubbed his eyes. "Oh, okay, great. When were you thinking of moving in?"

"How does tomorrow sound?"

"Sounds fine. We'll work out the details tomorrow then."

"I didn't mean to call you so late. I was just excited to tell you my decision. Hope I didn't wake you."

Ethan cleared his throat. "Yeah, no. It's fine. See you tomorrow." He clicked End on the phone and tossed it onto the table. When he laid his head back down on the pillow, he was asleep in seconds.

Chapter Four: Krista

She watched as Trevor packed two suitcases. Now that he was finally doing it, finally moving out, she felt a strange sense of loss. She hadn't wanted him to leave, not really. But she couldn't get over this betrayal until he was gone. "Is that all you're taking? Clothes?"

He fastened the last clasp on the suitcase and looked up at her. "It's all I need. He's furnished everything else. I have a bed, a dresser, and a closet already there. Brand new stuff. I'll be the first to use it, he said."

There was nothing else for her to say, she supposed. They had argued the pros and cons of this move, and—although she felt he should move farther away than across the street—there was nothing stopping him from doing just that.

He had been hurt, she recalled, when she said it wasn't far enough away. She simply meant that with him moving across the street, it would be too easy to call on him. She needed to be alone and not know that he was right there to bail her out if she stumbled. He always took what she said the wrong way. It had been part of their dysfunction. She was partly to blame for this—she could easily reword her thoughts, make them clearer—but she would never admit this to him.

In the end, they both decided the move was a good idea.

Trevor lifted the two cases, and she followed him out to the living room. Demy stood near the doorway, waiting for his dad. When he saw the suitcases, tears flooded his eyes. Krista felt something in her chest break, and realized it was her heart.

Am I causing those tears? Should I tell Trevor to stay, for Demy's sake? Am I being selfish? No, she would stay strong. Demy would get through this. He was a tough kid.

Demy used his hands, and spoke to his dad. "Don't go."

Trevor didn't respond in words. He dropped the suitcases and knelt in front of Demy. They hugged, crying silently. When they pulled apart, Trevor said, "I've got to do this, sport. It won't be that bad, you'll see."

Demy sobbed loudly and rushed past his father. A moment later, Demy's bedroom door slammed shut.

The sound was like a stab to Krista's chest. She was thankful that Trevor didn't turn around. He stepped out the door and was gone.

Once Trevor was across the street, Krista released a miserable sob.

When she gained control of her emotions, she went to Demy's door. She opened it and peered in. Demy was face down on his bed, sobbing into his pillow.

She entered the room and sat down on the edge of his bed. She felt him stiffen at her presence. She touched his back.

Demy rolled over and leveled a look of fury at her so strong, she flinched. He spoke and his hands flapped like angry birds. His arms were wildly swinging branches caught in a windstorm. She let him have his say.

This is your fault. You sent him away. Why do you have to be so mean?

When he was calm enough to read her lips, she responded.

"Your dad has just as much blame in this as me. I'm sorry you can't see it this way, but it's true. Someday, maybe you will be able to see this is the right thing to do."

"Doe." *No.* "I nehber see orr sigh." *I'll never see your side.*

"It's not just my side. It's your dad's side, too. He agreed to leave."

He spoke with his hands again. *You made him leave.*

Krista slumped, defeated. Demy dropped his face back down onto his pillow, though this time he didn't cry. She stood and exited the room, feeling it wise to give him space so he could deal with this in his own way.

The house suddenly seemed as silent as a tomb, and when the phone rang, Krista jumped. She answered it on the third ring.

"Hi, Girlfriend." It was Wendy.

"Hello." Krista huffed as she sat down.

"What was that for?" Wendy's words were steeped in hauteur.

"Nothing. Trevor just left, and—I don't know. I guess I thought I would be happy when he moved out, or at least relieved, but he's only been gone five minutes, and I'm already missing him."

"What?" Her voice was a sharp retort in Krista's ear. "I thought he wasn't moving out until next month."

"He found something sooner, and took it."

"And you're okay with that?"

Krista huffed again. "Yeah, I guess I am."

"Sweetie, get your behind over here and let's talk about this. You shouldn't be alone at a time like this. Besides, I want to hear all about how you finally kicked his cheating ass to the curb. Anyway, Missy's been asking about Demy."

Krista hung up the phone and opened the door to Demy's room. He was sitting on the floor in front of his train set. He wasn't playing with it, just staring at it. *He knows. He sees that his father bought that train set as a consolation gift. He is such a smart kid. My kid.*

This last thought made her smile.

Demy glanced up at her.

"Hey, Kiddo. How would you like to go over and visit Missy?"

Without responding, Demy stood and followed his mother out of the room. She grabbed her purse, and they headed out the door. She noticed Demy looking—dare she say—longingly at Ethan's house. She concentrated on strapping him into the car. He sat in the backseat with his head down, looking at his hands in his lap.

Krista pulled out of the driveway and drove toward town. She pulled up to the curb on Race Street and turned the car off. She glanced over as Wendy waved at her from the doorway. Missy waved at Demy, who had seemed to lose some of that gloom. He unstrapped himself and climbed out of the car. He and Missy disappeared into the house.

Krista climbed out of the car and met Wendy at the door.

"I put on a pot of coffee."

Krista nodded and followed Wendy into the house. They walked to the kitchen. Krista took a seat at the table as Wendy poured the coffee into two mugs, and placed one in front of Krista. She picked it up and sipped.

Wendy took a seat to Krista's left and stared at her, coffee mug untouched. Wendy's smile stretched across her face, slow and measured. "Spill, girl. Tell me what's going on."

Krista rolled her eyes. *I'm in misery over this, and she's ready to throw me a party.* She already knew not to defend Trevor. That would get Wendy started on how she, Krista, was enabling Trevor to be a *lowlife muthafucka,* to use Wendy's colorful vernacular.

"I worry how this move is going to affect Demy. He's really distraught over his father moving out."

Wendy sat back. "Sweetie, he's a kid. Kids are resilient. He'll get over it. You know this is good, right?"

Krista nodded. "I do. It is. But that doesn't mean it isn't hard."

Wendy gave a wistful shake of the head. "You only just sent him packing. You need time to process it. Give it a week, and you won't even think twice about him. You'll wish you'd done it ages ago." She leaned in with a conspiratorial wink. "You might even start dating again."

"I highly doubt that." Krista leaned back, removing herself from the circle of secrecy Wendy had inferred.

Wendy sat up straight. "Don't be so quick to count that option out." She sipped at her cup.

Krista shrugged, but said nothing.

"Where did he go, anyway?"

Happy to change the subject, Krista's expression softened. "He has a new friend named Ethan Edwards. Ethan moved into the house across from us, and Trevor is going to live there."

"Ethan Edwards, you say?" Wendy tapped a finger on her chin, thinking.

"Yes. Why?"

"I've heard of him. He bought the Garlock place, right? Plans to turn it into a country B&B?"

Krista said, "Yes, why?"

Wendy placed her hands flat on the table, as if she was going to use them to stand, but instead she leaned forward. "I've been hearing stuff about him that's been going around town. Not good."

She was afraid to ask. "What kind of stuff?"

Wendy leaned back, and her hands returned to her lap. "Let's just say, if you wanted to get back together with Trevor, you might not want him living there."

"Get to the point, Wendy. What are you going on about?"

"How can I say this gently?" Apparently, there was no way around it. "I've heard that Ethan is . . . what my grandmother would have called a Peter Puffer."

Krista recoiled in disgust. "That's absurd. What proof do you have? I have no interest in gossip."

"Well, I'm just saying, if you want to get back together with Trevor, do it now before he's . . . converted."

Krista wanted to stand and walk out. This was nothing she felt ready to talk about, and especially not with Wendy, the town gossip.

"First of all," Krista said when the anger had drained out of her. "Trevor is definitely not gay. Nor would he be susceptible to being . . . converted." She used Wendy's word back at her with a sarcastic lilt. "Second, who cares if Ethan is gay, straight, or indifferent? He's entitled to be who he is without ridicule. And you're silly if you think Trevor could be *turned* gay."

Wendy only shrugged.

It was time to put Wendy on the spot. "Trevor told me he stopped by and Bill gave him the cold shoulder. Was that your influence?"

Wendy shook her head. "No, not at all. If Bill brushed him off, it's because he didn't want to get in between what's going on with you two."

Krista wasn't convinced. "He has no reason to believe that being friends with Trevor would in any way have an effect on what's going on with Trevor and me. He needs to grow a pair and stop being pushed around by you."

Wendy giggled, clearly not the least offended by what Krista said.

Krista groaned inside. She had come to get away from the strain of her situation, but instead Wendy had increased that weight. She sipped her coffee and tried to banish the thoughts wriggling like worms inside her head.

"Tell me what's new with you." *Quickly, before I get up and walk out.*

"What's to tell? We have a camping trip planned for later in the summer. We're going to stay in a cabin at Green Lakes State Park. But other than that, we have no plans." Wendy looked away for a moment, then turned back to Krista. "Did you hear about Evelyn Sykes?"

More gossip? "No."

Wendy either ignored Krista's bored tone, or she didn't pick up on it.

"She was found wandering the streets," Wendy said. "Naked. They committed her to the hospital for a psych eval." She lowered her voice. "Seventy-two-hour watch." She spoke normally again. "They want to make sure she's not a danger to herself, or others, I'd imagine. She once told me she was taking medication for schizophrenia. Sounds like she stopped taking her meds."

When Krista realized she was being sucked into a gossip fest with Wendy, she drank the last of her coffee. She stood and placed her cup in the sink, glancing out the window.

The kids were in the backyard playing on the swings. Krista didn't think Missy knew sign language, but there never seemed to be a communication barrier between them. She had been thinking she would grab Demy and go, but he was having too much fun. Looking at him, she couldn't tell he had been sobbing into his pillow only a half hour ago.

Krista turned to face Wendy, staying near the sink.

"I don't have to be happy about the current status of my marriage, you know."

Wendy whipped her head around to face Krista. "What?"

"Getting a divorce is the last thing on my mind. I want to work it out with Trevor, if I can. I want to forgive him. If you were my friend, you'd support whatever stance I take on the subject."

"Sweetie, you know I support any decision you make. I'm just trying to make light of a tough situation. But you have to realize that whatever problems caused Trevor to wander still exist. That means the wandering could happen again. Why would you want to subject yourself to that all over again?"

"That's why we're separating. I think the lines of communication will be open again once we're apart."

Wendy huffed. "To me, it just seems like you're giving him what he wants."

"And what's that?"

"Space, freedom."

Krista took her seat again. "We both want that."

"He's a man. He wants it more." Wendy tittered a little with this comment. She sipped from her coffee cup.

Bill entered the house from the front entrance, but when he saw the women sitting at the kitchen table, he changed direction and headed toward the stairs.

"Bill, come in here." Wendy's tone gave no room for dissension.

He entered the living room with his head lowered.

"Afternoon, Kris." He offered a chagrined smile.

"Hi, Bill."

Wendy said, "Krista thinks I told you that Trevor is to be shunned. Tell her it's not true."

"This isn't necessary, Wendy—"

"Yes, it is. Tell her."

Bill turned to Krista. "Look, he showed up out of nowhere and caught me off guard. I didn't know what to say or do. I didn't mean to blow him off like that. I'm really sorry."

"It's fine. He's fine. But if you want to hang out with him, don't let what's going on between him and me stop you. He still needs friends, you know. You should talk to him. Tell him you and he are fine."

"Sure, sure." Bill took the opportunity to slip away.

"You shouldn't be so concerned about his well-being, you know." Wendy caught Krista's eye and held it. "Concern yourself with your own well-being. Hear what I'm saying?"

"I do." Krista felt a twinge up her back, which she identified as guilt. But what did she have to feel guilty about? Trevor brought this on. She was the victim.

And then it came to her. The thought of caring about her own well-being caused her remorse, because she wasn't the true victim in this. Her eye moved toward the window where she had seen Demy and Missy on the swing.

She needed to take care of herself, of course. But it was Demy's well-being that meant the most to her. He was the real victim here, and there was nothing she could do to prevent his pain. He was a victim of his parents' behavior. When she showed concern for Trevor, it was for Demy's sake.

Well, mostly. She also did still have feelings for her husband. She hoped he still had feelings for her, as well.

"No matter what the situation is between us, he's still my husband, and I'll always care about him, if not love him, and his well-being will always be a concern for me."

"You should be more concerned with yourself, is all I'm saying. This is the time you should do what you want. He's had no problem taking care of himself until now." Wendy's mouth turned down as she spoke.

I've hurt her feelings. That was not my intention. Krista reached out and touched Wendy's hand. "I appreciate your concern, and I'm glad I have someone looking out for me, even if I forget to look out for myself."

Krista smiled, and Wendy smiled with her.

"I will always put you first."

"I know, and I love you for that." Krista pulled her hand back.

The back door opened, and the children raced through the kitchen. Wendy stopped Missy.

"You should wash up for dinner. It's almost ready."

"Okay, Momma." Missy raced off, long, snarled hair whipping behind her in a golden wave.

"I have a roast in the oven, if you and Demy want to stay for dinner."

"Thanks, but no. I was going to treat him to a little dinner out, and an ice cream at Dad's."

"Sounds good. Enjoy!"

Krista stayed for another half hour, but headed out before the family sat down to dinner. She took Demy to Subway and bought him a meatball sub. As he downed half the foot-long sub in only a few bites, she wiped sauce off his face.

"Would you have preferred to stay and have dinner with Missy?" Krista said when he was looking at her.

He shook his head violently, then he pointed at the remains of his sub. He used his red-stained fingers to speak. *This is much better.*

Krista handed him a napkin so he could wipe off his hands.

Fingers of his right hand shot to his mouth, *Thank you*. He continued eating, but more carefully this time.

When they finished with their subs, Krista drove him to Dad's for ice cream. She watched his expression change as they pulled into the parking lot from contentment, to confusion, and then to fear.

When she stopped the car, he turned his fearful expression toward her. His hands fluttered. "Why are we here?"

"For ice cream, silly."

"But Dad brings me here."

"And now I do, too."

Then it dawned on her. *He thinks he's never going to see his dad again, and now I feel obligated to do what his dad did.*

"Tell you what. We'll keep this place where you and your dad go, and you and I will come up with our own place. How does that sound?"

Demy's expression of fear softened, and he shrugged. "Okay."

"Should we find somewhere new now?"

He shook his head. He spoke with his hands. "No, just get ice cream here."

She nodded and climbed out of the car. He followed.

Krista found it odd that the window was unmanned. It seemed darker inside the store than normal, as well. The screen was down. She shielded her eyes and struggled to see inside the store. She saw movement.

"Hello, could we get some ice cream?"

Something dark and unseen shuffled quickly past the window.

"Hello? We need help out here. Are you open?"

A face appeared in the window, darkened by the screen. The girl, about sixteen years old, stared out at her.

"Are you open?" Krista asked.

"What do you want?" The voice was dark, low, and raspy. The girl's eyes were bloodshot, and there were dark circles under them. The effect made her look twenty years older.

She looks . . . sick.

The girl lifted the screen and leaned her head out the window. Krista stepped back, thinking she was going to climb out. Without the screen to shade her, the girl looked even worse. Pulsing red veins streaked her skin like angry vines. Her eyes leaked pus at the corners. Krista felt a chill down her back, and her throat closed. Her hand flew to Demy, pushing him behind her.

She was only minimally aware of Demy pulling frantically at her sleeve, surely curious to know what was going on. Krista remained focused on the girl in the window.

"If you want to come inside, I'm sure we can accommodate you." The girl seemed to be talking through a damaged larynx, as if she had been smoking for twenty—no, fifty—years.

Krista's attention was drawn to the left when someone stepped out of the doorway. The man standing there was dressed in a white business suit, not so different than the costume worn by KFC's Colonel Sanders. He had white hair, and a white mustache and goatee. She would have laughed at the sight, if the man's hazy stare didn't frighten her so much.

The man's head was lowered, but his eyes were turned up, giving the effect that he was looking at her through his bushy, white eyebrows. A shiver ran through her when he lifted a hand, so she hoisted Demy into her arms and rushed to her car when he took a step forward.

She didn't wait for Demy to buckle himself in. She rushed around the back of the car instead, and clamored into the driver's seat. She didn't look up to see if the man had continued to approach her. She slammed the gearshift in reverse and backed out, spitting stones in her wake. She put the car into drive and sped toward home.

No ice cream today. Maybe, no ice cream ever.

She realized her hands were shaking, and she white-knuckled the steering wheel to try and get them to stop. She glanced back, half expecting to see the white-clad figure racing down the road, following her at preternatural speed. But there was nothing.

She adjusted the mirror to see if Demy had buckled his seatbelt. She saw that he had, and relaxed. By the time she arrived home, she wasn't even sure why the incident had scared her.

She pulled into the driveway, and parked. She took a few calming breaths, and climbed out. She came around and closed Demy's door when he exited the vehicle. She held his hand as they headed into the house.

She knew he was looking at her with a worried expression, but she tried not to face him. She didn't trust herself to confront what she was feeling yet. She would ease his fears, though.

As she entered the house, her first instinct was to call for Trevor, but the empty, silent house reminded her that Trevor wasn't there. She turned and bolted the lock. Her hand lingered on the latch of the deadbolt, and she moved the curtain on the door aside with her other hand, looking out the small window. Of course, no one had followed her. What was she thinking? She spared a glance at the house across the street.

He's only next door. I should go over there and tell him . . .

Tell him what? She still couldn't articulate what had scared her so badly. How foolish would she look if she ranted about some Colonel Sanders-looking character at the ice cream parlor?

An insistent tugging at her side caused her to look down.

Mommy, why are you scared? He used the quick tapping of his thumb to his chin—his sign for mommy—which he only used when *he* was scared. His wide eyes stared up at her.

She led him to the sofa, and they sat together. She hugged him. As they separated, she spoke. "Mommy's being silly. I didn't mean to frighten you. The ice cream store was closed, that's all. We'll get ice cream another time."

Demy nodded.

"Go to your room and play. I'll come for you when supper is ready."

The boy scampered off. Sitting alone on the sofa, Krista realized she was still shaking.

"I need wine." She spoke to an empty room, but that was nothing new. She stood and headed for the kitchen. She poured the wine, and with her first sip she felt her nerves snapping back to their natural position. She sat back on the sofa and let the wine work its magic.

She tried to forget the events at the ice cream parlor, but her mind's eye kept showing her that girl with the ruined face. She realized she knew that girl. She was the owner's granddaughter. She had seen the girl on several occasions, with a bubbly, infectious smile, and a kind word to everyone. This girl was not anything like the girl she had known.

Something is rotten in Denmark. She didn't know what that saying really meant, or from where it had originated, but it surely fit the situation here.

She sipped her wine.

An hour later, she went to bed.

Chapter Five: Trevor

He unpacked slowly, his mouth dry. His stomach clenched a sense of unease. He tried to postpone having to go out to the living room and face Ethan, but he wasn't sure why. No, he supposed he knew why. He was afraid to make this real. When he spoke to Ethan again, there would be no turning back.

There's no turning back now. It was true. He was no longer in control of his own life. Ethan was his landlord now, and Krista was his ex. He couldn't just pack his things back up and say, *Sorry, but I've changed my mind. I'm heading back to my own home, with my wife and son.*

This was his new home—for as long as Ethan would have him—and there was nothing he could do about that now.

He folded his last shirt and placed it in the drawer. With all the clothes refolded and put away, Trevor supposed he had no other choice but to head out of the room. He walked down the hallway.

As he entered the living room, he heard Ethan in the kitchen, probably preparing to cook something by the sound of it. Trevor looked around, unsure of what to do next.

Ethan came out of the kitchen and retrieved something from a hook near the door. They were a set of keys, Trevor noted, and they were offered to him. He took the keys, but just stared at them.

"That is your set of house keys. You'll need them, because I probably won't be here when you get home from work tomorrow."

"Thank you." Trevor cleared his throat. "Do you suppose we should work out some kind of agreement or something? A rental agreement, I mean."

"I could have my lawyer whip something up. I guess we should discuss how much I should charge. I was thinking four hundred a month. Is that too steep?"

" Are you kidding? It's half what I was going to pay at the apartment I had chosen, and that place wasn't half as nice as this place."

"Okay then. I'm glad to have that out of the way."

"I'm glad you offered." Trevor glanced around the room. "It's a nice place. Nicer than any of the apartments I looked at."

Ethan took a seat in a chair that Trevor could only describe as artistic. He took a seat on the sofa. The pattern on the chair matched the sofa. The plush rug under their feet complemented the furniture in a way that made Trevor think either Ethan had a female decorator or, Ethan himself had an eye for color.

When the silence stretched on between them, Trevor repeated himself. "A really nice place."

"Thank you. I made some nice real estate investments, made a butt-load of money, and used it to buy this place and the Garlock farm. I took interior decorating classes in school, and have a deep love of old, rustic buildings. I drove by that house and fell in love with it. I bought it up without realizing the problems that would come with it."

"What kind of problems?" Trevor wanted to encourage the conversation.

"For starters, it's literally falling down around me. A lot of structural damage, so I need a crew to come in and restore its foundation. But before I can do any kind of renovation, I have to remove all the asbestos they found in its original building materials. I thought that doing the removal myself would be cheaper than hiring professionals, but that's turning out not to be the case. In time alone, it's going to be very costly. Not to mention all the money I'm spending on decontamination equipment. I'm losing my ass to this project."

"Sounds like a real money pit."

Ethan nodded in agreement.

"If there is anything I can do to help, don't hesitate to ask."

"That's kind of you. But for now, your rent will be a big help in getting my project up and running. You saved my life agreeing to live here. I was afraid I would have to sell—try to sell—the farm, and give up on my dream."

Trevor chuckled nervously at the dramatic praise. "We won't let that happen."

There was another lengthy pause between them, and Trevor felt an uncomfortable sense of intrusion on this man's life. What was he thinking coming to stay here? *This isn't good. I should have gone to the apartment.* But Ethan spoke again, and that sense of not belonging was swept away.

"I hope you don't think me too forward, but I'm hoping to ask you about Demy. How long has he been deaf?"

Trevor smiled. He loved talking about Demy. "All his life. He was born without the ability to hear."

"I might have mentioned before, I'm not sure, but I had a sister who was deaf. She, too, was born without the ability to hear. The fine hairs in her ears were developed too short, and as a result she was deaf from birth. She was my twin. We actually both had this defect, but I was unfortunately spared from deafness."

Trevor frowned. "That's an unusual way to phrase that. Why do you say you were unfortunate?"

Ethan leaned forward, chuckling. "It's because I always felt a rift between my sister and me. But it was me that caused that rift, not her. We still had our own altered version of twin-speak, but I felt a sense of shame over being the one who could hear. Before she died, she did manage to make me understand that there was no reason for me to feel guilt over that. But I guess, in a way, that guilt is still with me."

"I'd like to hear how your sister died, but we can save that conversation for another time if you like."

"I would very much like to tell you about her, but right now I'm more interested in Demy. He reminds me of her so much. I hope he will be spending time here with us. I want to get to know him better."

"I hope so, too." Trevor laughed. "Ultimately, it will be up to his mother. I was thinking about that as I was unpacking. I should probably work out some kind of sleeping arrangement for him when he stays overnight. Assuming, that is, his overnights are allowed."

Ethan sat up straighter in his chair. "Of course, it's allowed."

"I didn't want to assume—"

"He's welcome here anytime he wants to stay."

"Thank you." *I think I offended him.* Trevor let a moment of silence lapse between them and spoke again. "I guess a small twin bed in the corner near the window of my room—"

"He can have his own room. There is a spare bedroom on the other end of the hall. You'll share the bathroom."

"That's . . . that's very generous of you. Thank you."

Ethan shrugged. "I'm excited to have him here."

Trevor let Ethan dip into a quiet moment of contemplation, perhaps recalling some special moment with his sister. His head bent down, and his face clouded over with shadows. When he looked up again, his eyes were a dazzling blue in his handsome face. He smiled. Trevor smiled back.

"So, what about you? I'd like to know what made you such a generous person." Trevor's posture relaxed, sitting back with his ankle on his knee.

"Well, I grew up in Fayetteville. My sister and I, and my parents, all lived in a comfortable house, and wanted for nothing. My parents were wealthy. Dad had an advertising business, and made great money; and mom had a sizable inheritance from her lawyer father. I wouldn't say we were spoiled children, but we got pretty much anything we could ever want or need.

"When Ellen got sick, they didn't hesitate to take her to the best doctors. But no amount of money could stop what happened. When she died, my mother took every cent she had and sunk it into a cult located somewhere in the Adirondacks. She said they were going to protect the world from the apocalypse. She said something was coming that would wipe out all human life, except, of course, her and her True Believer friends. When we refused to be swayed, she seemed to mourn, not only my sister, but my father and I as well.

She cut all ties with us, and I haven't heard from her since."

"I'm sorry to hear that. I'm sure the loss of her daughter was hard for her."

Ethan smiled solemnly and shrugged. "It was hard on all of us. Anyway, she's not who I want to talk about. My sister is what is really important to me. She accepted me for who I am, and never made me feel less than I was. She made everyone feel comfortable around her, even putting at ease those in the general public who seemed uncomfortable around people with disabilities."

"She sounds like Demy in that respect. He has a way of drawing people in, and they never see his disability as a social block. He's amazing like that."

Trevor stopped talking because Ethan seemed lost in thought again. He was smiling, but his eyes seemed glassy, far away. When Ethan's eyes refocused on him, Trevor continued.

"Demy's hearing loss is caused by certain bones in his ears not forming. It's a hereditary issue. You mentioned you and your sister shared the same defect, but you could hear and she was deaf. Can you explain that?"

"I can try. But even the doctors can't understand it. I'm a miracle of modern medicine." He laughed. "We were born without the fine hairs in the at—"

"The stereocilia."

Ethan paused, nodded. "Right. We were born without these fine hairs. Cochlear implants could rectify this, but my parents were dead set against it. They didn't want Ellen feeling like a freak, I guess. Besides, she didn't seem to need it. Deafness never held her back. She didn't know what she was missing, so she never pushed for the surgery."

"And you? What's your story? How did you gain your ability to hear?"

"Quite simply: I could always hear. The doctors were at a loss. The way they explained it is my body found a way around the hearing loss with a sort of natural cochlear implant."

"I see. That's very interesting. And you've never had trouble hearing?"

"None at all." He laughed. "My parents used to talk to me in sign language, and I wasn't sure why. The first time I responded to them when they were under the illusion I was deaf caused my mother to go into hysterics. She was sure it was some kind of sign from God. I think I felt guilty that I could hear and Ellen couldn't, so I hid it from her, and from my parents."

"When the truth came out, was your sister disappointed that you could hear? I mean, knowing she couldn't?"

Ethan chuckled soundlessly. "No, she was excited for me. She asked me what sounds were like. I described what I could hear, and having my unique perspective, I was able to make her understand what I was hearing."

"That's so nice. How horrible life is to take her from you."

Tears glistened in Ethan's eyes but did not fall. He took a deep breath. "I'm just glad for the time I did have with her."

"Oh, I almost forgot." Trevor bolted from his spot on the sofa. He snatched up his keys and dashed out the door. He crossed the road in the fading light of day to his car. He hopped in and started the engine. After a brief time, he backed out of the driveway and pulled his car into Ethan's yard. He turned off the engine, started back into the house, but paused. He returned back to the car and pulled the sack of potatoes out of the backseat. He entered the house as Ethan opened the door for him.

Ethan laughed. "What's that?"

"A gift from a friend. I'm hoping you can use them. There's too much for me to eat in a month, and seeing that you can cook . . ."

Ethan laughed again. "Yes, I'll put them to good use. Thank you." He took the sack of potatoes from Trevor and carried them off to the kitchen. When he returned, Trevor was walking around the living room, picking up objects to look at, and setting them back down again. "I'll have to get creative to use them up before they start growing in my pantry. They make a very unusual housewarming gift, though I appreciate your generosity."

"The real generosity came from Mr. Moroney on Chestnut Ridge Road. He just randomly placed them in my car."

"They are from a local farm?" Ethan sat back down and invited Trevor to join him.

Trevor placed the elephant figurine he was holding on the table and took a seat on the sofa again.

"You'll have to introduce me to the locals. When I buy produce and other necessities, I want to buy local. Think you could help me get some good deals?"

"I might know a few people who could help you out."

"That would be great."

"So, tell me about this place you're working on. Why haven't I been invited to tour it?" Trevor laughed.

"As soon as I get through this asbestos mess, you'll have an open invitation to stay there whenever you like."

"Hell, if you need help stripping the place, let me know. I'd like to help in any way I can."

"Watch yourself. I might take you up on it."

"I wish you would."

Ethan shook his head. "No, I don't think you should. It's hard, strenuous—dangerous—work. You'd be exposing yourself to fibers that could kill you. Mesothelioma is a long and drawn-out, painful death."

"I'd trust the equipment to protect me from getting sick. Just like you."

Ethan said nothing more on the subject.

Trevor glanced out the window. The sun was starting to dip low enough to cast elongated shadows of the trees. Some of these shadows caused dark patches on the windows, mingled with the glittering brightness of the sun, as if the day's light was battling with the cold dark of night for supremacy on the glassy surface. When Trevor turned back to Ethan, the man seemed on the verge of saying something more, but remained silent. Ethan smiled and looked away.

"So," Trevor said, just for something to say in place of the silence. "What was life like for you growing up?" He was thinking that he wanted to know what life was like for him after his sister died, but didn't feel brave enough to phrase it that way. Ethan seemed to understand.

"Life without Ellen was hard, but I managed to get by. I made good friends in high school, and stayed out of trouble . . . mostly. I was always the helpful kid. There was one teacher, in fact, that probably owed her entire career to me."

Trevor said nothing, and Ethan continued.

"She was a shy substitute, and couldn't have been more than twenty-five. Probably fresh out of graduate school. She just sat at the head of the class and let the students have the run of the place. When she tried to take roll call, her voice quaked with obvious trepidation. The kids just walked all over her, ignoring her. The principal came to the classroom and informed her that she would have to take the position full time, as the teacher she had been subbing for would not be returning." Ethan stopped and cleared his throat.

Trevor waited for him to continue.

"After the bell rang, and all the kids cleared out, I hung back. I was picking up some papers I had dropped and was bent over. She didn't know I was there. She had started crying. I slowly stood up, and when she saw me, she looked startled. She tried to compose herself. I told her I wasn't going to say anything to anyone. She smiled.

"Then I gave her a bit of advice that she seemed to take to heart.

"And quite literally, I created a monster."

Trevor had leaned forward, absorbed by the story. He almost asked Ethan to go on, but didn't have to.

"I said, 'You should keep in mind that you are in charge here. You are giving up your authority to these kids, and they are walking all over you. Stand up. Use your voice. Show them who is in charge.'"

"And she did?" Trevor asked.

Ethan laughed. "Did she ever. She came in the next day, and screamed at the top of her lungs for the class to Shut. The. Hell. Up. When one kid refused to take her seriously, she came around the desk, grabbed him by the ear, and dragged him into the hall. After class, the boy came back into the room, and all through the halls, she could be heard screaming at him. He never acted up again. In fact, future generations called her the Bitch in English Class."

Ethan laughed again.

Trevor leaned back, smiling. "Did she ever thank you for your words of encouragement?"

"She never did." He added an afterthought. "Nor did she ever show me that kind of treatment. I took that as a sort of 'thank you.'"

Trevor shrugged. "I guess you could look at it that way."

The silence in the room stretched between them again. What is it, Ethan? What are you trying to say? Ethan dropped his gaze to the floor, then over to the wall, then at Trevor, not as though he didn't know what to say, but as if he didn't know how to say it.

Finally, Ethan seemed to get the nerve to say what was weighing on his mind.

"Okay, so there is something I should tell you. I guess it would be better for you to hear it from me rather than hearing it on the street, I suppose. Something I probably should have told you before you agreed to move in. I guess I was just hoping I could tell you without it influencing your decision to move in here. It's something about me that might be circling around town. And something better heard from me rather than in a string of gossip, where the truth of it would be torturously stretched."

"I never listen to gossip," Trevor said. "But you can tell me anything."

"Yeah, I need to tell you this." Ethan sighed heavily. He wiped his hands on his pants. "Whew, saying it out loud is harder than I thought."

Trevor tried to keep his face expressionless, but there was a sinking feeling in the pit of his stomach, as if he was about to be told he had a terminal disease. What else would be this bad?

Oh, man. He's going to tell me he was convicted of murder.

"You see, I want to tell you that—"

Ethan wasn't allowed to finish. Before he could end his sentence, a heavy rapping issued from the front door. The sound was so sudden, and insistent, it startled both men.

Trevor threw a troubling glance at Ethan. "You expecting someone?"

"No."

When the quick succession of taps came again, Ethan stood to answer the door.

Trevor thought of the story "The Monkey's Paw," and suddenly had the urge to tell Ethan not to answer it. The moment of anxiety passed as he told himself he was being ridiculous, and he stayed quiet. He followed Ethan to the door.

Trevor was shocked by the figure at the door, and he thought Ethan might have been even more shocked. Ethan stepped back, and Trevor took up the space directly in the doorframe. Krista had been turned away, as if she were heading back to her home, but now she turned to look at him. Her eyes darted in the direction of Ethan. She held a sleepy, pajama-clad Demy in her arms. Demy reached out. Trevor pulled his son into his arms. He scowled at Krista, more confused than upset.

"I'm sorry to bother you," she said. She turned and looked back, then looked at Trevor again. "I didn't know what else to do."

"Please, come in," Ethan said.

She followed Ethan and Trevor into the living room. Trevor sat on the sofa with Demy curled up in his lap, the boy's head resting on his shoulder. Krista sat next to him, and Ethan returned to his designer armchair.

"What's this all about?" Trevor tried not to sound annoyed, but failed. Truth was, he wasn't trying very hard. He was annoyed, and he thought she should know it. He rested a hand on Demy's head, gently rubbing his soft yellow hair.

When Trevor saw her run a shaking hand through her hair, he calmed down. *She's scared. No, she's terrified.*

"What happened?" He managed to sound less . . . aggressive this time.

Krista sighed, closed her eyes, and when she opened them again, she began. "It started this afternoon when I took Demy to Dad's for ice cream." She took a shaky, deep breath. "The place looked deserted, but just as I was about to give up, a young girl came to the window. It was the owner's granddaughter. I didn't recognize her right away, but you know the girl I mean? With the long blond hair? She always gives Demy extra sprinkles."

When Krista stopped talking, Trevor coaxed her to go on. "Okay, yeah."

"Well, she looked sick, or something. Maybe not sick, but dirty somehow. Strung out."

"So, you caught her on a bad day."

Krista shook her head. "No, it was more than that. Her skin was blotchy. Like it was covered in lesions. But veiny, too. She looked hideous. But it wasn't just her appearance. She acted like a whole other person entirely. She was . . . nasty. She scared me so badly that I backed away."

She stopped again, hesitating. Her voice was low, ominous. "Then he appeared."

Trevor's skin prickled. "Who appeared?"

"I don't know who he is. A stranger. At least, no one I've ever seen before. He was dressed in a white suit. He had white hair, and a white goatee. He stared at me in a very scary way. Smiling. Like he knew something I didn't. I was so scared I grabbed Demy and left without getting ice cream."

Another pause.

"But that's not all. Just a half hour ago I saw him again. He was standing on the street looking at our house. That same stranger had followed me home . . . or something. I don't know. But I saw him again."

Ethan brought her a hot tea, and she took it, steadying it with two trembling hands.

Demy squirmed in his father's arms, perhaps feeling the tension in the room.

"Are you sure it was the same guy?"

"I'm sure."

Trevor said, "Where is he now?"

Ethan went to the window and pulled back the curtain. "I don't see anyone out there."

Krista shrugged. "I don't know where he went, but when I saw that he was gone, I came running over here. I'm sorry. I don't want to upset what you have going on over here. I just don't know what else to do. I . . . I'm afraid to be alone."

Trevor studied her, then looked at Ethan.

Ethan spoke up. "You should stay here tonight, then."

"No, I couldn't—"

"I insist. I have a pullout sofa in the guest room. You and Demy can sleep there for the night. In the morning, we'll sort this out. And maybe find out who this man in white is."

"I'm so sorry to impose."

"You're not imposing." Ethan sounded much more convincing than Trevor had.

She glanced around. "So, what was the topic of conversation before I intruded?"

"Ethan was about to tell me something important about himself." Trevor looked at Ethan.

Krista glanced over at Ethan as well.

"Oh, no worries. That will keep for another time."

Ethan rushed off to fix up the guest room.

Chapter Six: Tessa

Tessa Whittlespoon stood on the deck of her boat and bent down to pick up a red-and-white-striped life vest. As her butt took center stage, obscuring the rest of her body from view of anyone on the dock, her husband, Gavin, whistled. She stood up again, knees creaking like old, rusty hinges, and turned to face him.

"Nice caboose." He laughed.

Tessa chuckled and threatened to hit him with the life preserver. "I hope you don't plan on talking like that when our guests arrive."

Gavin stood on the dock winding a rope around his arm. When he reached the end, he draped it on a hook jutting from a post. She watched him work, loving him more and more as he showed such obvious pride for the well-being of the area surrounding their boat. She loved him more today than she had the day she met him, if that was even possible. He had taken such good care of her over the years, and now, as their days on the earth grew to a close, she supposed it was time to take care of him.

Gavin enjoyed having sex with her, still, even after all these years. But since her change of life had occurred—her menopause—sex had become painful. Still, she didn't deny him that pleasure. Doing so would only cause her undue distress—like she wasn't living up to her end of the bargain, or something. She knew that if she told him about the pain—a horrible, burning sensation—he would stop. But she didn't want him to stop. She was afraid that if he stopped enjoying sex, he would die. In fact, she would rather he died on top of her than to have him die of old age.

Her friend, Gladys, gave her a solution of sorts. "Why don't you let him put it in your behind? I hear that's all the rage with the young folks these days." Gladys had giggled.

Tessa had gone red. She put a hand to her mouth, speechless at the thought. Even now, recalling the memory, Tessa felt a tightening in her chest, and her stomach lurched. Never.

"What are you glaring at, old woman?"

Tessa snapped out of her thoughts. "I'm looking at you, old coot. I'm amazed you can still *bend* over."

"I can bend *you* over."

She tsked. "What did I say about that dirty mouth of yours?" *I won't tell him what I was thinking.* She laughed.

She watched as he pulled the power washer out of the shed at the end of the dock. He attached the hose and turned on the water. She held her ears as he started the power washer and it roared to life. He commenced spraying the barnacles off the hull, and she ducked down below deck, where the noise of the machine wasn't quite so loud. The sound of the water smashing into the side of the boat drowned out the roar of the engine.

Tessa hummed a tuneless song—something she remembered from childhood—as she cleared away breakfast dishes and wiped down the small table. She halted when the sound of the power washer stopped and glanced around. Everything seemed to be in order. It was amazing how homey the place was. Pictures of hunting dogs and lighthouses hung on the walls of the sitting room. A thick carpet lay under her feet. A faux fireplace crackled with real heat. The heater wasn't there for heat. They had found that a strange, moist chill permeated the boat, which the heat kept at bay. She supposed it also kept mold from cultivating in the fabric and rug. It wasn't hot in the yacht's parlor, but just the right temperature. She returned topside.

"How does that hull look?" she asked.

"She looks like a brand-new boat." Gavin stood back, admiring his work.

"I want everything to be perfect for our outing. He deserves it." She knew he understood who she was referring to, but she clarified anyway. "Demy, my sweet, sweet boy, deserves only the best."

"I agree." Gavin climbed on board.

She offered Gavin a hand, and he took it. She helped pull him up onto the boat. It wasn't that he needed the help—nor did she, for that matter—but they helped each other as a matter of courtesy, and because they enjoyed the excuse to touch. If he had been on the boat, he would have helped her. Similarly, when Demy and his parents arrived, they, too, would be helped up and onto the boat. For those youngsters it was out of courtesy, yes; but it was also because they were landlubbers, and didn't have the sea legs for a graceful entry onto the deck.

Tessa had been brought up on boats. Gavin bought their latest sea vessel in the same year they were married, dubbing it *The Whittlespoons*. The name was engraved on the outer hull at the back of the boat.

They usually launched their vessel into the Atlantic, from the shores of New Jersey, but in this early stage of the summer, they sailed the waters of

Oneida Lake. They invited Demy to sail with them—his parents, too, of course—on the lake.

They met Demy at the grocery store of all places, two years ago. He had been reaching for something on a high shelf, and his mother was preoccupied with reading the label on a can. Tessa had asked if he needed assistance, but the boy seemed to ignore her. She asked again. When he still did not respond, she tapped him on the shoulder.

She recalled how he had jerked around, startled. She had been taken aback, unsure if she should have been helping him. She suddenly felt like a predator, out snatching kids to put in her oven.

But the boy had calmed, no longer frightened. In the next moment, Tessa understood everything.

"I gont weech."

The boy's words were slurred, nasal. The boy was deaf.

"You poor, dear child," Tessa had said and pulled down the box of cereal he had been jumping at. He took the box and ran to his mother, who turned and looked up at his approach. After a bout of sign language that Tessa had no hope of understanding, the boy ran back and took her by the hand. Laughing, she let him drag her over to his mother.

The woman looked mortified. "I'm so sorry. He said you helped him and he wanted to thank you. He clearly has no boundaries. I—"

When the woman stumbled over her words, clearly too flummoxed to continue, Tessa intervened.

"Don't give it another thought, dear. I'm Tessa."

The woman extended her hand. "Krista." The woman looked down at the boy. "And this little demon is Demetrius. But we call him Demy."

"Demy." Tessa repeated the name.

Tessa asked if he liked boats. When he shrugged, Tessa gasped. "Oh, my. Either one loves boats, or one doesn't. How can a shrug suffice?"

The boy's hands fluttered. His mother translated. "He's never been on one."

Tessa's hand flew to her mouth.

She invited the family to her boat that day, and the rest—as they say—was history. They invited Demy's family out on the lake twice a year, in the beginning of the summer, and at the end, before storing it away for the winter.

She and Gavin had had no children of their own—and thus, no grandchildren—but they had grown to love Demy and his parents as though they were blood kin. And so, with pride and unbridled excitement, the Whittlespoons planned to announce to the Burnettes, that they—the aforementioned—would be put in the older couple's will. The younger couple would be getting everything—the cars, the houses, and the boat. As well as all the money. There was nearly two million in stocks and equity. They could sell off everything if they wished, and invest it all in Demy's future.

Of course, they hadn't done any of it yet. They were planning to tell the couple first. Gavin insisted on getting their approval before any papers were signed. Tessa wanted to surprise the couple with the news, but in the end, she knew her husband was right. They needed to be aware, and they needed to approve.

Sure, they would insist at first that the offer was too generous, but Gavin was a master sweet-talker. He would convince them to accept their gift. And it didn't matter anyway; they were doing this whether the couple approved or not.

When Tessa finished tidying up the lower deck, she sprawled out on the bed and dozed. The lakeside breeze and the slow lulling of the yacht on the waves conspired to make her drowsy. She woke at four in the afternoon. She jumped off the bed and rushed to the top deck.

"Dammit woman, you fell asleep again, didn't you?" Gavin wasn't really mad, though a passerby might have thought he was serious.

"I can't help it if this damn, rocking boat makes me sleepy."

"You should be tested for narcolepsy. For Christ's sake, our guests will be here any minute."

"It's fine, you old coot. Dinner's ready, and just has to be heated. I do that once they get here."

She couldn't remember when they started yelling at each other instead of just carrying on a normal conversation—maybe they had always done it—but it was the norm for them, and neither meant any of the bitterness they expressed in their words and tone. In fact, he might think she was leaving him if she ever spoke nicely to him. She'd never leave the crotchety old bastard. She loved him too much, and besides, where would she go? She didn't know any other life besides next to him.

The family arrived a little after five. She had suspected it would be later in the day when they arrived. Trevor worked till three. It took time to come home, get ready, and make their way to the lake. She preferred these later afternoon get-togethers during the week, as opposed to the weekend visits. She liked the weekends to be just for her and Gavin.

When she heard Gavin calling out to their visitors, she quickly shoved the prepared roast into the oven of the small kitchenette and went topside to meet her guests. Gavin helped Krista aboard, and Tessa stepped up to assist Demy. As Tessa inspected the boy, Trevor boarded without assistance. She led them to the seats at the front of the boat.

"Dinner will be ready in about an hour," she said as the family took their seats, and Gavin pulled the boat away from the dock, heading for the open water of the lake. Tessa stood near the boy and put out a hand to Krista. The woman took her hand, and Tessa squeezed it gently. "I'm so glad you could join us again." She smiled at Trevor.

Tessa's smile faltered at the sight of Trevor's distracted, uncomfortable face, but replaced the smile to her lips before the family could see that she had noticed the tension among them.

"How have you been?"

Gavin's question knocked Tessa out of her thoughts. She looked at her husband. *Does he see it, too? No.* She decided he was just asking an innocent question, probably to fill the void of dead air that surrounded them, even if he didn't know he was doing it. She looked back at the young couple. They shared a glance at each other before Trevor responded.

"We have been just great, Gavin. Thanks for asking. And yourself?"

As her husband went into an elaborate tirade of recent aches and pains, and a general list of complaints, Trevor listened with such rapt intensity Tessa couldn't help but believe the man was not hearing any of it. And an awful truth struck her. *He doesn't want to be here.* Her cheeks flushed, and her breath caught in her throat. She looked to see if anyone had noticed her dismay. She thought she must have recovered in time, because neither of the young adults gave her a second glance.

But the boy was another matter.

When she glanced down at Demy, he was frowning at her. He was confused by her distress. She quickly smiled at him.

"Oh, Manny, no one wants to hear about your woes. Hush." Manny was an endearing nickname she had given to her husband for reasons that only made sense to her. She turned back to Demy. "Are you ready for some deep-water fishing, child?" She laughed at his joyful affirmation.

She had managed to turn a near cataclysmic moment into one of happiness and comradery. The conversations turned casual and natural after that. She was happy to see that the night wasn't going to be a disaster after all.

While Demy and the men stayed topside, and took inventory of the fishing equipment, Krista followed Tessa to the kitchen and helped with dinner.

As Tessa removed the roast from the oven, she tried to sneak in a conversation that might help to reveal what was not being said by her guests. "I trust all is well with you and yours?"

"Yes. Thank you for asking."

"That's good to hear. But I can't help but notice that you and Trevor have been a bit distracted lately. I hope there isn't an illness, or anything like that, you are trying to protect us from."

Though she didn't look up from her task of basting the meat, Tessa could feel Krista's eyes on her.

Krista sighed. She sounded tired. "Trevor and I have been going through a bit of a rough patch lately, but it's nothing to be concerned about."

"And Manny and I haven't done anything to offend or upset you?"

"God, no. You've been nothing but wonderful to us."

"That's a relief."

"No, it's all good between us. And the stuff happening between Trevor and me isn't something to be concerned about, either."

"Okay, I'll take your word on that." She didn't want to pry. "The important thing is you're here. We'd hate for things between us to get . . . strained."

Tessa turned to Krista when the younger woman reached out to her. They embraced.

Krista whispered into her ear. "We appreciate all you've done for us. And for the joy you've brought into Demy's life."

They broke the embrace, and Tessa went back to the task at hand. "That's what's really important, isn't it?"

Krista answered even though the question was rhetorical. "Yes."

Five places were set around the small table, with Demy situated between his mom and dad. Gavin cut the roast into servable slices, and everyone helped themselves to the meat. Casually, and avoiding detection, Tessa watched the young couple's interactions with each other.

Something was wrong.

Krista turned to Demy and used her hands to say something. The boy nodded, and his mother poked a fork into a potato. She placed it on his plate. He tapped the table and held up two fingers. She gave him another.

Trevor poured lemonade into the boy's glass without any sign that he had asked if that was what Demy wanted. Still, the boy picked up the glass and took a drink. *They know him so well.* A feeling not unlike joy caused her heart to swell. *The boy is so dearly loved by both parents.* Whatever is the matter on that side of the table, it has nothing to do with him.

The parents, though; that was another matter. Neither of them spoke to one another. They didn't even glance at each other. They might as well have been strangers to each other.

Tessa tried to put that out of her mind—*none of my business*—and started in on her own dinner.

And though she had convinced herself their troubles were none of her business, they were still friends, and she cared about them. If they were having money troubles, perhaps Tessa's and Gavin's news would be more welcome than originally suspected. Maybe the young couple would jump at the chance to inherit the Whittlespoon fortune. And if need be, an advance in the inheritance could be arranged.

No, the couple did not have to worry about money.

Tessa was tempted to blurt it out over the dinner plates. *Don't you worry, babies. We plan on providing for your future. We are giving everything to you.*

But she did nothing of the sort. She knew this was not the right moment. She would know when the right time came. Or, perhaps, the right moment would not come, and she would have to blab the news in a breathy rush in order to get it out. That moment was not now, however.

Tessa finished her meal and began collecting empty plates and used utensils. Krista jumped up from the table.

"Please, let me help you with that."

"Oh, pish. I've got this." She dropped a fork.

With the dishes stacked in the sink, Tessa bent down to pick up the errant piece of silverware.

Gavin whistled. "Second time today I got a look at that sweet ass."

Tessa popped up with a gasp and swatted at the dirty old man. "Please, not in front of the company."

But when she turned embarrassingly toward the young couple, she saw that they were laughing . . . and looking at each other. The moment didn't last, but she had glimpsed it, and it caused her heart to swell at the sight. She smiled and hugged Gavin, though not even he knew the real reason why. *Thank you, dirty old man, for bringing a smile—however brief—to their otherwise grim faces.*

As Tessa returned to the sink, Krista came to stand beside her. "I insist, please let me help you."

Tessa hugged her with one arm, and handed her a drying towel.

"That's right. You women-folk fiddle round in the kitchen while us men retire to the deck. Come on, Trevor. Those fish aren't going to catch themselves." Gavin led the way up the flight of steps to the upper deck.

When the dishes were cleaned and dried, Tessa and Krista headed up top. They took their seats on the cushions along the back of the boat to watch the men fish. Gavin and Trevor sat in folding chairs at the railing as Demy stood between them, struggling to cast his line into the water. Gavin helped the boy by straightening the line, but let him cast on his own. The bobber landed in the water a couple of yards out. Smiling, Demy turned to his dad.

"Nice cast." Trevor spoke the words aloud to the accompanying hand gestures. He rubbed at the boy's hair, making his small head wobble. They all laughed.

Demy turned to glance at his mother, smiling. She smiled back.

"He's a natural fisherman," Gavin said. "Born for the open water. He'd do well on a hauler, I think."

"He's doing fine on this boat," Tessa said. She turned to Krista. "He would enjoy spending more time here, I think. A lot more time." She waited for the younger woman's reaction.

Krista didn't look at her. "Is that your hint that you want us to come around more often?"

This wasn't going to be easy. She tried again.

"Actually, I was thinking more along the lines of him owning the boat."

Now Krista did look at her. "He's only eight. What would he want with a boat?"

Tessa tried to bridge the gap. "Well, it wouldn't be his boat at first. It would be for—"

"Demy, you've got a bite!" Gavin helped the boy secure his fishing pole, and assisted with the task of reeling in the catch.

Krista and Tessa's conversation dropped away as they concentrated on Demy's progress.

Tessa forced herself to smile—happy that the boy was having so much fun, but disappointed as well that the opportunity to discuss the will had been snubbed.

Oh, well. There will be another chance soon. Or so she hoped.

She sat forward as the boy's progress intensified. She cheered, even though she knew Demy could not hear her.

Once the fish was dangling over the railing, Gavin used a net to bring it onto the boat. He deftly removed the hook from the animal's lip, and laid it on the deck at Demy's feet.

The boy looked up at the old man, smiling broadly. "It's a walleye," Gavin said.

The boy nodded.

"What do you want to do with him?" Gavin asked in his usual slow, methodical way he always spoke to the boy.

Demy looked down at the fish. He glanced at his father, and then his hands began to work. Gavin looked to Trevor for an interpretation.

"He wants to throw it back."

Gavin stared at Trevor for a moment, blinked. Finally, he shrugged. "Okay, if that's what he wants to do."

Demy nodded vigorously.

Demy watched closely as Gavin lifted the fish and let it drop over the side of the boat. The boy leaned over and watch the fish disappear into the murky depths of the lake.

Trevor sat back down. "He likes to catch them, but not to keep them."

No one had been requesting an explanation. Gavin said, "Okay. To each his own, I guess."

Gavin sat back down.

As the night wore on, Tessa took a seat next to Demy at the edge of the water. She only minutely became aware that Trevor and Krista had ducked out of sight when she decided it was time for some dessert, and they weren't nearby to ask them for their opinion on the choices.

She tapped Demy on the shoulder. He glanced up at her with droopy eyelids. She spoke. "What would you say to some ice cream?"

His eyes popped wide open. His mouth dropped, and he met her with a toothy grin. He nodded vigorously.

She had a thought that she had caught him just in time. He hadn't had a bite in hours, and she suspected that in another few minutes he would have been fast asleep, slumbering so deeply he would probably have to be carried off the boat when they docked.

She supposed she should get permission from his parents before filling their child with sweets, but she still wasn't sure where they had gone. And besides, she had promised him, hadn't she? She was obligated to fulfill that oath.

The mystery to where the young couple had gone resolved itself as she headed down to the lower deck, and heard a whispered conversation. The tone of their voices, though hushed, was decidedly heated.

They're arguing.

She turned to head back up the steps, intending to give them privacy, but one word stopped her cold. She froze, fully aware she was eavesdropping, but unable—or unwilling—to stop herself.

Divorce.

And then there was a pause from the two downstairs.

Krista said, in a breathy voice, "So there it is. You said it."

"Yeah, I said it." He went silent again.

Krista's expression grew defiant. "You want that? You want to give up on us?"

"Isn't that what you already did? You all but kicked me out of the house. And what was that nonsense about someone following you? This man in white? What kind of shit was that?"

"It's true." Her voice was defensive, maybe even a little hurt.

Trevor huffed. "I wasn't even out of the house one day, and you couldn't give me that. I feel like you were just trying to check up on me. You embarrassed me in front of Ethan. He probably thinks he made a mistake letting me stay with him. I'm sure he thinks you're going to be moving in next."

"I don't know what I saw, but it scared me. It scared me enough to swallow my pride and go running to you for comfort. Doesn't that mean anything to you?"

"What means something to me is my space. You need space from me? Well, I need space from you. Yeah."

Krista grew silent.

"Just remember, this is what you wanted. You wanted me out."

"But I never once mentioned divorce. You went to that all by yourself." She sounded desperately pained.

Tessa placed a hand to her heart, feeling Krista's sadness.

"Next time you see ghosts, call someone who cares."

Tessa stifled a gasp at the harshness of his words.

Trevor's next words sounded more tired than angry. "We never should have come today."

"We came because it means a lot to Demy to come. We did it for him."

"I know. We should have rescheduled, is all I'm saying."

Tessa had heard enough. They hadn't wanted to come. There was a tightening in her chest that threatened to cause her to black out. *That's all I need; my fat body rolling out into the hall so they can see I was snooping.*

She returned to the others. Demy looked at her with a furrowed brow. Gavin said what the boy couldn't.

"Where's the ice cream?"

"The ice cream, yes." She spoke too loudly and hovered just shy of hysterical. She was near tears. "Coming right up."

She returned to the stairwell and stomped on the steps, grunting and being as loud as she could. She entered the kitchen and glanced at the couple. They were standing at opposite ends of the room, turned away from each other. They hadn't been having a conversation, no. They were just two people in the same room.

"Sorry to intrude," Tessa said. "The fishermen want ice cream. I hope it's okay if Demy has—"

"Yes," Trevor said. "It's fine."

"It's kind of late for him to be eating heavy sweets." Krista addressed Tessa, but Trevor responded.

"It's fine."

Tessa looked to Krista for approval. The boy's mother nodded, relenting. Tessa quickly pulled three ice cream sandwiches from the small freezer and rushed back up top.

Tessa unwrapped Demy's ice cream and held it out. Her hand shook, and she snatched it back as soon as the boy had taken the treat.

It was too late, though.

"You're upset," Gavin said. "What's wrong?"

She shook her head at him. "I can't say—not now. But we have a lot to talk about after our guests leave."

Tessa glanced down to be sure Demy wasn't "listening." He was turned toward the water finishing off his last two bites of the ice cream, and what the boring old adults had to say was the least of his worries.

He's such a good boy. It's a pity his parents are splitting up. She smiled at him when he looked at her. He smiled back. *So happy. I'm glad we could give him that much, anyway. Who knows what his future holds, with his parents getting a divorce . . .*

When Trevor and Krista rejoined the group, Demy filled them in on what they missed. The adults conversed with little being said other than trivial topics such as the weather, and what plans had been made for the summer.

"We're heading out to the Jersey shore in a few weeks," Gavin said. "You should think about joining us some time. There's nothing like ocean breezes to clear your head."

Tessa's throat closed. *I should have warned him about the breakup.* But then, he was only making small talk. They had no obligation to accept. But what he said next caused Tessa's stomach to clench.

"I mean, after all, we are planning to leave you the boat in our will."

Tessa's face heated, but if her reaction was noticed by the younger couple, they didn't let on.

The two looked at each other.

Trevor turned to Gavin and smiled. "That's a mighty generous offer. You sure about that?"

Tessa gasped—or thought she did—when Gavin spoke again.

"Sure, we are. In fact, we thought it over, and we decided we would leave it all to you—and Demy, of course. The money—everything. On account of the fact that we have no kids of our own to leave it to."

Krista stammered.

Tessa glanced down at Demy. The boy had fallen asleep with his head on his daddy's lap. She turned to her husband, aghast. He showed no discomfort. She supposed he wouldn't. After all, their shocked faces were exactly what she and Gavin had expected when the couple heard the news. Gavin was the only adult on board who didn't know about the divorce. Knowing what she knew now, Tessa felt this was probably not a good time to spring the news on them.

"Oh, my God," Krista was finally able to say.

When Krista turned to look at her, Tessa forced a smile.

Trevor resolved the tension, and Tessa loved him for it.

"That's a very generous offer. We'll take that home with us and consider it. We'll get back to you before you go away, and tell you our decision. Thank you so much for the offer."

"You take as much time as you need," Tessa said when she could finally trust her voice. "But right now, I think you should get that beautiful boy of yours home to bed. He's exhausted."

The couple agreed, and they disembarked as soon as the boat was back in the dock. Tessa and Gavin watched as the couple and their son drove back up the dirt road to the main drag, Route 31.

Tessa turned toward a neighboring dock and what she saw caused her eye to linger. There was a man standing there, under the glow of a lamplight. The man was dressed in white. Her next thought caused her heart to beat heavily against her chest. It was what Krista had been chastised for. She had told Trevor a man dressed in white had been following her.

When Tessa looked away and then turned back, she could have sworn the man was looking at her.

A hand flew to her mouth.

Gavin stood beside her and placed a hand on her shoulder. She turned to her husband, thinking she should tell him about the man. But when she looked back to the other dock where she had seen him, the dock was empty.

"You look like you've seen a ghost." Gavin smiled at her uneasily.

"I think I might have." She turned and hugged him. "I've got a lot to tell you about our little visitors, so let's get downstairs. I suddenly don't like being up here anymore."

Chapter Seven: Jennifer

Jennifer scowled at the way the woman treated the child in her care. If the woman was the girl's mother, Jennifer would have to say something about her parenting skills. She was far from a perfect mother herself, but dragging the child by the arm like that—nearly pulling the poor little arm out of its socket—just wasn't right. But it wasn't her place to say anything.

Her friend, Lanelle, reminded her of this. "Don't, Jenn."

"Don't what?"

"I see you working yourself up to cause a scene. Ignore it."

"Ignore what?" She was playing dumb on purpose. Once it was out there, spoken aloud, so to speak, she would feel obligated to speak up.

"Ignore whatever it is that has your face twisted up in a knot."

"You mean I should ignore the abuse that horrible woman is inflicting on that innocent little girl?" Jennifer's voice carried down the length of the store, and the woman looked at her. Jennifer did not look away. Her eyes said, *Yes, I'm talking about you.*

When the woman looked away, Jennifer turned back to her friend. "She knows I'm watching now. She'll behave."

"You're so loud. Has anyone ever told you that?"

"I hear it all the time. Especially from you. In fact, you've said it several times today already. What's your point?"

Lanelle sighed, and Jennifer laughed. She liked getting reactions from people, even the exasperated expressions.

"I can't change who I am."

"Nor should you," Lanelle said quickly. "I'm just saying you can talk more softly. Not everyone in the store needs to hear what you have to say."

Jennifer shrugged. She let the subject go. And she all but forgot about the woman yanking her kid around the store. Until, that is, she saw it happening again.

Jennifer heard Lanelle gulp down a warning, even as they made their way over to the woman.

"Is this your daughter?" Jennifer stood just out of the woman's reach.

The woman nodded.

"Well, you're a horrible mother."

"What?" The woman seemed angry, offended, but yet, confused. "Who are you to judge?"

"I watched you drag that poor child, nearly pulling her off her feet, around the store, and just now you slammed her in the grocery cart as though she were a bag of groceries. Aren't you worried you'll leave bruises? Something we can use to have you arrested?"

"You really should mind your own business, and leave me alone." The woman turned away from her.

"Oh, I can do that. But I wanted to let you know I saw what you did. You're nothing more than a bully, picking on a baby. Horrible."

The woman turned back. "You have no right to judge me. She's been giving me nothing but grief since we walked in this place. Am I supposed to let her walk all over me?"

"No, but there are better ways to handle the situation than tearing her arm out of its socket. Did you even try talking to her? Using your words?"

When the woman opened her mouth to speak, Jennifer ignored her and turned, taking the child—a girl about two and a half, or three—by the hands.

She spoke, not talking down to the child. "What's going on here?"

The girl lowered her chin to her chest. She pouted. "I want a candy bar, but Mommy said no."

"Okay, Sweetie. Look at me."

The girl looked up at Jennifer. Unfallen tears sparkled in her eyes.

"There is not going to be any candy, do you hear me?"

The girl sobbed, but nodded.

"You aren't going to pout because you didn't get your way, right?"

She nodded again. She did not cry.

"Okay. Be a good little lady for your mommy, and I'm sure she'll be nicer to you. Do we have a deal?"

The girl nodded again.

Jennifer addressed the mom. "Was that so hard?"

She glanced at the white-knuckled grip the woman had on the grocery cart, and it made her smirk.

"You practically made her cry," the mother said. "How is that any better than what I did?"

"She's sad because she's not going to get her way. But she's doing what I asked and she's not physically harmed in the process. That's the behavior we're looking for. When I tell my daughter to clear her room, she gripes, and she complains, but she cleans the room. I don't concentrate on those negative behaviors if she's doing what I want. I've learned to pick my battles. It's a much better way than beating on them."

"I never—"

Jennifer and Lanelle turned and walked away as the woman bombarded the back of her head with insults.

Lanelle giggled.

"So that's off my chest. The mom will either heed my advice, or lose her kid. It's no longer my concern. I did what I could."

"Jenn, the Child Whisperer."

They both laughed at that.

Jennifer stopped. "I don't even remember what I came in here for." Then her migraine began to throb. "Right. Headache medicine."

She found the correct aisle and searched the shelves. She found the bottle she was looking for and snatched it up.

She turned to Lanelle. "Do you need anything?"

Lanelle placed a finger to her chin, thinking. "Soda."

Jennifer followed Lanelle to the soft drink aisle. As Lanelle collected what she needed, Jennifer glanced around. She had the distinct feeling she was being watched, and it unnerved her.

At the opposite end of the aisle, Jennifer located the source of her malaise. She stared at the stranger in white for some time, and he stared back at her. *What do you want?*

"Okay, I'm set."

"Lanelle, look at that guy over there."

Lanelle glanced at Jennifer and then turned in the direction Jennifer was pointing. But even as Jennifer turned back and faced the man, she saw no one there. She dropped her hand.

"What guy? Was he cute?"

Jennifer was distracted, but she answered. Her voice was a whisper. "No, he was old. Handsome, but old."

As she reached the checkout line, Jennifer smiled at the Widow Bowers in line ahead of her. "Hi, Mrs. Bowers."

The elderly woman scowled. "Hello."

Jennifer knew the old woman didn't approve of her status as an unwed mother, but it was hardly any of her business. Jennifer liked to show off her happiness and pride of her lifestyle to the old woman. *Prove she doesn't get to me with her disapproving glares and backhanded comments.* She giggled when the old woman turned away.

Mrs. Bowers turned to her shopping companion, someone Jennifer didn't know.

"Some people like to flaunt the fact that they had children out of wedlock. They like the fact that they have a house full of bastards."

"Excuse me." Jennifer stopped smiling and turned her full attention to the old woman. "Was that comment directed toward me?"

Lanelle placed a hand on Jennifer's arm. "She's not worth it."

Jennifer shrugged away from the hand. "You can say what you want about me, but leave my children out of it. You have no business calling my children names. Who do you think you are, anyway?"

The old woman glanced at her briefly but didn't respond.

"I really think you should let this one go," Lanelle said. She stepped in between Jennifer and the woman.

"No, I won't." Jennifer peered around Lanelle. "You need to shut your mouth, you withered old prune. How are you still alive? Aren't you like a hundred, or something? I swear the rotten ones live the longest."

When the cashier finished bagging Widow Bowers' groceries, the old woman and her companion exited the store.

Though the woman was gone, Jennifer's soured mood lingered.

Lanelle followed Jennifer out to the parking lot.

As they reached the car, Lanelle walked around to the passenger side and waited for the doors to unlock. Jennifer dropped her keys, cussed. She reached down and picked them up. When she looked across the hood at Lanelle, she saw *him* again, and she felt her blood drain from her face. Shivers traveled up her back, and her skin prickled with icy veins.

"He's back." Jennifer spoke through her clenched teeth, trying to be inconspicuous.

"What?" Lanelle said. "Who's back?"

Jennifer dropped the pretense and spoke normally. "The old man I saw in the store. He's behind you."

Lanelle turned and looked. Jennifer flinched. *He'll see you looking.* She couldn't mouth the warning in time.

Why am I so afraid of him? I'm not afraid of anything . . . except clowns. Yet this harmless looking old man frightens me more than if he were wearing a rainbow wig and a big red nose.

Lanelle turned back to Jennifer. "That guy in white? He looks like he should be holding a bucket of chicken."

Colonel Sanders, right. He looks like Colonel Sanders, and it's freaking me out. "Will you be able to stay at my house tonight?"

"Sure, but why?"

"No, even better. Take my kids and get out of town. Will you do that?"

Lanelle scowled. "Yeah, I guess. If it's what you really want."

"It's what I really want. Take them to my mother's. No, wait. Don't tell me where you're going. I can't explain it, but I need you to do this one thing for me."

"Okay. I'll do it."

Jennifer opened the car, and they both climbed in. She drove past the man as she exited the parking lot, and he watched her the entire time.

"Creepy," Lanelle said.

"I have a bad feeling about him, and I don't want him anywhere near my kids if he shows up at my house, or something like that. I can't shake this feeling he's following me."

"Why don't you leave, too?" Lanelle's fear was evident in her voice.

Jennifer shook her head. "I can't. If I'm right, I'll lead him right to you and the kids."

Lanelle made a strange noise in her throat. "You're scaring me."

"Good. Then maybe you'll take me seriously, and do as I ask."

Lanelle did go, and she took the kids. Jennifer said she would call her as soon as the man was apprehended, or however the ordeal would be resolved. She intended to make sure this man was no longer a threat before she let her kids be near him. The kids—bored, unhappy—were nonetheless compliant.

After they were gone, Jennifer began to rethink her decision. *Why am I being so rash? Surely, there's no danger here.* But even as she tried to convince herself she was being silly, she knew she had done the right thing.

She dropped the rationalizing, and replaced it with physical activity. She cleaned her kitchen for the third time, wiped down clean counters, and rearranged the sugar, flour, and tea containers until there was nothing new she could do with them. Then she moved them back to their original position. *They were fine the way I had them.* She stood back in the empty room and stared at them, laughing.

A noise in the living room caused her to gasp. She laughed again. The cat. She had forgotten about Boots.

The cat would be fine. Once again, she was being irrational. She went in search of the little troublesome furry beast.

But the cat was nowhere in sight.

The room was quiet, empty. Perhaps she had imagined the sound.

She glanced out the front window at the street beyond. She saw nothing. No one. The street was as quiet as her house. The sun was setting just beyond the trees behind the houses on the other side of the street, and strange shadows stretched like dark fingers over the town. Jennifer shivered and pulled the curtain closed. She checked the door, confirmed it was locked, and sat down on the sofa.

She turned on the television set, but the noise of sitcoms and infomercials was more disturbing than the quiet, so she turned it off again. *I need to hear him approaching.*

This thought jarred her. *Do I really expect him to come into my home?*

She assured herself the thought was foolish. *I'm stupidly trying to scare myself.* She lay down on the sofa, propping her head up on a throw pillow. *Maybe the migraine is messing with my emotions as well as my head.* She doubted very much she could, but she fell asleep within minutes.

Mommy, wake up.

Her kids were home already? She hadn't given Lanelle permission for that.

What are you doing home? she said without opening her mouth. She didn't open her eyes, either.

Wake up, Mommy. Wake up!

Her daughter's voice was so urgent she opened her eyes and looked into the girl's sweet, round face. *She's so pretty. She's going to be –*

Her daughter's eyes turned to the back of her head, and a man's deep voice bellowed from her little girl's mouth. "Wake up."

Jennifer snapped her head up and looked around. The room was empty. Dark. The sun had set, and with the curtains drawn, even the lights of the streetlamps couldn't enter the room.

No sign of her kids. Her daughter wasn't there. She had clearly dreamed it.

But I could swear I was awake. Another shiver passed through her body. She hugged her knees until it passed.

She recalled the dream, and shivered again. She tried to remember the deep male voice that had come from her daughter's tiny pale lips. Was it their father? No, he hadn't been in the picture for a very long time. And he never frightened her. No one frightened her. The voice had been unfamiliar. A stranger, maybe? Someone she had heard speaking in a random moment of passing?

She decided she might never know.

She didn't dare turn on any lights, and stumbled around in the dark until she reached the kitchen. She poured herself a tall, icy glass of lemonade and took it back to the living room. She set her glass on the coffee table, using a coaster. She picked up her cell phone and stared at the dark screen. *I should call Lanelle and have her bring my kids back. I miss them. I'm being ridiculous.*

Another strange noise outside the front door caused her to drop the phone. She stood and walked to the door. She engaged the chain lock and opened the door a crack. "Hello?" she said into the darkness.

No reply.

She unhooked the latch and opened the door. She stepped out onto the porch. A light breeze caused the glider to swing, squeaking lightly. She turned toward the side railing and peered over. There was no one squatting there, waiting for her. She glanced down the street. She saw Herbert Shaw standing on the porch, having a cigarette in the dark. He waved to her, and she waved back.

Everything was normal.

She giggled at her nervous energy.

As she turned to go back into the house, the man in white appeared from nowhere and stood beside her.

She tried to run, but he shoved her into the house. She lost her footing and staggered, knocking over a table holding a small potted fern and a framed photo of her children. She steadied herself against the wall and dropped down onto the arm of the sofa, her legs refusing to move, to run as she wanted. Nor could she speak.

The stranger entered the house, closing the door behind him. When he spoke, she recognized the sound at once as the male voice her daughter used in the dream.

"I've been waiting for you."

She didn't know what that meant. She glanced around, looking for an avenue of escape. Finding her voice again, she tried to take control. "You're breaking and entering, dude. That's jail time."

The man chuckled, as if amused by the ruminations of a naïve child. "You soon won't see it that way." The man looked around. "You sent your family away. Why would you do that?"

Jennifer glanced at the coffee table, looking for her cell phone. It was gone. She had dropped it, she remembered, but had not seen where it had gone.

"To keep them away from you."

"Strange that you would know to do that, but no matter. It's probably for the best. This usually doesn't end well for the relatives."

The man leaned over Jennifer, looking into her eyes.

"It's time for you to come over with us." He reached out toward her face, but she knocked his hand away. He straightened. "You fight with such vigor. If only you knew how powerless you really are. Perhaps you'll finally understand when it's done." He reached out with snake-like reflexes and touched her ear.

Jennifer screamed.

She heard the sound of her own scream, and it relaxed her. As the man stepped away, she sat up, looked around. She stood, and her foot crunched on something. The ruined cell phone.

Yes, it was a pity the kids weren't there to take part in this. But, as the man said, it was probably for the best.

As the man strode out the front door, Jennifer followed.

Chapter Eight: Dan

He used his key in the lock, sighing before opening the door and pushing through. The house was dark—no surprise there—as he closed the door behind him; doing so as quietly as he could. He walked through the living room without turning on the light. He entered the kitchen, flicked on the switch, and headed to the fridge. Empty. He didn't know what he had expected. Linda hadn't gone shopping—hadn't left the house—in over a week.

He heard her walking around upstairs and cringed. A moment later her voice carried down the stairs to him.

"Darling, is that you? You're home late."

Of course it's me, you dumb cow. Who else would be looking through our empty fridge and bare cupboards, for food that doesn't exist? Good thing he wasn't really hungry. He sat down in a chair.

"I was worried. You've been coming home late more and more often." Her voice sounded closer.

She's coming down here.

He considered running out the back door, but she entered the kitchen before he could stand. She stood in the doorway with her arms folded across her chest.

"There's no food," he said.

Her face contorted into a pout. "I haven't been able to get to the store. Why are you so late all the time?"

"I'm swamped at work. We are in mandatory overtime. I don't have a choice."

"Why didn't you call? I shouldn't have to sit home alone, wondering if you're lying in a ditch somewhere, or worse."

"Why can't you get dressed and run to the store once in a while? There's no food in the house."

"You're having an affair, aren't you?" She sobbed.

"What?"

"You're sleeping around on me. You're leaving me, aren't you?"

"You're crazy. I don't have the time, or the energy, to sleep around."

She sniffed. "Can't deny it. I can smell the whore's perfume on you. Didn't even have the decency to wash it off."

He was so tired. He didn't have time for this nonsense. "I'm going to bed."

"Not in my bed. I don't want that sleazy perfume soaking into my sheets."

"The only thing you can smell on me is my own B. O. I'm taking a shower. It's been a long day."

She sniffed him again as he brushed past her. Whatever phantom perfume she thought she smelled did not belong to any woman he knew. He hadn't had sex in almost a year. He didn't even think he could get it up anymore. Linda had doused that fire when her paranoia took hold and settled in for the duration.

She didn't stop him, and she said nothing as he strode to the bathroom and shut the door. He turned on the shower until the water was good and hot, stripped, and stepped into the scalding spray. It hurt—it burned—and it felt so damn good. He felt as though his neuroses were burning off him. He stood in front of the spray, letting the water wash over him. Steam rose up all around, filling the room and covering the windows, the mirror, and obscuring all views.

It took the hot water tank twenty minutes to drain, and when the shower started to turn cold, he got out. He dried off and stepped into a pair of sweatpants. They were baggy, so he tied them around his waist with the drawstring. He exited the bathroom and walked down the hall to the living room.

Linda was not there. She must have returned to the bedroom. He watched the television until he fell asleep on the sofa.

He woke to the sound of Linda shuffling around the house like a clumsy wraith, but when he looked around, he saw nothing. He was sure the sound that woke him had been close. He stood and entered the kitchen. She was not there, either. *Okay, so maybe it was a dream.*

He returned to the living room, and froze.

The front door was wide open.

Had it been open when he woke? He didn't think so. He was sure he would have noticed. Had she gone out? But why? She hadn't been outside the house, as far as he knew, in days. Why all of a sudden, in the middle of the night, no less, would she have chosen this time to leave the house? And leave the front door wide open?

"Why is the door open? Did you go out and forget to close it?" Her voice came from the stairs to the second floor.

Dan turned and stared at Linda who stood on the steps, about halfway down. She was dressed in a nightgown and slippers. Her hair was a mess. For a moment, he saw the beautiful woman he had fallen in love with all those many years ago. She looked vulnerable and afraid. She needed protecting.

Then the vision was gone.

"Goddamn it, you fool. Don't just stand there with a stupid look on your face, answer me. What the hell are you doing? Are you trying to leave me?"

He opened his mouth to speak, but the sight of the stranger stepping out of the shadows caused him to lose his words. He stared, awestruck, as the man dressed in white stepped toward him.

"Who is this now? This your lawyer? You divorcing me? I—"

Dan thought to turn and run, but his body wouldn't respond to the command. He lost all interest in Linda. He stood motionless as the man walked up to him. He only flinched when the man reached out and touched him on the ear.

And then he heard the sound of a million bells, all held by the delicate hands of angels, ringing. But the sound changed, morphed into a million damned souls, screaming in unison.

An amber glow came over his sight, and it all became clear to him.

He turned to Linda, standing on the stairs, and she was still protesting.

Dan turned to the man. "Do we have to bring her with us?"

"Not at all," the man said.

Dan nodded and smiled, then headed to the kitchen to retrieve a butcher knife. He wanted something big, and sharp, and capable of doing a lot of damage.

Chapter Nine: Trevor

He pulled into the driveway of Ethan's home, but his eyes were on the driveway across the street. *She's not home.* He didn't know why he thought she would be—or should be. She was free to do as she pleased, especially now that they were—for lack of a better term—broken up.

Trevor climbed out of the car and stood at the end of the driveway. He hadn't seen her, or Demy, since the boat. He had wanted to apologize, but even more importantly, he wanted to discuss the offer that had been made to them. He felt it was worth a discussion.

I haven't seen much of them lately.

Trevor shielded his eyes from the sun and glanced in the direction from which a voice had come. After a moment, he saw her. Mrs. Kennedy stood just inside the shadow of the screened-in porch, a shadowy figure hidden among the leafy canopy of plants that hung on hooks, or huddled on tables in pots. She held a watering can in one hand, and was hydrating a row of ferns.

"Demy used to come over every day to see me. Now I'm lucky if I get a glimpse of him as she rushes him into the house."

"She's been a little on edge lately. She thinks someone is following her. She's probably keeping a closer eye on him. I'm sure it'll blow over and he'll come around and see you again."

"Oh, I truly hope so." Then she added, "I miss him."

As do I. He thought it would be in poor form to acknowledge how little of his son he had seen in the past few days.

Trevor was about to turn away from the road and head inside, but Mrs. Kennedy stopped him.

"Did you hear about that poor woman's murder?"

Trevor stopped and stared at the old woman's shape behind the screen for a moment, then he crossed the road and stood just on the other side of the porch. "I didn't."

Mrs. Kennedy let out an exasperating gasp and set her watering can down. She crossed the porch and opened the screen door. She stood in the doorway, holding the door open. Trevor didn't know if she was coming out to stand with him, or inviting him in to her house. He stayed standing where he was.

"Linda Reed, her name was. Butchered in her own house. Twenty-seven stab wounds." She let out that exasperating sob again. "They think her husband did it. He's nowhere to be found."

"You don't say." He didn't know what else to say.

Mrs. Kennedy continued. "There's been reports of people coming up missing all over town. Strange things are happening here."

Strange, indeed.

There was a moment of silence between them, and Trevor thought this would be a good time to say his goodbyes and duck out. But another thought came to him. *Mrs. Kennedy is a nosy old gal. If a stranger has been coming around, she might have seen him.*

"Diane, have you seen any strange men coming around the house lately?" He pointed to the home he once shared with his wife and son.

She blanched. "Strange men?" She glanced around. "I..."

"I don't mean someone Krista might be seeing romantically. That's none of my business. I'm talking about a man dressed in white, who might be secretly watching the house."

She sighed heavily, clearly relieved. "Oh, a strange man." She thought a moment. "No, not that I've noticed. But if there is a problem, I can keep a lookout if you wish."

"Don't go to any trouble, but if you happen to see a stranger walking around, dressed in white, and sporting a white goatee, can you let me know?"

"Oh, is this the reason why Krista is afraid to let Demy out of her sight?"

Trevor didn't respond—mostly, because he thought the question was rhetorical, but also because he didn't want to get more entangled in the conversation. Instead, he said, "Thank you, Diane. Enjoy the rest of your day."

Trevor walked away before she could respond. He heard her screen door squeak shut.

He let himself into Ethan's house and looked around.

He hated an empty house.

The clock on the wall said ten after four. Ethan would still be at the farmhouse, working on stripping asbestos. On a whim, Trevor exited the house and drove to the Garlock farm. He parked the car on the road and climbed out. Now that he was there, he didn't know what he thought he was doing. He couldn't enter the house, unprotected, and he couldn't call Ethan out. He stood next to his car, leaning against the bumper. He didn't wait long.

The form dressed in an orange hazmat suit came out the front door, onto the porch, and stood there for several seconds, unmoving. Then the hands came up and the helmet came off. Ethan cocked his head and stared at Trevor for another few seconds before speaking.

"What are you doing here?"

Trevor stepped forward. "I came to see if you needed any help."

Ethan held his helmet under one arm. With the other, he put up a hand. "I wouldn't come any closer. You're not protected."

Trevor stopped. "I'm sure it's not as bad as all that."

Ethan nodded. "It's pretty bad."

"Where can I get me one of those suits then?"

"Why do you want to help?"

Trevor shrugged. "Bored, I guess. I just do, that's all."

Ethan stood unmoving, quiet, for a long time. Then he sighed. "If you truly want to help, I have an extra suit in my car."

Trevor smiled broadly, and headed for Ethan's car. He put the suit on over his day clothes, and Ethan inspected. When they were both properly protected, they entered the house.

Trevor gawked at what he saw inside. The house was a shell. The walls had been pulled out, shelving had been removed. Insulation had been taken out of the walls and discarded, but a Shop-Vac sat unused nearby.

Through the muffling material of the hazmat helmet, Ethan said, "If you would be so kind, I need all the partitions of each wall to be vacuumed thoroughly. It needs to be precise, because if one fiber is left behind, I'll have to do all this over again."

Trevor voiced his own muffled reply. "I can handle that."

They worked for another three hours before Ethan finally called it quits for the day. He inspected Trevor's work.

"Impressive," he said. "I'm glad you came by. I thought I was going to have to redo everything you did today. I won't need to. My apologies. You were very thorough. Thank you so much."

"I'm glad you approve." Trevor couldn't wipe the smile off his face. *That's what you get for underestimating me.* "If it's all right with you, I'll come back and help out again . . . and for as long as you can use my help."

"I wouldn't mind that at all. I welcome your help."

Ethan led Trevor to the side yard where they took turns hosing each other off using a special chemical in a container attached to the nozzle. A foamy orange substance sprayed from the hose and covered their suits. Then the foam was turned off and clear water washed away the contaminants. When they were cleaned and dried, they removed the suits and packed them away.

"So, I guess I'll meet you at home."

Ethan nodded, climbed into his car, and drove away.

Trevor climbed into his car as well, but didn't start it up just yet. He thought about the prospect of going into business with Ethan. Surely, he could be of use around the new place. He found that working with his hands, doing something that required more than a computer and a calculator, was much more satisfying than sitting behind a desk. But could he afford to quit his job?

And something occurred to him.

He had just been given an opportunity to inherit millions. What if he accepted the Whittlespoons' offer, and asked for an advance on the money to help Ethan get his business up and running?

No, he couldn't ask for an advance.

But what if he made them an offer . . . they could loan him the money to buy half the B&B business, and give them the opportunity to become partners.

How would Krista feel about this? He would just have to ask her. He squeezed his eyes shut and fought back the anger that came over him at the thought of her ruining this.

He drove home.

He pulled his car into Ethan's driveway, and saw that Krista's car was in her driveway. When he climbed out of the driver's seat, he headed across the road instead of going inside Ethan's house. He walked up onto Krista's porch and knocked. After a moment, she opened the door.

"Daadee." Demy rushed him the minute the boy saw him, and threw himself into Trevor's arms. He lifted his son into a great big bear hug.

"May I come in?"

Krista moved aside and allowed him to enter.

Trevor carried Demy into the house and placed him back on the sofa with a kiss on the forehead and the sign: I love you. And then another: forever.

He turned to Krista.

"So, to what do we owe the pleasure of your company today?"

She tried to sound annoyed, but couldn't stop the pleasure of seeing him shine through.

She misses me. He almost laughed.

"I've been thinking—and before you make a wise crack about the idea of me and thinking, hear me out."

She laughed, and nodded.

"I was helping Ethan today on his B&B, and let me tell you what—I've never felt so alive. I know why he's doing this. There's something freeing about working with your hands, creating something new. I want to help him get this thing off the ground. I want to see if I can be a business partner."

"Okay, I'm glad you found something you care about so passionately. What does that have to do with me?"

"Come have a seat."

Trevor sat down on the edge of the sofa. Demy wrapped an arm around him, holding onto him. Krista hesitated for a moment, but gave in. She pulled Demy off Trevor and spoke with her hands. "Go play in your room."

Demy didn't argue. He kissed Trevor on the cheek and scampered off to his room.

Krista took the seat adjacent to Trevor's spot on the couch. The irony wasn't lost on him that this was the exact positions they had been in when he had told her about the affair. *It took an affair for me to realize I still love her, but by then it was too late.* He had to tell her. He couldn't take the chance that she would find out another way. *Did I do the right thing?* He needed to believe he had, though it had cost him his marriage.

Trevor pulled himself out of his own head and looked into Krista's patient eyes. He placed his hands on his knees and leaned in.

"I want to accept the Whittlespoons' offer. And I want to ask them for a loan to make up the amount of money Ethan is short from fulfilling his dream of opening this country bed and breakfast place."

He waited for her to tell him how crazy he was.

She said nothing for a long time. When she spoke, she shocked him.

"I think it's a great idea."

"Really?"

"Yes. How much does he need?"

"He said he is short ninety thousand."

"Only one thing. I want in. Have you gone over this plan with him yet?"

"No, he has no idea I'm planning this."

"Well, we'll have to sit him down and see if he is willing to go along with this. If he says no . . . if he says he doesn't want partners, it's all for nothing, right? But if he's willing to do this—if he's willing to accept this money, and our partnership, I think we should ask the Whittlespoons if they want in on the partnership too. If they have no interest in owning a B&B, well, I am almost positive they would loan us the money. If we offer them a silent partnership, we won't have to pay them back for a loan. I think this will appeal to them."

"I have to admit, I'm a little shocked you're so accepting of this. I expected you to be—"

"Combative? Resistant?"

"Yes."

She laughed. "I can be reasonable sometimes, too."

Though he felt awkward, he leaned closer and hugged her. He took in her clean-scented skin. She used Ivory soap, and he always loved that smell on her. He lingered until it didn't seem so awkward. He pulled away when she did.

"I can't tell you how much it means to me to have your support. I think this will really help us with what we're going through. Don't you think?"

She shrugged. "Maybe. We can hope. Though, an estranged couple going into business together could get messy, as well."

"I think we can handle this."

She smiled. "So do I."

Chapter Ten: Brody

Brody stepped out of the brightly lit house to get away from the noise, and to smoke a cigarette. His sister, Sarah, refused to allow him to smoke in the house. He'd only been staying with her for four months now, but her rules were already getting on his nerves. That was fine; he could deal. He had to. He had nowhere else to go.

He stepped off the porch and lit his cigarette as he walked across the yard to the road. He glanced up and down the street. No one was out. He looked up at the dark, night sky. No stars. The moon moved in and out of a blanket of clouds. The streetlamps were on, which offered enough light to see by.

He took a puff of his cigarette and blew the smoke out through his nose. The thing tasted like a wet dishrag. He wondered if his sister had tampered with his smokes, made them taste bad on purpose. He didn't care how nasty they were, he'd smoke them anyway. He needed them to calm his frazzled nerves. He couldn't use the real drugs he wanted, so he'd smoke the acceptable one instead.

Brody looked across the street at the house directly across from his sister's place. He had seen the older couple who lived there looking at him, studying him, judging him. There was a single lamp on. Someone over there was awake.

He glanced down the street again, and this time he saw a figure walking along the sidewalk. Perhaps walking a dog; although, he didn't see a dog. Then again, he was too far away to see the figure closely.

Brody took another long puff from his cigarette then dropped it to the sidewalk, crushing it out. He lit another. He usually smoked only one cigarette at a time, but he wasn't interested in going back to the house right away.

His sister had taken him in after he had been released from rehab, and he appreciated her devotion, but she had two young children, and he hated kids. She had put him in a bedroom away from the hub of the main part of the house, and that, too, had been appreciated. But the seclusion of his room was pointless when she constantly complained that he was being unsociable. So, he watched TV with the family. He put up with the constant bickering between the two siblings. And he accommodated her no-smoking-in-the-house rule.

But it was all killing him. He needed out.

And then there were the two nosy neighbors that thought he didn't deserve a second chance. He didn't know that for sure, but he guessed that was what they were thinking. He blew out another puff of smoke then dropped the cigarette to the ground and stomped this one out as well. *Damn things taste like a used tampon*. He didn't know what he would do if he couldn't smoke anymore. There wasn't much left in his life to do. His sister had seen to it to take away almost everything that gave him pleasure and now he supposed smoking would be added to that list. He caught himself lighting up another cigarette and stopped. He jammed the pack back into his pocket.

Another glance up the street, and Brody could see that the night-walking stranger was getting closer. Now he could see that there was definitely no dog. Just a tall stranger wearing white, swinging long, dangling arms, and pumping swiftly moving legs. The stranger seemed to be coming directly at him.

He would let the stranger walk on by. He had no interest in striking up a conversation, and he definitely didn't want to make new friends. Hell, he didn't want the friends he had already. Not that he saw too much of them these days. They were all drug addicts, pushers, and dealers. He supposed he was done with that crowd, whether he liked it or not.

He looked back toward the house, and considered going back inside, but the truth was he just wasn't ready. He wanted to wait outside a little while longer. Maybe for most of the night. He figured once the kids were in bed he might go back inside, and with a little luck Sarah would have gone to bed as well. The one good thing about being at his sister's place was the breakfasts. She knew how to feed a man—Tom, her husband, was a lucky dude. She made hearty, delicious breakfasts of steak, potatoes, and eggs that were worth waking up for.

The stranger on the street was practically on top of him now. Brody moved off the sidewalk, to give the man free range to go by without having to interact. Brody hated talking to strangers. That was another good thing about his sister taking him in. He had stayed at halfway homes and homeless shelters before, and there was always someone wanting to talk, ask him questions, get to know him. He hated that. He felt obligated to play nicely. But no matter how nice they sounded, he knew they were only there for one thing.

They might say, "How are you feeling today?"

But what they really wanted to know was, "Are you a threat to yourself or others?"

They might ask, "What do you like to do?"

But what they were really asking was, "Are you a social deviant?"

But he could understand their concerns, and so he played along with the game. And he couldn't say he truly missed the life, either. He hated feeling sick all the time. He hated feeling the *need* to get high. He loathed himself for the things he would do just to score a high.

There were things in his past he would just as soon forget ever happened if he could; things he would never admit to, or divulge to anyone. These were moments he had a hard time forgetting, no matter how much he wished he could.

He had gotten down on his knees in front of another man to perform an act on a promise to score heroine. And after doing it, and getting the drugs, he had taken more than he normally used, secretly hoping for an overdose.

After waking up from that high, Brody made the decision to take his sister up on her offer. He made arrangements to enter rehab. And unlike previous failures, he used that most humiliating moment in his life to stay on track.

Who would have known staying sober would be this hard, though?

In the past, when the need got to be too much, he simply gave in to it. That option no longer presented itself, however. He would be strong, and he would endure. He had to, because the alternative—returning to the drugs—would mean his death. He was sure of that.

Now, his sobriety depended on the strength of his will to live.

The strange man had reached the sidewalk in front of Brody. The man in white stopped walking and turned to face Brody. They stared at each other.

"Can I help you with something?" Brody struggled to swallow a lump that had caught in his throat. A chill raced down his spine, settling in his groin. His breath grew ragged, and he struggled to take in air.

"Brody Sutter." The man spoke his name, not questioning, but as though taking roll call.

Brody choked on his own saliva.

"How do you know my name? Do I know you?" Brody's instinct told him this was an old dealer, coming to tempt him, but he didn't think so. This was something else.

Something more sinister.

The man seemed harmless enough, dressed all in white, with a white goatee and white hair cut short. He looked like a kinder and more handsome older brother of Boss Hogg.

"You don't know me." The man's voice was soothing, with a slight, southern lilt. "But you're about to."

The man stepped off the sidewalk and crossed the yard, heading for Brody. The grass rustled under his feet.

He's real. It was a strange thought, but it was what Brody thought before the man reached him. He had another: *I should run.*

Brody's legs refused to move.

The man stood before Brody, hovering. In another instant, his hand shot out, quick as a snake, and reached for Brody's ear. Brody flinched. He raised a clenched fist and readied to hit the man—old or not. But in another instant, Brody heard the siren sound, and his hand dropped back to his side. The old man stepped back.

"We have a lot of work to do."

Brody nodded.

"Shall we start with your family?"

Brody turned and looked back toward the house. "If you don't mind, I want to be free of them right now. Can we do this later?"

The old man chuckled. "We have all the time in the world. Their time will come. If you wish to delay their initiation, we'll delay."

Brody turned to the old man. "Thank you."

The old man nodded.

Brody turned his attention to the house across the street. "I want to go there first."

The old man turned to the little white house on the other side of the road. "They are elderly, and may be hard of hearing. If they can't hear the song, they won't be affected."

Brody shrugged. "So, we'll find out."

The two men crossed the street. As Brody crossed the yard to the house, the old man (who was not an old man at all, Brody now realized) stayed on the sidewalk.

"You know what to do if they can't hear the sound, correct?"

Brody nodded.

Ignoring the front door, Brody circled round to the back. The door was locked, but it was nothing to him. He twisted the knob until it broke. The locking mechanism gave out, and the door swung inward on squeaky hinges. Brody entered. He was in the kitchen. There was the sound of a television on low, and voices that were not coming from the TV set.

After a moment, the elderly man in the other room entered the kitchen. He spotted Brody and froze in place. The aged face reddened—either in fear or in anger, Brody couldn't be sure—and the man stepped forward.

"What are you doing in my house?"

Brody didn't answer. Instead, he approached the man and reached out to touch his ear. The man brought his hands up defensively, to protect his face. Brody hesitated and continued his trajectory. He touched the mottled earlobe.

"Holden, what's going on?" The raspy, hesitant voice came from the woman in the other room.

"Stay where you are, Betty." Holden turned his head slightly to speak to his wife, then turned it back again. He stared at Brody. "What are you doing in my house, you hoodlum? I knew you would be trouble the minute I laid eyes on you."

"Now wait a minute, old-timer. You have this all wrong. I'm here with a message." He touched the old man's ear again—this time cupping it with the palm of his hand.

Holden knocked the hand away. "Betty, call the police."

"Nothing, huh? Not even a little bit of the buzz?"

"Get out of my house."

"It's a glorious sound. You hear none of it?"

"I'm not going to tell you again." Holden lunged to the right and gripped the handle of a butcher's knife and held it out defensively in front of him. Betty entered the kitchen. He moved backward, toward his wife. "Did you call the police?"

"Oh, no. Holden, what's happening?"

"Do as I say, woman."

Brody stepped toward the elderly couple and held out his hands, placatingly. Holden leapt at him, lunging with the knife. Brody caught the knife by the blade. The elderly man pulled the knife back, cutting through the skin on Brody's palms. Blood flowed between his fingers and dripped to the floor. He held out his hands to the man. The cuts were deep.

The old man blanched as Brody brought his bloody hands to his lips and sucked at the blood. He dropped his hands away and laughed, spitting blood. He let his bloody, dripping hands dangle at his sides. The old man glanced briefly at the hands—the blood—but quickly looked back at Brody's face.

Holden looked into Brody's eyes. His Adam's apple bobbed beneath the loose, weathered skin of his neck. His voice came out in a whispered croak. "*What* are you?"

Brody moved so fast that the elderly couple had no time to react. He gripped the old man's neck in both hands and squeezed. He squeezed until the pink tongue protruded from the toothless mouth, and the bones cracked. The body went limp, and Brody let it drop to the floor.

The old woman gasped and turned to run back into the living room. Brody didn't bother letting her hear the song. He took her by one wrinkled hand and spun her around. She stared at him through tear-filled eyes as he pulled her into a tight embrace. He released her only after hearing the brittle snap of the bones in her back.

Brody didn't turn to look back at what he had done. He exited through the broken kitchen door and returned to the man on the street.

"I take it the elderly couple won't be joining us?"

"No," Brody said. "No, they won't be joining us."

Chapter Eleven: Evelyn

They were all bastards, the lot of them. How dare they lock her away? Even though Evelyn had been released from the institution long ago, she still could not deny the truth. The horrible truth. Didn't they understand the danger they were in, all of them? They had locked her away for seventy-two days, claiming it was for her own good, but they were liars. She was not the liar. She was not in denial. They did it because they didn't want to deal with the truth.

They were all in danger. It was coming for them. If they didn't listen, they would all be doomed. She had seen it, dreamed it. She knew what was happening. Instead of taking her seriously, they called her crazy. They locked her up. They would be sorry. She learned in those seventy-two days to keep the truth a secret . . . no one wanted to hear it. But she could never forget.

Evelyn had been normal, once upon a time. She had had a husband, and she had kids. She had had a boy and a girl, both now grown. When her husband died—killed by a drunk driver while coming home from work one day—Evelyn had been devastated. She had withdrawn into a shell of protection. When she emerged, her kids were gone, and she had been committed to a home for crazy people. After she began to show signs that she could function on her own again, they had let her go.

But during that time of self-reflection, Evelyn had been given the gift of sight. In one of her visions, she saw the monsters that were coming.

There are monsters out there.

She had told people the truth, but no one believed her. She had felt the burning fire, and had stripped out of her burning clothes. She ran from the house and down the road to escape the fire. She had not understood it was a vision until the neighbors found her, naked and curled up in a fetal ball in the middle of the road. That was when they put her in the looney bin for the second time. This time they did not shut her away because of her grief . . . they locked her away to protect themselves from the truth she carried. Her omen.

That was then, though, and this was now. She would let that go. The past was in the past. She cut up apples for her pie, and let the memory slip away.

She was making a pie to give to her daughter. Sally would be arriving soon, and she wanted the pie finished by then. She wanted to show her daughter how well she could still cook. Her daughter stood by her when everyone else abandoned her. Sally was a good girl, and loved her mother.

Evelyn peeled another apple, and removed the core. She chopped the remaining chunks into smaller pieces and placed them in the pie crust. When she had enough filling, she rolled out another crust and placed it over the pie filling. She enjoyed pressing a fork along the edge of the pie to create the border.

She placed her creation in the oven and closed the door. The mess around her was too much to consider for the moment, so she left it and went into the living room. She sat in her recliner and relaxed. When the timer went off it would wake her up, and the pie would be done. She and her daughter could clean the kitchen together then, like the days when Sally was a young girl.

Evelyn dozed.

-:-:-:-:-

She woke to the shrill sound of angels singing.

The room was full of smoke, and she coughed. The angels were the smoke alarms, and Evelyn felt a moment of disappointment. She had hoped the angels had come to save her from the doom that was coming to town.

There was another person moving through the smoke. Evelyn stood and worked her way to the kitchen. She moved to the table and picked up the knife she had used to cut the apples. The form hovered at the oven, removing the burnt-out husk that had been meant to be a pie for her daughter.

That's for my daughter. You can't have it.

Evelyn lifted the knife over her head. She coughed, then, and the form turned around. Evelyn dropped the knife to cover her mouth.

"Mom, get out of the house. This thing in the oven caught on fire. How could you have been so careless?"

Sally tossed the pie in the sink and ran water on it. She then turned and ushered Evelyn toward the front door.

Evelyn struggled away from her daughter and returned to the kitchen. With burning and watery eyes, she searched the floor until she found the knife. She slipped it into the pocket of the apron she wore. She returned to her daughter, and together they exited the smoke-filled house.

Sally moved Evelyn to the road, and they both turned to watch smoke pour out of the cracks in the door, seen billowing under the glow of the porch light like a plume from the underworld.

"I don't think there was any damage, but we can't go back in there until the smoke clears. Mom, what were you thinking?"

Evelyn turned to the woman standing next to her. She smiled. "Oh, Sally. Darling. When did you get here?"

Sally fixed Evelyn with a blank, dumb stare. "Mom, you nearly burned your house down—with you in it. Why aren't you concerned about this?"

Evelyn turned back to the house. "I was cooking you a pie. Oh, dear. I hope it's okay. I should go in and check on it."

Sally turned Evelyn by the shoulders. The older woman allowed her daughter to guide her so they stood face to face. Sally shook her.

"Mom, you nearly died. If I hadn't come when I did, you might have died from the smoke."

Evelyn wiped the tears from her daughter's eyes.

Sally grabbed her mother's hands and pulled them away from her face, forcefully. "No. Mom, you can't just wish this away. You are a danger. I'll have no choice but to have you placed in a . . . facility."

Evelyn's head snapped back as if she had been slapped. "A facility? Do you mean the looney bin?" Evelyn shook her head violently. "I won't go back there. I won't."

"No, Mom. Not there. But I think you would do well in a place where people can look after you. I'm not able to care for you like I should, and I'm sorry. But it's clear to me you can't be on your own anymore."

"You want to take me from my house?"

Sally nodded, her eyes sorrowful. "I'm sorry, Momma, but you can't be left on your own anymore. Don't you understand that you could have died today? This is not acceptable."

Evelyn looked up at the night sky. She saw no stars. *It's odd to see a night without stars. Such a sad sky.*

"I'm going to go back into the house and open windows. You wait out here." Sally touched her mother on the arm and walked away.

Evelyn watched her daughter walk toward the house. When Sally disappeared into the home, Evelyn turned toward the road. In the distance, she saw the stranger in white walking up the street toward her.

He's coming for me.

Evelyn moaned. She had hoped to postpone his coming until she could prepare, but now her time was up. She turned and ran into the house.

She found Sally in the kitchen opening the window over the sink.

"He's here." Evelyn's voice wavered with despair.

"The firemen are here?" Sally moved to the next window. "I wonder who called them. The fire wasn't that bad."

Evelyn wrung her hands. "He's going to steal our souls. We have to go. We have to go now!"

Sally ignored her mother.

Evelyn sobbed. "Oh, Lord. Where art thou?"

Smoke alarms continued to blare.

"Mom, take a towel and wave it around to clear the smoke. Let's see if we can get those detectors to stop screaming."

Evelyn turned and watched as the stranger in white entered her house. She yelped and ran to Sally. She wrapped her arms around her daughter's waist. She cried into Sally's blouse.

"Mom, I can't—"

Evelyn looked up and stared into her daughter's face. She could see that Sally was looking at the stranger.

She turned and stood as a blockade between her daughter and the man in white. She stood with her arms out and spread her feet apart. "You can't have her."

The stranger said nothing.

"Mister, who are you? Why are you here? If you saw the smoke, I can assure you, we have everything under control." Sally tried to move her mother out of the way, but Evelyn wouldn't budge.

"I'm not here because of the smoke." The stranger glanced at the air around him. "Seems to be dissipating, at any rate."

"He's here for us." Evelyn's voice was a hoarse whisper.

"Mom, please. Stand aside. I need to—"

"You can't have my daughter. I won't let you take her." Evelyn pulled the knife from her apron pocket and held it out defensively in front of her. She waved it at the stranger, attempting to look threatening.

The man laughed.

"Mom, where did that come from? Give that to me."

"You can't hurt me with that," the stranger said.

Tears streamed down Evelyn's cheeks. "Our Father, who art in heaven, hollowed be thy name—"

"Your prayers are useless. If you sensed my arrival, old woman, you must have sensed that, too."

"I did." Evelyn wiped at her eyes with her empty hand. She cast a devilish smile at the man. "But I can still beat you."

The man tilted his head, curious. "What do you mean?"

Evelyn spun around and jammed the small paring knife into Sally's neck. She twisted the blade, and pulled it out again. Blood jetted from the wound, covering Evelyn's face. She laughed and blood filled her mouth.

Sally dropped to the floor, dead.

Evelyn turned and glared at the stranger. "You can't have us."

The stranger frowned. "For all that, you still haven't won the day."

"No?" Evelyn smiled and moved toward her own neck with the blade.

The stranger stepped forward and slapped the knife out of her hand before she had the chance to use it. Evelyn stared dumbly as the knife soared toward the kitchen sink. When she turned back to face the man, he brought a hand up and touched her ear. The siren rang out, drowning out even the wail of the smoke detectors.

Evelyn's expression grew blank. Her gray eyes turned to a soft amber. She looked down at her daughter's corpse.

The stranger's voice broke through the singing echo in her ear. "Let's go. And bring the dead girl with you."

Evelyn obeyed, and draped the corpse over her shoulder.

Chapter Twelve: Sarah

"Joshy, stop fidgeting and stand still." Sarah struggled to fix her son's tie. The seven-year-old groaned and twitched. When she finished, she held him out at arm's length and inspected her work. "Good enough."

"I don't want to go." Josh kicked his feet at the floor and pouted.

"Too bad for you. They are our neighbors, and we have to show them respect."

"Their grandparents died." Josh's sister poked her head in the room to divulge this bit of information.

"That's enough, Dakota." Sarah tapped Josh on the behind as he scurried off.

Barry came out of the bathroom, dressed for the calling, and hugged his wife. "They don't get it."

She sighed and leaned into his shoulder. "It's so disturbing. They were murdered a mere five hundred yards from our doorstep. What if the killer had come to our house instead of theirs?" She shuddered in his arms.

"They didn't."

She looked up, and peered deeply into his eyes. "You think there was more than one?"

He shrugged. "Maybe." He led her to the bed, and they sat down next to one another. "I'm just using the most ambiguous pronoun I can. I don't want to assume it was a man, or a woman. Could have been either, could have been both. We just don't know."

"They were crushed. Had to be a man." Sarah cringed.

"They were old, fragile. It could have been accidental."

Sarah huffed, and stood. "Holden had his throat crushed. That's no accident. And I'm not being sexist, but to me that's something only a man could do."

Barry stood and took his wife by the hand. He swung it back and forth like a schoolboy. "We are okay. Focus on that. We need to be strong for the Sanfords. Emma and Sam need us. They lost their grandparents. We can't think about what might have happened. We need to show them we are here for them."

She nodded.

Sarah glanced at the digital clock on the bedside table. "They'll be here in a few minutes. I should go wait for them." She turned to leave the room, but stopped and looked back at Barry. "Do you think we should have offered to host this gathering somewhere else? I mean, their grandparents' bodies were found right next door."

Barry sat down to pull on a pair of socks. "It's too late to worry about that now. Besides, they said it was fine."

She nodded. He was right. She turned and exited the room.

The guests started arriving minutes after Sarah entered the living room. She greeted them as they entered, and directed them to the living room. Hors d'oeuvres were laid out on a table in the dining room.

When Emma and Sam arrived, she hugged them each in turn. "I'm so sorry for your loss."

They thanked her for her kindness.

She led them into the living room, where they mingled with the other guests, and were away from the front window. They would not be able to see their grandparents' house from in there.

The Sanford elders had an abundance of friends, and it was good that her house was big enough to accommodate all of them. Still, Sarah couldn't shake the feeling that it had been a mistake to have the gathering there. *We should have rented the American Legion banquet hall.*

Sarah stared out the front window. She studied the little, one-story house with the yellow police tape blocking the door. She didn't know if it was a blessing that Brody had chosen this time to run back to his old life, but she was glad he wasn't there at the moment. After this mess was sorted out, she would have to start all over again with him. She wouldn't worry about that now.

She wondered if she should worry about him at all.

Realizing people might see her staring at the empty Sanford house, Sarah stepped away from the window, and joined the crowd. She commenced with the usual pleasantries, offering condolences, and accepting those offered to her.

"Such a shame, what happened to them," Mrs. Martin said as she studied Emma from across the room. The woman turned and spotted Mrs. Martin staring at her, obviously talking about her. Emma waved, and Mrs. Martin waved back. "Such a shame."

"Yes," Sarah said. "A shame."

Sarah looked for an escape route. She would have welcomed a drunk or high Brody coming in at that moment, anything to pull her away from this woman.

She nodded with everything Mrs. Martin said. When she could take no more, she forced an exit.

"Yes, this is all very fascinating, but I must be moving on." She gripped the woman's hand and shook it. "So nice getting to chat. Perhaps we can meet up again before long." *But not too soon, I hope.*

"Yeah, sure. We—"

Sarah scurried away, snickering at the confused expression on Mrs. Martin's face. She sought out Barry, and located him in the kitchen.

"What were we thinking?"

"Huh?" Barry pulled the can of soda away from his lips.

"There's too many people here. I can't handle it. And with Brody going AWOL on me... How is he going to explain this to his parole officer? He'll go to jail this time for sure."

"He'll turn up."

Sarah rolled her eyes at her husband's optimism. When she scanned the room, she giggled at the sight of Josh getting mauled by the gnarled hands of old Mrs. Brubaker. She loved pinching his cheeks with those bony fingers of hers. She always left marks, but she was harmless.

Sarah's attention was drawn to hearty laughter coming from the dining room. She looked over at Mr. Humphreys holding his signature Jack and Coke, laughing too loudly, with a face much too red to be healthy, standing near Tom Yeager; and she prayed he wouldn't have a stroke until after the gathering ended.

She should save Tom from an afternoon of feigning interest in stories that were anything but interesting, but chose not to, fearing she would be pulled into the trap. Tom would have to fend for himself.

A headache began to form behind her eyes. Just another unwanted guest to add to the rest. She closed her eyes and pinched her nose, but the trick she had learned in college wasn't working.

She glanced at the clock, which seemed to be running backward. She blew a lock of auburn hair from her face and made another round through the crowd. Mercifully, no one stopped her. She nodded politely and shook hands. She placed a comforting hand on Emma's back, and the grieving woman offered her a tired, sad smile.

"How are you holding up, Emma?"

Emma's full lips quivered. "It's hard, you know? It's just so senseless. Who would do such a thing? Why?"

Sarah hugged her. "Don't torture yourself with such questions. There are no answers. Even if they found the bastards who did this, they may never say why. There might not even *be* a *why* that makes any sense. Do what you can to get through this, and let me know if there is anything I can do to make things a little easier for you."

"Thank you."

"How is Sam? I know how much he depended on your grandparents. He has to be taking this pretty rough."

"He's holding up. There are times when he wanders around like a lost puppy, but he's a trooper. I pitch in with his needs when I can."

"Did he find a job yet?"

Emma shook her head. "Not yet. But he's still looking."

Sarah smiled at Emma. *I'm sure he's not trying very hard if you're willing to support him.* She felt sorry for Emma. The woman was a hard worker, with a husband and a baby, and now she had this new dead weight.

She looked up and saw Sam staring dumbly at the wall. She felt bad for him, too. It was just as much his grandparents' fault as his for the state of his life. A thirty-year-old should not depend solely on his grandparents for his well-being.

When the wall lit up with flashing red and blue lights, Sarah rushed to the window. Two police cruisers had pulled up in front of her house. Her house . . . not the murder scene across the street. Her heart pounded in her chest as the thought that something had happened to Brody passed through her mind. *They found him dead of an overdose.*

Sarah rushed to the door to meet the police as they approached. Two cops climbed the front porch steps as two cops stayed back by the police cruisers. Another thought came to her. *They're looking for him. He's gotten himself into some kind of trouble.* Her headache spread to the entirety of her head.

"Good afternoon, Ma'am," the handsome male cop said.

The female officer stood a pace behind him, looking around.

She isn't fooling anyone. She's scoping the place out. She expects trouble.

The young man in uniform continued. "Is this the residence for one Brody Sutter?"

Sarah stepped forward, aware that a crowd had gathered around her. "He's my brother, and yes, he's staying here with me."

"Could we speak with him?"

"He's not home at the moment. What's this about?"

"We would like you to tell us where we could find him, please."

"I'm not sure. What is the issue? Is he in trouble?"

The female officer stepped forward. "He's wanted for questioning at the moment, Ma'am. We really just need his whereabouts so we may talk to him."

Sarah's hand rose to her lips, and she could see that it was shaking. She quickly dropped it to her side. "Tell me what you believe he's done."

"We aren't saying he has done anything, Ma'am."

"Stop calling me Ma'am, goddamn it." It came out harsher than she had intended. She took a breath. "I just need to know what it is you want to question him about."

"We're not at liberty to say—" The male officer stopped abruptly when his female counterpart cut him off.

"Ms…"

"Mrs.," Sarah said. "Mrs. Sarah Richfield."

"Sarah, if I may be so bold?" The officer waited for her nod of approval before continuing. "Quite frankly, your brother's DNA was found at the murder scene across the street. We need him to come in and answer some questions."

At the mention of her grandparents' murder, Emma stepped forward. "What are you saying? Did Brody have something to do with my grandparents' murder?" Emma was screaming now, aggressively throwing herself into the conversation.

The female officer placed her hand on the butt of her gun, and held out a hand to stop the woman from coming any closer. "Who would you be, Ma'am?"

Emma ignored the police officers and turned to face Sarah now. "Sarah, did Brody kill my Nana and Papa?"

"No!" Sarah was suddenly overwhelmed, and struggled not to slip into hysterical laughter. This was all insane. "No, he had nothing . . ." She shivered. It was all so surreal. People were looking at her. She stepped back. The police tried to push into the house, but Barry was there to prevent them.

"We'd like to come in and look around if you don't mind," the male officer said.

"Actually, we do mind." Barry blocked the police from entering.

"We will be back with a warrant."

"That's fine. Come back when you have it. But for now, this conversation is over."

Blood rushed to Sarah's head until she thought she would pass out. She was dimly aware of the police cars leaving. She heard Emma's voice screaming at her that her brother better not have killed her grandparents.

Emma and Sam stormed out of the house. The guests quickly followed until the only car left in the driveway was their own minivan.

The house was so abruptly empty that her ears had begun to ring in the silence. She snapped her head around when Barry spoke.

"Honey, they're all gone. It's over."

Sarah tried to stand, but her legs wouldn't hold her weight. She dropped back into the chair.

"Is it over?" Tears filled her eyes. *Where is he? Damn it, where is Brody? What has he done?*

"I'm sorry, honey," Barry said. "It's not."

"How did this night go so wrong? How could the police say those things? Brody had something to do with the murders? It's not possible."

"They seem to think they have evidence he was in the house."

"He would have no reason for going over there. No reason to do what the police say he did."

She stared at Barry, waiting for him to explain all this, but he just stood there with a dumb look on his face. She turned away from him, disgusted.

"How could they just come here and bust our gathering up like that? Where do they get off ruining my night?"

"They are the police. They have a job to do. They can't not do it because we had a few cars in our driveway."

Sarah turned back to him. Her look of disgust turned to hatred. "Is it their job to make my life hell? Is it their job to come here with outrageous accusations about my brother and embarrass me? Is that their job?"

Each mention of the word *job* held more disdain in her voice than the previous instance.

The police returned as promised with a warrant. Sarah had calmed down by then, and didn't make a scene as they turned her house upside down. She stood against the wall and held her kids at her side as Barry followed the police through the house. She felt the fear radiating off her children like heat.

By the end of the search, the female officer who had come earlier that night approached Sarah.

"We'll be leaving now. If Brody happens to come back here, please encourage him to turn himself in."

Sarah sent the kids off with Barry to another room. When she was alone with the officer, she let her guard down.

"Please tell me what you found. What is it you think Brody did?" Sarah thought if any officer would talk, this one would.

The officer sighed. She glanced around. They were alone.

"We found a knife at the scene. The couple fought back. Blood recovered at the scene belonged to your brother. Now this information is going to be released to the public, and we'll try to keep your brother's name out of the papers until he is located and has an opportunity to explain his role in this, but I can't make any promises. We are hoping he will come forward before the information is released. We need your help. If you hear from him, please do what you can to get him to contact us."

Tears streamed down Sarah's cheeks. Her anger melted away. She nodded to the officer. "Thank you. I'll do what I can."

When the police were gone, Sarah found Barry in Josh's room, cleaning up the mess the police had left behind.

Josh and Dakota huddled together on the bed, wrapped in each other's arms like waifs from a Charles Dickens tale. Sarah helped Barry straighten the room. When they were finished, they moved to Dakota's room, then to their room last. They decided not to touch Brody's room until they located him. Sarah was afraid of what she might find in there. *What if I see something incriminating that the police didn't realize was important?* She knew it was silly to think the police wouldn't be so thorough to take away anything that might have been evidence, but still she couldn't face going into that room. Not right now, anyway.

The children followed their parents from room to room, and when the house was at least semi-recovered, the family settled down on the sofa to rest. They were sitting there still, asleep, when Brody returned.

Sarah was the first to wake. She heard the front door close, and she snapped awake, thinking Barry had gone outside. She looked over at Barry as he sat sleeping on the end of the sofa, with Josh leaning against him. Josh, too, was still asleep; as was Dakota. She lay cuddled up against Josh. At once the sight filled her with both joy and dread. She felt joy at seeing her children—who are normally at each other's throats—in such peaceful repose; and she felt dread because . . . who, then, was at the door? Sarah stood and turned toward the front doorway.

She stared at Brody, who stared back at her. After the initial shock of seeing him, it dawned on her that Brody was not alone. She turned toward the blonde standing next to him.

"Where have you been?" Sarah's voice croaked, whether from sleep or fear, she could not say. When

Brody didn't respond, she continued. "Who is this?" The blonde standing to her brother's right did not look altogether . . . healthy, to say the least. She looked like she was dying, in fact.

Brody turned and looked at the blonde standing next to him, as if seeing her for the first time.

"Oh," he said at last. "This is Jennifer."

Sarah stepped toward her brother. "She has to go."

The blonde laughed. Her eyes were wide and wild.

Sarah stopped her approach, suddenly leery of the woman.

"The police were here," Sarah said, turning back to Brody. "They think you killed the couple next door."

Brody stopped looking at Jennifer and turned toward Sarah once again. He tilted his head and studied her as if she were an insect under a glass.

Sarah swallowed hard. "Did . . . did you kill them?"

His simple answer stopped Sarah's heart for a single beat. "Yes," he said. "I did."

Silent tears streamed down Sarah's cheeks. She heard a whimper from behind her, and she turned. Dakota and Josh were sitting up now, and turned to look back at their mother and their uncle . . . and the mysterious blond woman.

Barry stood and joined Sarah.

"Brody, buddy," Barry said. "We have to call the police. You have to turn yourself in. It's the right thing to do."

"No, it isn't." Brody approached Barry and Sarah in a few swift steps. Jennifer giggled behind him.

Barry stepped in front of Sarah and balled his hand into a fist. "I'm warning you, Brode. Stay back."

As Brody came within a few inches of them, Barry swung his fist. Brody caught the fist and held it. He squeezed the fist until Barry moaned and dropped to his knees. Dakota screamed.

"Brody, stop!" Sarah's sharp retort silenced the giggling girl, and ended Dakota's scream.

Brody dropped Barry's fist, and the kneeling man pulled the injured hand to his chest. Sarah helped Barry to his feet, and inspected his hand for injuries.

"It's not broken, is it?"

Barry shook his head. "I don't think so."

So quickly that even Brody didn't see it coming, Sarah slapped her brother across the face. His smirk vanished, as did the twinkle of amusement in his eyes. He placed a hand to the cheek Sarah had slapped.

"That was uncalled for." His hand fell away from his face.

"I want you out of here. I don't care if you go to the police, or if you spend the rest of your life on the run, but I want you out of my house and don't ever come back." She turned to Jennifer. "And take your crack whore with you."

Jennifer giggled again.

"Sarah, my dear, sweet sister. I'll be going, but I'll be taking all of you with me. We're all going away." Brody looked down at his feet.

Sarah looked down as well. His shoes were covered in swamp muck. A glance at Jennifer's feet told Sarah that this woman, too, had been strolling through muddy terrain.

Brody looked up at his sister again. "As for the neighbors, well, you see, they couldn't hear the call. They were not gifted with the sound, so they had to be eliminated. You, my dear, dear family, will be allowed to join us."

As Brody reached out toward Sarah's face, Barry grabbed him by the throat. It was too late. Brody touched her ear, and she heard the sound. It filled her head, and as it all became clear to her, she touched Barry's ear. A tingle ran up her arm as the sound was transferred to him. As he heard the siren call, his hands fell away from Brody's neck.

Brody rubbed at his neck, then twisted it roughly to the side until it cracked. He smiled. "That's better."

Brody turned to the children on the sofa. Barry turned to face the kids as well. When Sarah turned to face her children, Dakota began to scream again.

Chapter Thirteen: Krista

As Krista and Trevor approached the boathouse, Krista took his hand in hers. He gave her a sideways, wary glance. "A united front, right?"

He shrugged and nodded.

With her free hand, she waved at the couple on the deck of the boat. Tessa smiled broadly, and returned an exuberant wave back at them.

They boarded the yacht, and each hugged Tessa in turn. Trevor shook Gavin's hand.

"No Demy to join us today?" Tessa asked, her disappointment showing heavily on her face.

"No," Trevor said. "Today we have grownup talk to do so we left him with a friend."

"Oh," said Gavin. "Does that mean you've made a decision about the will?"

"We have." Krista touched Trevor's arm, a gesture that clearly stated *let me do the talking*. "May we have a seat?"

"Of course." Tessa stepped aside. "Follow me." She led them down to the living room section of the boat. Krista and Trevor took a seat on the sofa as Tessa sat down in the plush chair, and Gavin took his seat in the recliner.

Krista glanced around. She felt strangely out of place, and stomach acid roiled inside her like a turbulent sea. She closed her eyes and tried to calm herself down with a few deep breaths.

When she looked back at the others in the room, she saw that all eyes were on her. She smiled. "We should get on with it then, I guess."

Tessa clasped her hands together in her lap. "Yes, please. Don't keep us in suspense. Tell us what you've decided."

Krista took a deep breath and spoke. "Trevor and I have decided to accept your offer."

Tessa and Gavin spoke the same words in unison. "Oh, good."

She continued. "We also have a request of you." She spoke tentatively at first, but soon her words were coming out in one long, flowing stream. "We don't want you to think us too forward, but we are here to ask you for a loan, and were hoping you would be willing to give us a loan."

Krista locked eyes with Tessa, but the older woman's stony eyes were impossible to read. She swallowed hard and continued.

"If you go into business with us, we could hold weekly meetings to keep you abreast of how things are going." She had a million other things to say, but for the life of her, she couldn't remember any of it. She sat back.

Tessa leaned forward. "You have me intrigued. What kind of business are we talking about here?"

Gavin stayed quiet.

Krista looked over at Trevor, then turned back to Tessa. "It's a country-style bed and breakfast. It could be up and running before the next Wizard of Oz Fest. But it's not like it would only be profitable in the summer. It's on one hundred acres of farmland. We could grow pumpkins in the fall, and host a haunted hayride for Halloween. In spring we could have strawberry picking. The possibilities are endless."

Tessa sat back. "Sounds like a marvelous venture. What got you going on this path?"

Krista looked at Trevor again, but like a good silent partner, he stayed quiet. She turned to Tessa. "We have a friend named Ethan. It's his business, and Trevor's been helping him. It was my idea to ask you for the loan to help him get his business off the ground."

Tessa frowned. "A bed and breakfast, you say? Who is this Friend named Ethan?"

"He's a neighbor."

Trevor spoke up for the first time since the conversation started. "He's a close friend of mine."

Krista glanced over at him. *He thinks I'm losing the edge on this discussion, and he might be right.*

There was a moment of silence during which the two couples stared at each other, or looked about the room. Tessa broke the still, uncomfortable air with a question.

"Speaking for the both Gavin and I, we wouldn't be able to make a decision on this loan until we met your…friend."

A prickle of unease passed through Krista's chest. She tried to smile but it felt too forced, so she let it ease off her face. "We can set up a meeting."

Tessa sat back. "Are you and Trevor working out your differences then?"

Krista frowned. "You know we were having difficulties? How? I don't recall us discussing it with you."

Tessa blushed a deep crimson and dropped her chin. When she spoke, her voice was hoarse. "I may have overheard your, uh . . . discussion the last time you were here."

Overheard? More like eavesdropped, no doubt. Krista smiled. "Well, rest assured, anything that was said then does not impact anything we are doing now. Our marriage couldn't be stronger. This endeavor has only strengthened our bonds." She reached over and squeezed Trevor's hand. She stared into his dazed face and tried to wordlessly coax him to play along.

After a moment, he seemed to understand. "Right." Trevor turned to Tessa. "Stronger than ever."

Krista turned away from him, praying his performance had been accepted as the truth.

Tessa seemed eager to believe. She giggled, and her eyes grew wet. "I'm so happy to hear that."

It wasn't a complete lie. Krista had grown excited by the prospect of working on this business with Trevor, and she had begun to toy with the idea of allowing him to move back in.

Her focus returned to the present when she sensed the people around her were moving. She stood and followed Trevor. She wondered what he thought of her comments about their relationship. Did he want her back? She had thought kicking him out would make her feel better, but it didn't feel good at all. Demy missed him. *She* missed him. And when he lived there with her, she had known how he felt about her. *Does he still love me? He told me he did, the night after the affair, but I refused to believe him, or even care how he felt. But now...*

"Since we're all adults here, I think some grown-up refreshments are in order." Tessa pulled a red wine from the cabinet and gave it to Gavin. He used a corkscrew to open the bottle and passed it back to her.

She took four rounded wineglasses from the cupboard and poured equal amounts in each glass. When everyone was holding a glass, Tessa proposed a toast. "To a future of possibilities."

The four glasses clinked together as the others cheered their agreement.

The group split up. Gavin and Trevor went topside to talk, and Tessa and Krista returned to the living room. Krista sipped at her wine, but was quiet. She glanced over at Tessa when the woman spoke.

"I'm happy to hear that you and Trevor are working out your issues. It was a blow when I heard you were separating. It's such a relief to hear that everything is going to be okay between the two of you."

Krista smiled and blushed at Tessa, warming to the older woman's desire to see her happy.

"This Ethan you speak of," Tessa said. Krista turned to look at the woman. Tessa continued. "He's not the stranger you've seen following you?"

Krista gulped. That man. Why did she have to bring him up?

"No." Her reply was a whisper. "It's not him."

Tessa patted Krista's hand. "Surely Trevor saw him this time, didn't he?"

Krista almost spilled her wine. "What? When?"

Tessa rocked forward. "The man in white was here, watching you leave the last time you were visited. Didn't you see him?"

"No, I never knew." Krista placed her wineglass on the table with a shaky hand. "You saw him? The man I've been seeing?"

"Yes. I recognized him because he was exactly like you described him. He was on the adjacent dock watching you drive off. I thought for sure you saw him, too."

"No." Krista's voice sounded foreign, even to her own ears. She was lost in thought.

Tessa giggled. "Sounds as if you might have a secret admirer."

"No, not an admirer."

Tessa continued talking, but Krista heard none of it. She dismissed herself to go to the bathroom, and spent most of the time in the bathroom with the water running, willing herself not to throw up. Finally, she exited the bathroom and announced she wasn't feeling well. She and Trevor said their goodbyes, and they headed home.

Krista pulled into the driveway, but neither she nor Trevor climbed out of the car right away. She waited for Trevor to say something. When he stayed quiet and unmoving, she decided to start. Her fear of the stranger loosened her bravery. When she thought about it, if she was being honest with herself, deep down, she had already forgiven him for his transgression. All that was left in her was a desire to punish. Even that notion had lost its thrill. She had begun to think that if she didn't invite him to move back in, she might lose him forever. Besides, kicking him out as a punishment had backfired on her. He seemed happy at Ethan's place.

"What do you think of us moving back in together?"

Trevor turned to look at her through the car's dim interior. He opened his mouth to speak, but only a garbled, stuttering squawk issued from his open maw. He blinked in the darkness.

"You don't like that idea?" Krista forced the quiver to stay out of her voice.

"It's not that. It's just so…sudden. What brought this on?"

"I guess I was just…" She didn't want to bring up the stranger again. But it wasn't just that. "I guess it's still a little too soon."

"How about this." Trevor turned to face her in the gloom. "After Ethan's meeting with the Whittlespoons, and he gets the money he needs to complete the B & B we can revisit this discussion."

"You're right." Krista reached quickly for the door handle, suddenly eager to be out of the car, but Trevor stopped her.

"Ultimately, that's what I want. You know that, right? It's just that I want to make sure it's what you want, too."

"Exactly, right. Yes." Krista pushed the door open and stepped into the cool night air.

Krista sprinted across the street to Ethan's front door. She heard Trevor clamoring behind her to keep up. He used his housekey to let himself in and held the door open for Krista to follow him in. Ethan had been sitting in the blue chair and stood as they entered. He stepped forward and smiled when he saw Krista.

"Hi," he said to her.

Trevor said, "I invited her in. I hope you don't mind."

"Not at all." Ethan stepped closer. "Please, come on in. I made coffee. Would you like some?"

Krista followed Trevor into the living room. "No, but thank you."

Trevor motioned for Ethan to return to his seat.

"We have something to talk over with you, my new friend," Trevor said.

Ethan paused, confusion clearly etched on his face, then returned to his seat.

Trevor and Krista sat next to each other on the sofa.

Trevor began. "You told me you are about one hundred thousand dollars shy of making your dream a reality. Is that the case?"

Ethan swallowed hard. "Y-yes. I plan to make a circuit of the banks once my money runs out. I—"

Krista took over the conversation. "What if we told you we found an investor who might give you the money you need? We could turn this farm house of yours into a real tourist destination. You would need to take on some additional stakeholders, but that would just include Trevor and me, and an older couple we know."

Ethan appeared to have trouble swallowing. When his voice returned to him, he spoke, soft and raspy. "You . . . you want to go into business with me?"

"Yes. Trevor convinced me your B and B idea could be a very lucrative investment. I have some ideas on how to expand it. If you're okay with that."

Ethan seemed not to understand. "You found investors that will provide the money needed to complete the project?"

"Yes." Trevor's voice was exuberant.

Ethan looked around the room. When he turned back toward the pair on the sofa, his eyes were wet. "Thank you so much."

Krista reached out and touched Ethan's hand. "They want to meet with you. Is that something you'd be willing to do?"

"Yes, definitely. I can't thank you enough for this." Ethan stood, and Trevor stood with him.

Ethan pulled Trevor into a bear hug. He broke off and pulled Krista to her feet, including her in the hug. After a moment, Ethan sat back down.

Krista and Trevor sat back down as well.

"Who is this couple?" Ethan asked. "And when can I meet them?"

"They're the Whittlespoons. And now that we know you're on board, we can set up a time for you to meet them."

Ethan rubbed his hands together as if warming them by a fire. "This is great. Scary, but great."

Krista's smile faltered. "Scary? Why is it scary?"

"I guess, it's just that I'm being given everything I've ever wanted, and I'm not used to things coming to me so easily. I've always had to fight for everything. I'm afraid it'll all be yanked away as quickly as it has dropped in my lap. That, and I've never had partners before. That's going to be interesting . . . in a good way. I won't have to depend on myself for everything anymore."

"No, you won't," Trevor said. "You have us to help you."

"And we'll do anything in our power to not let this deal fall apart on you," Krista said. "Believe it. Now, if you gentlemen will excuse me, there is a little boy who may have exhausted our exceedingly kind neighbor."

Ethan laughed, and stood to walk her to the front door. As she hit the sidewalk, she turned to see Ethan and Trevor watching her cross the street. She waved, and they waved back. She entered Mrs. Kennedy's yard and knocked on the door leading to her screened-in porch. The woman and the boy met her at the door and opened it for her to enter.

Krista looked around. She was surrounded by greenery, making her feel as though she were in a private jungle. There was a wet warmth on the porch that was, at once, comforting and disturbing. She couldn't quite put her finger on how it felt to be enclosed by all those plants. It might have been her imagination, but she thought she was having trouble breathing.

How can she stand being surrounded by all this vegetation?

When Mrs. Kennedy spoke, Krista turned to her. "What? I'm sorry, I didn't hear you."

Mrs. Kennedy repeated herself. "Did you and Trevor get your task accomplished? If you don't mind my asking."

"Oh, no, it's fine. And I think we did."

Mrs. Kennedy clapped her hands together. "I'm glad to hear it."

Krista looked down at Demy. His lids were at half mast, and he yawned. He leaned against her arm, his pinked cheeks warm against her cool skin. "I should take this one home. He's run you ragged, no doubt. I'm tired, but you must be exhausted as well."

"Oh, I'm fine. He was a delight, as usual. But you look beat. You should really get home and get right into bed."

Krista laughed. She did feel tired. "I doubt that will happen. I still have so much to do tonight."

"Oh, pish. It'll keep till tomorrow. Get some sleep."

She couldn't tell the woman she wasn't able to sleep much these days. Vivid and terrifying dreams woke her up, and kept her from falling back to sleep. She was lucky if she got an hour and a half of truly restful sleep a night. She took Demy by the hand. "Thank you for watching him. How much do I owe you?"

Mrs. Kennedy waved an impatient hand at her. "You don't owe me anything. Except to keep bringing him around. He's a cure for loneliness."

"Are you sure I can't give you something?" Krista reached for her purse.

Mrs. Kennedy grabbed her by the arm and pulled her to the door. "Get your buns out of here now, and stop trying to give me money. I won't take it."

Krista hugged her, kissed her cheek, and took Demy's little hand again. She led him out to the street and into their house. She used her hands to tell him to get ready for bed.

She performed her nightly ritual of walking the house and ensuring all windows and doors were locked, then she, too, slipped into a pair of sweats and one of Trevor's old T-shirts. She poured herself a glass of red wine and sat down on the sofa. She fell asleep before she took a single sip of the wine.

Chapter Fourteen: Loretta

She leaned over and sniffed the aroma steaming from the pot of soup. Nothing was too good for her little girl. Loretta used a ladle to fill Hannah's bowl. She placed the bowl on the bed tray and turned her attention to the sandwich. She cut the bread in a triangle and removed the crust, just as Hannah preferred. She poured Hannah's drink of choice, Ocean Spray cranberry juice, into a glass and set that on the tray as well.

Loretta glanced over her shoulder. Satisfied no one was around, she returned to the task of fixing Hannah's lunch. She reached into the cupboard over the sink and took out a small container that looked like a plastic shot glass with a lid. She added a few drops of the liquid—her special little ingredient—to Hannah's drink, then returned the tiny cup to its hiding spot in the cupboard.

She stirred Hannah's drink. She placed the spoon in the sink and lifted the tray. She carried the food into the dining room and up the stairs to Hannah's room. She tapped lightly on the door and pushed it open.

Hannah was a tiny series of lumps under pink My Little Pony bedsheets. The girl turned to face her mother. Damp, oily hair clung to her face. The child's complexion was pale and waxy. She smiled and struggled to sit up.

"I have your lunch, honey." Loretta spoke softly as she carried the tray to the bed and placed it in front of

Hannah, so its legs surrounded the frail girl's hips. She tucked the napkin into the neck of the girl's nightgown and sat down on the bed next to the tray. Too weak to lift the spoon, Loretta helped her, using the napkin to dab at the drip of broth running down the girl's chin. She fed Hannah a few more spoonsful of the soup, but then the girl turned away from the food.

"That's all I get? What's the matter? Don't you have an appetite?" Loretta tried to get the child to take more soup.

"My tummy hurts." Hannah tried to sit back.

Loretta pulled her forward. "At least have some juice. You're dehydrated."

"I don't want to, Mommy."

"I insist. Drink." Loretta lifted the glass to the girl's lips.

The girl only seemed to pretend to take a drink, which was not good enough for Loretta.

"I'm not going to stop trying until you take a drink, young lady."

Hannah moaned and guided the glass Loretta held back to her lips. This time Loretta could see the neck muscles moving as the girl drank. A satisfied smile stretched across Loretta's face as she placed the glass on the tray.

Hannah closed her eyes and let her head drift back down to the pillow. She lay there only a few seconds before her head came back up and she twisted to the side. Loretta pulled the bucket up from the floor to Hannah's face just in time to catch the vomitus as it spilled over the young girl's lips.

When the girl seemed confident that she was finished, she sat back, weak from the exertion. Loretta placed the bucket back on the floor.

"I need you to drink again."

Hannah moaned. "I can't."

"You must. Do it for mommy." Loretta lifted the glass to Hannah's lips.

"Yours is too sweet. I like how Daddy makes it. It stays down when he gets me a drink."

"It's not the drink that's making you sick, it's the failing kidneys and the dialysis doing that. My juice is the same as Daddy's. Now drink."

Hannah took a drink without further complaint. This time it stayed down.

"It burns my tummy."

"It's just the acid in your stomach interacting with the nutrition you're putting in there. It's a normal part of digestion, and nothing to be alarmed about." Loretta removed the tray from the bed and set it on the floor. "How can I make my baby feel better? Want me to rub your belly?"

"No, I just want to sleep."

"Okay, Lovey. I'll let you sleep. You need your rest. We have to meet with the press tomorrow. They are going to interview you for the news. You're an anomaly because the doctors can't pinpoint why you're so sick. This is very important, sweetheart. We have to tell the world that healthcare is not very good. We have to speak for all the people who are sick, and can't speak for themselves. You are very special."

"I know, Mommy. I'll do what you want."

Loretta ran her hand over her daughter's damp hair. "Such a sweet, brave girl you are."

She stayed with Hannah until the girl's soft, steady breathing indicated she was asleep. Loretta leaned over and kissed the girl's clammy forehead, then stood. She bent over and picked up the tray.

She whispered. "I'll leave the juice here for you in case you get thirsty when you wake up."

Loretta placed the drink on the stand next to the girl's bed and took the tray with the half-eaten lunch downstairs. As she passed the living room, she saw her husband sitting in the dark room. She stopped and stared at his silhouette.

"I didn't hear you come in, Clifford. Have you been home long?"

The man stayed seated in the chair, unmoving.

"I asked you a question. Are you going to answer me?"

The head turned, but it was so dark, she couldn't be sure if he looked at her or away from her. Still, he did not speak. She watched the shadow for another moment, and opened her mouth to say something more, but thought better of it and remained quiet.

It's Clifford – of course it is – has to be him. Who else would it be? But it doesn't feel like him. It feels like there is a stranger sitting there.

She shivered.

She concluded she had to speak. She needed to confirm—if only to calm her racing heart—that it was her husband sitting there in her darkened family room.

"You should go up and say hello to your daughter. She misses you."

A soft, melodic voice responded. "I'll go in just a minute. I have a few questions for you first."

The voice belonged to her husband—she had no doubt about that. It was his voice, but it sounded different. It was not his normal whiny, nasal tone. The voice was husky, sexy. If he had sounded like this more often, she would gladly have had sex with him. She would have sex with him now, if he asked her to.

That new voice spoke again. "Where is it?"

Loretta was hypnotized by the sound of her husband's voice. After a moment, it came to her that he had asked a question.

"Where is what?" She could see him more clearly now, though he hadn't moved. She supposed her eyes were becoming accustomed to the darkness around him. She wasn't sure, but he looked *stronger* somehow, more . . . masculine. That sexual attraction was back.

"Where is the poison?"

She swallowed hard and tried to speak. To regain her composure, she laid the tray in her hands on the nearby sideboard. Still, her voice croaked when she finally responded, "What poison?"

"The poison you've been giving our daughter."

Loretta's blood turned to ice in her veins, and she stumbled back as if struck. Her voice was soft, broken. "What are you talking about?"

Clifford's voice became louder and more forceful. "You've been poisoning our daughter." He stood and walked toward her.

Loretta's knees nearly buckled under her. She stayed standing, however she took a step back.

"It's a matter of time before the tests come back."

"Wh-What tests?"

He was nearly on her now. "The doctors have suspected for some time that you've been giving

Hannah something to make her sick. They suspect antifreeze because of the kidney damage. They asked me for permission to test her for ethylene glycol poisoning. I begged them to do the test immediately."

"You . . . you can't do that without my permission. I am her caregiver. Only I can authorize such tests."

"They couldn't very well ask you, now. Could they?"

She no longer backed away from him. She would sue that hospital for defamation of character, and her new and improved husband would go down with them. Who did they think they were? She had politicians in her pocket. She had the press on her side. She was Mother of the Year in the eyes of the public. She was so devoted to her sickly daughter that she made other parents cry with shame. She was the most powerful mother on the planet.

"If they go public with those test results, I'll sue."

Clifford stepped into the light of the hallway, and Loretta almost gasped. His face was covered in purple veins, and his skin was pale. His eyes . . . his eyes looked different as well. They were sharp and amber.

He laughed. It was a mocking sound. She didn't know if he was laughing at her threat, or at her reaction to his appearance. It could have been both, perhaps. She placed a hand to her chest, and took another involuntary step away from him. She backed into the wall and a framed picture fell to the floor. The protective glass shattered.

She glanced down. If he came any closer, she would pick up a shard and cut him. She waited for him to move again.

She shivered as his knowing smile told her he knew what she was thinking. He brought his hands up with a quickness that caused her to scream.

She wouldn't be able to move fast enough to retrieve a piece of glass before he had her, so instead, she moved down the wall away from him.

When he turned and headed up the stairs, she ran to the kitchen. She retrieved the small cup of special ingredient and poured it down the sink. She rinsed the cup and tossed it in the trash. They could accuse her of anything they wished, but there wouldn't be any proof.

Tests. How dare they run tests on her daughter without her permission? She'll own that hospital when she's done with them.

And as for that husband of hers . . .

Loretta glanced around the kitchen and saw nothing left that could incriminate her. On the off chance they did find something in those tests, she would put the blame on *him*.

Oh, my poor baby! She would cry to the press. *What had he been giving her, and for how long? Oh, the horror of it all!* She smiled as her clever plan came together. All she had left to deal with was that husband of hers.

She turned to the kitchen door, intent on going to Clifford and confronting him with the evidence against him, but froze when she saw a small figure standing there. She took a calming breath.

"Hannah, Sweetness, why are you out of bed?"

Hannah stood in the doorway, still wearing her nightgown, her head down, but her eyes were turned up. She was glaring at Loretta with an intense, piercing stare. Her hands were behind her back. Loretta took a step toward her daughter.

"Let me help you back to—"

Hannah's hands came out from behind her back. She was holding something out to her mother. A glass full of purple liquid.

Loretta's mouth went dry, and she felt something slip inside her. She thought maybe it was her sanity slipping away. She nearly laughed, suddenly giddy with the absurdity of it all.

Hannah held the glass of juice out to her mother.

"Honey, let me have that. I'll pour you a fresh glass." Loretta reached out to take the glass, but stopped when the girl pulled it back.

"Drink it." Hannah held out the glass again.

Loretta swallowed hard. There was an obstruction in her throat making it difficult to breathe. She placed a hand to her throat. Tears welled in her eyes.

"Hannah, Sweetheart, I—"

"Drink it, *Mother*." Hannah spoke the last word with a venomous lilt.

Loretta's lips quivered. "No, I can't."

Hannah rushed forward, and splashed the liquid in her mother's face. Loretta screamed, throwing her hands up for protection but it was too late. She tasted the juice on her lips. So sweet. Sickly sweet, one might say. She had heard antifreeze tasted sweet, and she now understood that it was true.

She sputtered and coughed, trying to expel the liquid that had gotten into her mouth. Hannah came at her. The girl smashed the glass on the sink, and jammed a broken shard into her mother's throat. Loretta froze. She reached up, and as she pulled the piece of glass away from her throat, a stream of red splashed across the floor. She looked down and saw a river of blood pouring from somewhere under her chin. She reached up and touched her neck. When her hand came away, it looked as though she was wearing a red glove. Blood dripped down her arm.

Loretta dropped to her knees. Her hands went to the floor to steady her, but they slipped in the blood. So much blood. Where did all that blood come from? *From me,* she realized with a sort of odd fascination. Loretta dropped to one side, staring up at her daughter.

Loretta tried to speak, but her lips only smacked together, and more blood sprayed from her mouth.

Through a blur of tears, Loretta watched Clifford enter the room. He stood behind Hannah, and they both stared down at her. They were watching her die. She blinked away the tears. She had trouble opening her eyes. She could no longer see them, but she could hear them.

Clifford said, "Go out to the shed, Hannah, and bring Daddy the hacksaw."

Please, God. Loretta prayed as she heard the patter of her daughter's bare feet skipping away. *Please let me die before they start cutting.*

Chapter Fifteen: Trevor

The car turned down Lakeport Road, and Trevor accelerated to 55 mph. He turned and glanced at Krista sitting in the passenger seat. She stared out the front windshield without looking in his direction. He glanced into the rearview mirror and saw Ethan and Demy tickling each other. Ethan caught him looking and offered a knowing smile, before returning to the game.

He's so calm back there, and my stomach is in knots. How is he not nervous? Trevor returned his attention back to the road in front of him. It was certainly understandable. This meeting with the Whittlespoons was the most important moment in his life, no doubt. If the couple backed out of this arrangement, Ethan's dream of starting a bed and breakfast was probably over.

Krista turned and glanced at the backseat passengers. From the corner of his eye, Trevor caught her sign, *don't play rough.*

"We're not, Mom." Ethan pretended to look abashed, and Demy laughed.

He's been so much happier since Ethan came into our lives. Trevor watched his son through the rearview mirror. *We're becoming quite the extended family.*

After a couple of minutes of silence, the car reached the end of Lakeport Road and turned right onto Route 31. He took the third left onto Horan Private Road. At the end of the road he pulled into a small, gravel-filled lot and parked the car. Demy wasted no time climbing out of the car and running to the dock where the boat was moored. The Whittlespoons were there to meet him, and he leapt into Tessa's embrace. She hugged him tightly.

The adults took their time walking to the boat. They were greeted by the older couple. Demy found a bucket of Legos and busied himself by building a scale model of the Whittlespoons' boat.

The five adults entered the living room.

"This is Ethan." Trevor turned his body in Ethan's Direction.

Ethan smiled and waved.

"Nice to meet you, Ethan," Gavin said.

Tessa said nothing and offered only the faintest smile.

The group sat, nervously looking around until Tessa broke the silence. "So, we're here to discuss an investment opportunity. Does someone want to tell me about it?"

Ethan took a deep breath. "I guess that would be me." He breathed out, heavily. "I bought the property on the corner of Quarry and Cottons roads."

Tessa shook her head. "The old Garlock farm? I know the place. Last I knew it was severely rundown and dangerous. Asbestos and all. Did you plan to tear it down and rebuild?"

"No, I want to restore it. I've already begun the process of removing the asbestos, and I'm having the state inspectors out next week to verify that I got it all."

"Who did you hire to do the work?"

"I did it myself. Well, Trevor helped."

Tessa glanced at Trevor, and he nodded.

"Impressive. No one can accuse you of taking the easy way."

"Thank you."

"So, let's say you restore the place, and everything is on course. What can we expect by way of profits?"

"Well." Ethan cleared his throat. "At first, probably not much. But with the business plan Krista and Trevor laid out, the possibilities are endless. My five-year goal is to bring in about five hundred thousand a year."

Gavin whistled.

Tessa glanced at her husband but said nothing. She turned back to Ethan.

"I don't ask about profits for me or my husband, you understand. We plan to leave everything we have to Demy, and his parents, of course. We want to know they will be taken care of for the future. We have no children of our own, and ever since meeting that boy, he has become our whole lives."

"And we appreciate that," Krista said.

Tessa gave her a loving smile and patted her hand. She turned to Ethan, and her smile faded. "Tell me what brought you to this decision, Ethan. Why do you want to open a B&B?" There was a toughness in Tessa's voice that caused the young man to swallow hard.

Ethan began. "I'm an interior designer by trade, and..."

"Interior decorator? That's an odd profession for a man, isn't it?"

Ethan blinked. "I…I don't think so." He cleared his throat and continued. "Anyway, it was something my sister and I dreamed of doing."

"Your sister." Tessa made a steeple of her fingers. "She died, right?"

Ethan nodded. He spoke slowly. "Yes."

"I'm sorry for your loss."

"Thank you." Ethan started again with his story. "I guess my interest in opening a bed and breakfast stems from my sister's love of being a hostess. I want to do this in her memory."

Tessa shifted in her seat. "You're married, Ethan?"

Ethan appeared to be in thought, and the sudden change of subject caused his head to tilt, inquisitively. "No, I…"

"Then it's safe to assume you have no children?"

Ethan stared at the woman. "No, I do not."

Tessa leaned back in her seat, as if contemplating what she had just heard. "Forgive my old-fashioned ways. I'm trying to wrap my head around this notion that a man with no wife, and no children wants to open a family business."

Ethan rocked forward, tipped his head up as if collecting his thoughts, and started talking again. "I have no love interests, and no prospects of starting a family any time soon, but let me assure you, my desire to open a family business is not diminished by my lack of family."

"Are you a homosexual, Ethan?"

Krista let out a squeaky gasp. Trevor looked at her, and then back at Ethan.

Ethan's eyes glazed over.

"Tess." Gavin's voice came out in a tight, soft whisper.

Tessa glanced over at her husband. She shrugged. "What? These are things I need to know if we're going to lend this man money, right?"

"This isn't something you should be concerned with." Gavin reached out to touch his wife's hand.

"No, you're wrong. If we're going to lend the money, I need to know if this man is a pervert, or that his intentions are pure."

Gavin opened his mouth to protect, but Ethan spoke first.

"Yes," he said. Every head in the room turned to face him. "I am gay, but I am not a pervert. I have nothing but the purest intentions for this endeavor. And I fail to see how any of this is pertinent to whether or not you loan me money."

Trevor watched as Ethan's face turned red at the sound of Tessa's mocking laughter.

When Tessa stopped laughing, her eyes narrowed and she focused in on Ethan. "It's pertinent because I say it is. I say who gets my money. I've gone over everything you've said, and I understand the game plan as you've laid it out to us, but I'm afraid we're going to pass on this investment. I'm sorry, but it's a no."

A stunned silence filled the room. Krista's mouth dropped. Trevor's stomach clenched, as if he'd been punched. Even Gavin looked shocked. Ethan sat, silent and calm.

When the initial shock of Tessa's reply wore off, he cleared his throat and said, "You're saying no because I'm gay?"

"Not at all." Tessa fussed at the pant leg of her track suit, as if wiping crumbs away. She folded her hands in her lap again, calmly, before continuing. "The way I see it, no matter what you do to generate revenue, the prospects of a bed and breakfast showing any kind of profit is negligible. I'm looking out for Demy's future here, and this plan is doomed to fail. In fact, I can only see it losing money in the long run. So, no. This is not an investment I'm willing to make."

Ethan listened to what she had to say, or perhaps only seemed to be listening. He nodded along with her, almost as if he agreed. When she finished talking, he did not respond right away.

Trevor saw the faraway look in Ethan's eyes. *He's giving up? Just like that?* Trevor glanced at Krista, but she seemed to be at a loss for words as well. *Please, Ethan.* Trevor's heart pounded painfully against his ribcage. *Please offer a counter claim that will make her see this is a good business venture.*

Ethan sat quietly for a long time.

When the uncomfortable silence became more than anyone could bear, Ethan stood abruptly. Tessa flinched. Ethan turned and walked out of the room. Trevor listened to his friend's footfalls as Ethan climbed the stairs and disembarked the boat. The sound of his shoes on wood ended as Ethan reached the end of the dock.

Demy had glanced up from his play when Ethan stormed by. The boy looked back at the adults, as if in search of an answer of why his friend had left the boat so quickly. He went to his mother, and she hugged him.

As he pulled away from his mother, his hands began working. *What's wrong with Ethan? Why is he mad?*

"He's not mad, Honey." Her hands worked to sign the words, even as she was saying them. "He's just a little sad at the moment. He'll be okay."

Demy didn't believe her. He sprinted away from her. She hurriedly stomped her foot, using the vibration to get his attention; but he wouldn't have it. Demy rushed up the stairs. Tessa made a gasping sound, and Trevor rushed after him.

Demy was already standing beside Ethan as Trevor approached. Ethan sat at the end of the dock, staring into empty space. He wasn't even aware of the pair of them standing next to him. Demy reached out and touched Ethan's shoulder. The man looked at the boy with eyes that were seeing him, but were still far away. Trevor stepped closer.

Demy's fist formed the letter "A" and he circled his chest in a clockwise motion. Ethan grabbed the boy's hand and stopped him.

He spoke so Demy could read his lips. "You have no reason to be sorry." He pulled the boy into an embrace.

"But I do." As Trevor spoke, Ethan glanced at him over demy's shoulder.

Ethan held Demy's face tenderly in the crook of his shoulder so the boy couldn't see them talking. He shook his head. "No, you don't. You tried to get me the money I needed, and I appreciate that more than you'll ever know."

Trevor had to choke down a sob. He had to stay strong for Demy's sake. But the truth was that Ethan's dream had become his dream, and Ethan's pain, though surely stronger than Trevor could ever fathom, was a shared pain.

Ethan's voice cracked. "Take Dem back downstairs, please."

Demy pulled away from Ethan's shoulder as the man released his gentle hold on the boy's head.

"Go back downstairs with your dad." Ethan spoke and signed.

Demy's head bowed in defeat, and he walked over to his dad. He leaned his head against Trevor's leg, and Trevor placed a hand on his son's shoulder, holding him in place. He looked at Ethan. "I'll be right back and we'll talk some more."

Trevor guided Demy down the steps and back into the bowels of the yacht. His head still spun with the confusion of it all. This was supposed to be a formality. Everything he had read in the couple told him they would accept this deal. They did everything right. They had it all planned out. Now, as he comforted his son, he wanted to scream. He wanted to break something.

He wanted to cry.

As he and Demy entered the living room, Tessa was clutching her throat and shaking her head. "I never wanted to upset the boy. I never wanted that."

Trevor felt weak. "No, I'm sure you never wanted that." He turned to Krista. "I think we should go."

Krista stood.

Tessa took her hand. "We'll want you to come back again. You know that, right? We'll want you to visit again."

Krista pulled her hand free and touched Tessa gently on the cheek. "Yeah, we know."

"It's nothing against you folks. You understand that, right? It's just…that man rubs me the wrong way.

It's nothing I can explain, but I just don't trust him. I don't think you should trust him, either."

Krista and Trevor said nothing, but turned and headed up the steps. Tessa stayed seated, but Gavin followed them up.

Once out of his wife's earshot, the old man said, "I don't know why she said what she did. Honestly, I thought we had agreed to fund the project. The amount you and your friend requested isn't a problem for us."

Krista took Gavin's face in her hands. "We know. It's a mystery to all of us." She kissed the corner of his mouth. "It's all good."

Krista dropped her hands away from his face and walked away.

Trevor tried to smile at the old man, but his face refused to obey. He gave a short wave. Gavin's mouth moved but only guttural utterings came out. He waved with a shaking hand.

Trevor doubted they would ever see the old couple again.

As the family headed back to the car, something seemed horribly wrong. Trevor didn't realize what it was until he looked into the car.

Ethan was gone.

Trevor had assumed that when he didn't see his friend sitting at the end of the dock, he would find Ethan at the car. But the car was empty. Trevor glanced around. The man was nowhere to be seen.

"Where did he go?" Trevor felt stupid for asking, but he was honestly perplexed. He turned to Krista. "You don't think he's trying to walk home, do you?"

Krista opened her mouth to speak, but before any words came out, something caught her eye, and she turned toward the windshield. "What's that?" She pointed to the piece of paper under the wiper on the driver's side.

Trevor pulled the slip of paper out from under the wiper and looked at it. It was a Burger King receipt with writing on the back. Trevor held it under the lamplight so he could read it.

Trevor, Krista

Thank you, both of you, so much for your help. I'm sorry this endeavor didn't work out for us, and maybe there will be another chance to make it happen, but for now I think have to be alone for a while. I hope to see you back at the house when I return.

Love,

Ethan

Trevor handed the note to Krista. He watched her expression turn from confusion, to worry, to downright panic. When she looked at him, there were tears in her eyes.

"Should we be worried?"

Trevor had no reply. He climbed into the driver's seat as Krista sat down in the passenger's side. Trevor glanced into the rearview mirror at his son. Demy was turned around, looking out the back window.

The boy turned and scooted up close to his parents. *Where is Ethan? We can't leave without Ethan.*

Krista answered him with words. "We don't have a choice. He already left. We'll see him back home."

"Doh." *No.* Demy shook his head angrily to emphasize his protest of the situation.

Krista tried to stop his protest by putting a hand on top of his silky head, and when he looked at her, she used aggressive hand gestures to make her point. *Sit down and buckle your seatbelt.*

Demy huffed, slammed into the seat, and buckled up.

Trevor drove out to Route 31 but stopped at the stop sign. He wasn't sure which way to go. "What should I do?"

Krista shrugged. "I guess we have to go home the way we came, and hope we run into him along the way."

Trevor turned right onto 31 and then left on Lakeport Road. They drove along slowly, with the lights on high. He thought he saw someone on the road at one point, but when he reached where the person would have been, he saw nothing. He drove the rest of the way home without ever seeing Ethan.

Trevor pulled into Ethan's driveway. Krista and Demy waited in the car until Trevor checked inside the house. They had hoped that maybe Ethan had called Uber for a ride home.

Trevor came out of the house. He shook his head. Empty.

Krista climbed out of the car and helped Demy out. Trevor followed them across the road and into their home.

"Will you stay until Demy falls asleep?"

"Yes, of course."

Trevor made coffee as Krista readied a bath for Demy. The boy seemed to forget about the adults' problems as he splashed and played in the tub. Trevor watched his son play, and couldn't help but laugh, and he realized he was the happiest he'd felt all day. He'd been a bundle of nerves before the meeting, and a basket case after leaving the Whittlespoons. There had been a point when Trevor didn't think he would ever feel joy again, but now, as he watched his son playing in the tub, he remembered what was truly important.

Krista came and stood next to Trevor in the doorway. She put an arm around his waist. He glanced at her, incredulous. But she didn't look at him. Ignoring his stares, she laughed and pointed at Demy. Trevor's eyes returned to watching his son, and they both laughed.

A half hour later, Trevor carried two cups of coffee into the living room. After getting Demy dressed for bed, and tucking him in, Krista returned to the living room as well, and sat down next to Trevor.

"You can stay the night if you want," she said after taking a sip of coffee.

Trevor held his cup to his mouth but didn't drink. He said nothing.

She placed her cup on the table and said, "It's up to you."

"Thank you." Trevor set his cup down.

Krista leaned against him and placed a hand on his chest. "I can't help but feel bad for Ethan. I had so wished this would be the silver lining to a dreary year. I wanted this to happen for all of us."

She tipped her head up, and Trevor saw tears in her eyes. He wiped them away.

She kissed him then. He kissed her back, passionately. She pushed herself into him, and he took her in his arms. He lifted her as he stood, still kissing.

He carried her to the bedroom, and they made love for the first time in months.

Chapter Sixteen: Ethan

As Trevor and Demy disappeared downstairs, Ethan walked over to the car. He tried the door, and it opened. He unlocked the glove compartment and found a pen under the crumpled-up paper bag. Something in the bag felt heavy, but he hadn't wanted to be nosy, so he didn't look. He used a scrap of paper from off the floor and wrote his note. After leaving the note on the windshield, Ethan sprinted down the road to the main thoroughfare, wanting to put as much distance between himself and the group as he could. He walked along Route 31 until he reached the road that led to home. He had nowhere else to go. *I'll retrieve my car from home, and then go anywhere . . . I just need to be away.*

The chance of the family catching up to him was greater if he took the obvious route home, and more than anything he did not want to face his only friends in his current state, but he didn't know any other way back.

As he passed a trailer park on his left, he looked back to make sure no one was coming. He continued down the road.

What he knew about Lakeport Road was that it was extremely long, and there were a lot of woods on both sides of the road. As the road crept closer to town, the fields near the road became more populated. But that would not be for a long time. First, he would have to walk the road for several miles of nothing but wooded emptiness. Only tall grass and trees.

Ethan tried to clear his thoughts of the last half hour, but his mind kept returning to the devastating and confounding meeting. *Why did I get my hopes up like that?* He didn't blame Trevor and Krista. He could tell they were just as shocked, and disappointed, as he was when that *bitch* told them all no. Who did she think she was to say his dream was garbage? He felt more determined than ever to make his dream a reality. He wouldn't accept her money now if she begged him to take it.

He was even more determined now than ever to do whatever it took to show that woman just how wrong she was. His bed and breakfast would make a profit. He would not only make a profit, but he would replace the inheritance Tessa offered with money from the business. He could look after Demy, and his parents. The won't need the Whittlespoon money at all.

Ethan stopped walking. He looked back, but still he saw nothing behind him. As he began walking again, he turned his thinking around. He could not begrudge Trevor and Krista if they chose to better their son's future with the older couple's money.

Where can I get the money I need? He had hit all the banks in town. The only bank willing to lend him any money would only grant a pittance of the amount he truly needed.

Sure, he could probably make do with the amount they offered, but there was no way he could make a profit without the full amount needed to actualize his dream for the B&B. If he settled for what he could get, that woman would be right. His dream would fizzle and die before it ever had the chance to shine.

The most the banks would loan him was ten thousand. He could probably raise, if he was lucky, another fifty thousand through crowdfunding, but that still left him at least forty thousand short of his goal.

He could sell his house.

His house was worth seventy thousand, but then he would be homeless. He could live in the bed and breakfast, he supposed. That was one way to get around this funding problem. But this still left a lot to chance. If he couldn't sell his house for what it was worth, or if the crowdfunding plan didn't pan out, he would be back in the same boat he was in now.

Boat.

Ethan thought of the yacht he had just run away from. That boat was worth easily as much as he had been asking for. The couple could clearly afford to pass along the amount Ethan needed if they wanted to. Even if the bed and breakfast lost money, which he didn't believe was the case, but even if it did, they wouldn't be rendered penniless.

Maddening!

Ethan heard a car and dipped into the tall grass, but the make of the car was not Trevor's. He brushed off his pants and stepped back onto the road. He resumed his darkening hike down Lakeport Road.

The sun had finally dipped below the horizon, and the dim light of day turned into the inky blackness of night. Ethan could still see the road, and where the gravel shoulder met the high grass, but not much else. In the distance, the tree line where the forest began was a black, jagged maw against the lighter gray of the sky.

The road had no streetlamps, and the only light came from the stars and moon, bright and high overhead.

When Ethan saw headlights approaching from behind, he ducked back into the tall grass. As the approaching car reached his location, it slowed. Ethan stared up from the grass at Trevor as his car slowed, searching the road for a walker. Trevor wasn't looking into the grass.

If he looks this way, he'll see me for sure. Ethan didn't move a muscle. He didn't want the grass around him to rustle. He held his breath.

After the car crawled out of his line of sight, Ethan dared to stand. He stayed in the grass as the red taillights faded to black in the distance. He returned to the road and continued walking after the red glow finally winked out.

He walked on.

I feel bad about ditching them like this, but I can't take their piteous looks, or their sympathy anymore. I don't want to be an object causing others' distress. I just want to be alone for a while. They will have to be patient and wait for me to come back to them.

And he would come back.

He understood they shared his desire to build the B&B, but in the end, it had always been his dream, not theirs. It was his failure, not theirs. He hoped they would understand that as time went on, especially if the B&B dream died. He still wanted to be friends with them. He needed Demy in his life. That boy was like having his sister back. He even thought he could teach Demy the twin speak that he and his sister had shared. It was basically American Sign Language in shorthand.

He was excited by the prospect of teaching it to him, passing on that special creation of his and Ellen's.

Ethan quickened his pace, and was watchful of any cars coming from ahead. It had just dawned on him that Trevor might circle around and come back looking for him. Trevor was nothing if not persistent. He had picked up on the work at the Garlock farm right away. If there was a task Trevor had trouble with, he kept at it until he got it right. Ethan admired that trait in his new friend. Working together helped Ethan get to know Trevor. The man was smart, and funny. He even shared with Ethan much of what had caused the breakup with Krista. Though he couldn't condone Trevor's poor choice, he could better understand what had led to the affair.

Ethan knew something else from listening to Trevor's story. The man was still in love with his wife. That fact was obvious. Trevor never spoke ill of Krista. Even as he described her as a cold and unfeeling lover, he kept his tone soothing, and his descriptions of her neutral. He was simply describing a pattern of behavior that led to the transgression with another woman. When Ethan suggested maybe Krista had been a controlling bitch, Trevor refused to agree. Ethan backed off then. He had no right to make that kind of judgment about someone he didn't know, and trusted Trevor's honest assessment. What Ethan took from Trevor's story was that he, Trevor, was solely to blame for his actions. Krista wasn't perfect, but she wasn't the cause of the affair. She was the victim, and Trevor stressed this fact. Ethan respected Trevor's stance and said nothing more against Krista. As it would turn out, after Ethan met Krista, he completely understood a simple truth: people are more complex than any snap judgments made about them.

Krista's ideas about making money with the B&B were inspiring. He had been listening to her with growing excitement, and he felt the dream moving closer to reality. Maybe that led to the overwhelming force of the devastating blow when the old woman turned them down. Still, that wasn't a mark against Krista. Even now, as he walked and breathed in the crisp night air, his head cleared. His animosity toward Tessa was lightening. He had been too quick to judge her, too. She was merely looking out for Krista, Trevor, and Demy, and he couldn't fault her for that. Even if she was wrong.

Ethan took a deep breath, forcing the tension that had been building up in his muscles to relax.

But now, as he released his anger into the night, a new problem developed. His feet hurt.

His nicest shoes were not made for long walks, and he hadn't had the foresight to predict this impulsive excursion that ensued when he received the bad news. He should have worn his sneakers.

It had been half an hour since Trevor had driven by. Ethan now felt confident the car would not be returning, which was a pity. His feet hurt so bad he might have given up his self-imposed exile, swallowed what was left of his pride, and accepted a ride home.

He concentrated on the road in front of him, trying to put his aching feet out of his mind, when he spotted something . . . strange. There was a group of people in the road up ahead. At first, he thought Trevor had returned, and had parked the car so he could walk back. But that was obviously not the case. There were too many people. At least five. Possibly more, if there were people behind the shadowed forms that he could see. He also couldn't be sure if they were walking toward or away from him. It didn't take him long to realize they were coming toward him.

Ethan felt the first stirrings of panic sting his guts as the group came within a few hundred yards of him. He slowed his pace, trying not to look directly at them. *Ignore them, and they will walk right on by.*

He could no longer fool himself into believing a confrontation was avoidable when the group stopped.

They are waiting for me.

The group spread themselves along the road like a barricade, making it impossible for Ethan to walk by without passing through them. He stopped and faced them when he was just a few feet away.

"I don't want any trouble." Ethan tried to think of anything he could use as a weapon. "I've had a really bad day, and I just want to go by."

"By all means, please pass." The man wearing the white suit stepped aside and invited Ethan to go through.

Ethan stepped forward, but stopped. His heart thudded in his chest. A memory surfaced that caused his knees to go weak.

This is the man Krista had been afraid of when he had first met her. She had come over that first day of Trevor's stay, and she was terrified that a stranger in a white suit was following her.

His foot took an involuntary step backward. He stumbled, almost fell.

The old man laughed. "There is really no need for you to be afraid."

"Are you a cult?" Ethan didn't know what else to say. He was just hoping to distract them. Each second counted now. If they weren't actively hurting him, maybe he could somehow escape.

"A cult?" the white-haired old man said. He glanced at the woman to his left, and then the man at his right. "No, we're not a cult."

Ethan watched as two children, a boy and a girl, stepped out from behind the old man. They smiled up at him. There was something about the children that scared him more than the old man did. He took another step back.

He bumped into something and spun around. There were more of them standing behind him now. He tried to work his way out of their reach, but they encircled him. He put his hands out in front of him. *There's no way out of this.*

Ethan saw all the events of the day playing out in his head. He understood how pointless his anger had been. He thought of Demy. He would never get to see the boy again. He thought of his sister. He could see her now, as if she stood in front of him. She was smiling. He loved how her eyes shined with an inner light when she smiled.

He realized he was smiling now. Tears formed in his eyes.

"I love you, Ellen." His voice was barely a whisper.

The old man stood directly in front of him now. He seemed to be studying Ethan, as he would a bug under a glass.

"Your life is not over. We will accept you." The old man reached out toward Ethan's face.

Ethan's hand came up, catching the man by the wrist. He pleaded with the man using only his eyes.

The old man sighed. He did not force his hand away, but after a moment, Ethan lost the urge to fight, and he let go of the old man's arm.

The old man's hand continued its trajectory, and he touched Ethan's ear. The siren sound burned through Ethan's brain. His hands flew up, and he pressed his palms to his temples. He squeezed his eyes shut. When the intensity of the sound settled to a dull buzz, Ethan's hands dropped to his sides. He opened his eyes and looked at the man.

"Now what?" Ethan asked.

"Now you are with us."

Ethan glanced around with new eyes. He could see clearly in the dark now. He counted twenty people with the old man. Three of them were children. The girl in the nightgown smiled up at him and nodded a greeting. He nodded back.

The group turned and started walking into the tall grass. They disappeared, one by one, into the woods around the road.

Ethan followed them into the trees.

Chapter Seventeen: Jennifer

The white building sat on the main street in town, at a place where the road curved from a southerly direction, and headed west out of town. A creek ran along the southern border of the funeral home property. The location was idyllic, with a finely manicured lawn, and a copse of trees the other side of the creek as a lovely backdrop for the mourners, more suitable, in fact, for a picnic.

Jennifer led the group of five past the low-cut shrubs, and the stately pillars, and up the steps to the heavy, wooden front door of the Taub Family Funeral Home. As they entered, a bell chimed faintly from within. They waited just inside the door as a man in an elegant black suit glided quietly down the carpeted hallway and stood in front of the guests. A tight, respectful smile garnished his face; no doubt, an expression that had taken years of practice to master.

"Welcome. May I help you? Do you have a loved one you would like us to take care of for you?"

Jennifer glanced down the hall at the Victorian reproduction furniture. Opulent chairs waited against the wall to receive mourners when the stress of grief became too much to bear. Gleamingly polished wooden tables held brimming boxes of tissues. *This is a place of tears and sadness, and this guy is all business.*

"Actually, no," she said. "We're here to make a withdrawal."

She laughed when the man's practiced smile faltered.

"Excuse me?"

Jennifer walked past him and started opening doors. "Do you have any fresh cadavers here?"

The man rushed to keep up with her. "I'm sorry, but we are not a storage facility. We only keep the ones who are planned for display. May I ask what your intentions are?"

Jennifer stopped opening doors and looked at the man. "We're robbing you."

The mortician stiffened. "I'm sorry?"

Jennifer went to the man and straightened his black tie, then teasingly caressed his chest. "You look like a helpful fella. Where do you keep the dead bodies? We need a few. Preferably, without embalming fluid. But we won't be fussy. We'll take whatever you have. We'll also want any that come in from now on. Oh, and you can trust me on this—"

Jennifer pulled him closer and whispered huskily into his ear. "Business will be booming."

She released him, and he stepped back, tugging on the bottom of his suit jacket.

When he had regained his composure, he moved to block her from going any farther into the building.

"Are there any mourners here now?" she asked.

The man looked over his shoulder, then turned to face her again. "There is no one here at the moment. I'm going to have to ask you to leave. This is not a place for trouble. It's a place of peace and rest for our dearly departed. I must ask you to leave now."

"Rest?" Jennifer huffed, incredulous. "Have you been paying attention to what's been happening around here? There is no rest. There is only the dead, or us. But believe me, no one will be getting any rest, not anymore. What happened to the others that were sent here?"

Jennifer held up her finger, and the man looked at it. He stared at the delicate tip, which glowed with a strange blue spark. It looked like she had captured static electricity on the end of her finger. She brought it slowly up and reached toward his ear. He did not move.

She touched his ear with the spark, and he screamed, clapping his hand over his ear. When the screaming stopped, the man dropped his hand and stared at Jennifer. He smiled.

"Do you understand now? Do you *capeesh*?"

"I do. And I will let you know if any fresh 'meat' comes through our doors." The mortician turned and walked away.

Jennifer watched him go. "I don't recall dismissing anyone, but okay." She turned and motioned for her followers to vacate the premises. This mission was complete. On to the next.

Brody and his sister walked beside Jennifer as they moved down the street, past several shops, most of which had somehow incorporated the Wizard of Oz into their names, such as the All Things Oz Museum. When they reached the park in the center of town, Jennifer sent Brody and Sarah down Arch Street. Jeffrey, with Dan, took Race street. Jennifer took the houses on Russell Street.

Jennifer turned the knob on the front door, and it opened with a mere touch. *Oh, the perils of living in a safe town. People are so trusting, they leave their doors wide open.* She stepped inside. The couple sat on the sofa in the living room, watching television. The man looked up at her, shock etched across his face. He had a lazy right eye that caused Jennifer to giggle. The man stood and rushed her, but she knocked him down easily. He crashed into the coffee table, breaking one of its legs. He scrambled to stand, bringing the broken leg with him as a weapon.

The woman began to scream.

"Stop that." Jennifer pointed at the woman, and she stopped.

The man rushed forward with the wooden table leg over his head. Jennifer slapped the weapon from his hand, and in the same fluid motion, touched him on the ear. The man stopped attacking and stood at attention.

"Who else is in the house?" Jennifer asked the man.

"My daughter is upstairs."

The woman on the couch lost her fearful expression and turned to her husband. "Why are you talking to this crazy person, Bill? Knock her out."

The man, Bill, turned to his wife. "Shut up, Wendy."

Jennifer ignored the woman and spoke to the man. "I don't have the spark in me right now. It's all used up for tonight. Take care of her—" Jennifer pointed to the woman. "And your daughter."

Bill nodded.

"It's your choice. Kill them or turn them. Either way, though, they come back with us."

"Got it."

As Jennifer exited the house, she heard the woman scream, a resounding thump, and then silence.

Jennifer turned and looked to her right. Her old house was nearby, and she followed the urge to go back there. She started up Russell Street, walked the hill to Lake Street, and turned right. She walked down to Boyd Avenue and turned right again. Her house was the fourth on the left. She stepped up to the front door. It was still slightly ajar, just as she had left it weeks ago. She entered.

"Hello?" She felt foolish calling out in her own home, like some bimbo in a horror movie. "But I'm the monster in this movie." She laughed.

Her laughter halted when Lanelle stepped around the corner from the laundry room.

"My God, Jennifer. Where have you been?"

Jennifer glared at her former friend. She seethed. "What are you doing here?" She glanced to the right. "Where are my kids?"

"I . . . they're safe."

"Did you bring them back with you?"

"N-no, they're not here." Tears came to Lanelle's eyes. She wiped them away. "Where have you been? I've been calling. You just disappeared. I've been so worried. I went to the FBI, but they wouldn't help me. I've been talking to a reporter here in town. He says there have been a lot of disappearances lately. And a lot of people have been killed."

"You shouldn't talk to strangers."

Lanelle's voice was sharp. "This is no time for jokes, Jennifer. Something really awful is happening around here. I thought you might be dead. Why haven't you been answering your phone?"

"I lost it." She had grown bored of the conversation.

"What's happened to you? Why do you look like that?" Lanelle pointed to her face. "Your skin is waxy, and I can see your veins. And what are those *things* on your forehead?"

Jennifer knew there was something growing on her forehead, but this was the first time she gave them any credence. She reached up and touched the two knobby protrusions in her forehead, about two inches above her eyebrows. She dropped her hands, giving Lanelle no explanation of what they were.

Jennifer studied Lanelle. She tried to see her former friend in a way that would make her recall old feelings for the woman. They had been best friends all through grade school, and then through college. When Jennifer met John, and she had had her kids, Lanelle stuck by her. Jennifer had been a single mother, but Lanelle helped raise her kids. Now as she looked at her friend, she realized she could kill her easily, without so much as a single tear shed.

She was still Jennifer, she had all of her own memories, but she was something else now, as well. And it was that something else that controlled her. The Jennifer that would plead for her friend's life no longer had any say in the matter.

Jennifer, or what passed as Jennifer, would have to kill her old friend now. Lanelle could have been given the spark, but Jennifer had no spark to give at the moment. It would not return for several more hours, and she didn't have that long to wait. She had to deal with Lanelle now.

Jennifer took a step toward the other woman. Lanelle stepped back. When Jennifer ran at Lanelle, the woman cried out—an unintelligible, guttural cry—and shoved at Jennifer. The momentum threw both women in separate directions. As Lanelle struggled to stand, Jennifer popped up instantly. She charged at Lanelle and grabbed her by the arms.

Lanelle screamed, and struggled to break free.

"Listen," Jennifer said. "Listen to me. I don't want to kill you, but I can't give you the spark right now. Come with me. We'll find someone who can give it to you. It's not so bad. It doesn't hurt. It's like a terrible case of tinnitus for a minute or so, but it passes. What's left is like this soft droning, like someone is constantly murmuring in your ear."

Jennifer let Lanelle go. The woman rubbed at her arms.

"What? Was I holding you too tight?" Jennifer reached out and snatched one of the other woman's wrists.

Lanelle cried out, and tried to pull away. The pain caused her to moan. "Please, why are you doing this to me?"

Jennifer pulled her through the house to the front door. Lanelle gripped the doorjamb with her free hand, but didn't have the strength to hold on. She stumbled down the steps to the sidewalk, tripping; but Jennifer kept her grip, and didn't allow her to fall. She yanked harder on the other woman, nearly pulling the arm out of its socket. Lanelle screamed. Jennifer didn't relent.

"Stop struggling. The pain will stop once you relent."

"Please." Lanelle continued to beg. Tears streamed down her cheeks. "Please, don't do this."

Jennifer pulled Lanelle into her, and grabbed her in a bear hug, lifting her off the ground. Lanelle squirmed in her grip.

"You're hurting me. You're crushing me." Lanelle leaned into Jennifer, throwing her off balance, and the two women fell to the ground. Lanelle rolled and struggled, pushing against her captor. Finally, Jennifer's hold broke. Lanelle scrambled away. Both woman stood, yards away from each other.

Jennifer took a step toward Lanelle, but Lanelle stepped back, refusing to yield willingly. When Lanelle ran, Jennifer—silent and swift—caught up to her and tripped her.

"Please. Just let me go." Lanelle panted, exhausted, lying prone on the ground.

Jennifer showed no ill effects from the struggle. She paced back and forth, keeping her eyes on the other woman. She seethed, and as the anger rose in her, her eyes burned.

Lanelle stood up and stared at Jennifer. "Your eyes . . . they . . . turned. They're amber."

Jennifer laughed. She stopped pacing and stepped toward Lanelle. The other woman seemed too shocked to move, and Jennifer took advantage of her confusion. She rushed forward and grabbed Lanelle by the shoulders. The terrified woman fought back, and with a scream that sounded like a primal yell, Lanelle broke free, and ran. Jennifer chased her, but the other woman's adrenaline had given her a burst of speed. Jennifer could have caught up to her easily, but she stopped instead, and watched Lanelle run away. Perhaps, there was a little humanity left in her, after all.

"Run," Jennifer said. "Run and hide. Don't come back. If you come back, you'll die. Don't come back."

Jennifer turned around and walked back toward town. She turned and looked over her shoulder, knowing that she could have gone after her. Lanelle's burst of speed had limits, and the woman would eventually slow down. Jennifer could have followed her and caught up to her, but something—maybe a shard of humanity that remained—kept her from going after the woman.

Jennifer caught up to Brody. He stopped and looked at her.

"Where have you been?"

"Never mind that." Jennifer walked toward the rest of the group who were gathering on the road at the end of town. "We have to get back. We've done enough for tonight."

She continued walking, and didn't look back.

Chapter Eighteen: The Reporter

The room was so full of people it looked more like a rave than a police station. It was wall-to-wall bodies, and they were shoving each other, shouting, and shaking their fists at the authorities. The police barely kept control of the situation. Ray leaned against the wall, away from all the others, and watched. He noted a couple near him who were acting calmer than the rest, but still showing clear distress. He stood and walked closer to them. They snagged a police officer as he walked past them, and Ray eavesdropped on their plea.

"Please help us," the man said to the officer. "We have missing people. We need help."

The officer shrugged them off. "Talk to the officer at the window. He will direct you to the proper department."

The woman grabbed the officer's arm. He gave her a stern look, and she let go.

"I'm sorry. It's just that we've already had the runaround. We need your help. Our friend . . . I mean, we had a friend come up missing a few days ago, and then just last night . . . people are disappearing all over town. What's happening? We need answers. We need to find our friend. He might be in danger."

The police officer sighed. His expression turned from stern, to concerned, and then to sympathetic. "Go over to that desk and have a seat. I'll be with you in a moment, and I'll take your statement."

"Thank you so much." The woman's voice cracked with emotion, but she managed to keep her composure.

The couple walked over to the desk the officer had indicated. The cop walked by Ray, giving him that same stern expression he had originally used on the couple, but when Ray didn't stop him, the cop moved on.

Ray moved closer to the mob, listening in on their individual complaints.

"My daughter never came back from her date late night. Her date is missing as well." The man who spoke pushed his way through the crowd to the police officer at the window. "What are you going to do to find my daughter?"

"Nothing." The cop at the window shifted his attention elsewhere.

"Bullshit. What the hell kind of answer is that?"

"I'm sure they just stayed at a motel and got their freak on. Go home and wait for her. One night is not a missing person. Move along."

As the cop's attention diverted to another complainant, the man spat at the floor in front of him and stormed away. Ray thought to go after the man for an interview, but by the time he made it through the sea of people, the man had gone out the door and disappeared.

Ray dipped back inside the station and focused on a new person.

Everyone had the same complaint: their loved one was missing, their neighbor was missing, their friend.

On and on it went. The police were doing very little to appease the multitude.

What else can they do? They are as stumped by the disappearances as everyone else. Ray decided to enter his own voice into the equation. He pulled out his microphone and held it out to a cop.

"Officer." Ray spoke louder to be heard over the din of so many people talking at once. "Officer, what is being done to appease the townspeople? Surely, so many missing persons in one place is highly unusual. Has the FBI been called in yet?"

The rumble of voices in the room died down so everyone could hear the policeman's reply.

The officer scowled at Ray, proving looks could not kill, and he was happy for that one fact.

"We have not deemed this situation worthy of the federal government's involvement at this time."

Someone in the crowd spoke up. "When will you deem it worthy? When there's no one else left to report?"

"Yeah." Another voice in the crowd added to the opposition. "You clearly can't handle this on your own. You need help. Get the government involved."

Another voice said, "We just want our loved ones back. Why aren't you doing anything to help us?"

As the rumble of every voice in the room started back up again, Ray felt a tug on his sleeve. He clicked off his microphone and turned around. He stared at another officer directly behind him.

"Come on, Buddy. Can't you see this is already a very volatile situation? We don't need you here trying to incite a riot." The officer pulled Ray by the arm toward the door.

"Riot? These people need help. I'm trying to make sure you give it to them, and not the runaround that you're passing off as help. I speak for the people. You can't silence us."

"I'm not trying to silence everyone, just you. Now get out of here, troublemaker, before I really get mad."

Ray looked over the cop's shoulder, and saw the couple from earlier leaving the police station. He ignored the police officer, and sprinted for the door. He pushed out the door and squinted at the bright sunshine. He spotted the couple over by their car. He raced to them before they could get away.

"Hi," he said, panting. "I saw you in the police station. I was wondering if you would be willing to talk to me?"

"Why would we want to talk to you?" The man crossed his arms.

"I'm a reporter for the Times. I was wondering if you'll let me interview you."

The woman stepped closer. "The Times? Chicago Sun, or New York?"

"Actually, just the Times. You know? The little paper here in town?"

The woman lowered her head and walked back to the driver's side door. "Why would we want to be interviewed by some rinky-dink local paper? We need national exposure."

"And I can help you get it. You have to start somewhere."

The man uncrossed his arms and opened the passenger door.

"Look, I don't see any national paper trying to interview you. If you have to start somewhere, why not with me?"

The man sat in the bucket seat but didn't close the door. *I have them. Now, to reel them in.*

"Look, just sit down and have coffee with me. Let me hear your story. I've been investigating these disappearances since they started a couple of weeks ago. Whatever is happening here, it's not going away any time soon. In fact, I think it's going to get worse."

When they climbed back out of the car, he knew he had his interview.

-:-:-:-:-

Ray led his guests to a booth at Darlene's Diner, and he ordered coffee for all of them. The couple glanced around nervously as Ray watched them. He cleared his throat. "Why don't we start with introductions. I'm Ray Sullivan."

The woman stopped looking around and faced Ray. "Krista Burnette."

The man nodded at him. "Trevor. Nice to meet you."

"Hello. Same." He shook their hands.

"Do you live here in town?" Krista asked.

He nodded. "No, I'm freelance, and in town only until this story is done. I'm in the motel on the edge of town. But we're not here to talk about me. I want to know what you know, and maybe I can help you with what I know."

Krista leaned forward. "What do you know?"

"We'll get to that. First, I want to hear your story. Do you mind?" Ray showed them the recorder. When neither of his guests objected, he turned it on and placed it on the table. He began. "You seemed upset at the police station. And I didn't get the impression you left there feeling like you had been helped by the police. Is that a true statement?"

"I'd say," Trevor said. "They were next to useless."

"Tell me about your situation."

It was Krista that spoke. "We have a friend out there somewhere that we haven't seen in several days." She sighed, and her shoulders sagged. "Granted, he *is* in a self-imposed exile after he received a bit of bad news, and as a result he took off without telling anyone where he was going. We haven't seen him since."

"I'm sorry, but that doesn't sound like a missing person to me. That sounds like someone who doesn't want to be found."

"We understand that, but still." Trevor heaved and let out a slow, even breath. "He left us a note saying he would contact us soon. I live in his house. He wouldn't just up and disappear. We were expecting him to return later that night or the next day."

"Do you have the note?"

Krista fished through her purse and pulled out the piece of scrap paper. She handed it to Ray. He looked the note over then read it aloud to record what it said. He handed the note back to Krista.

"I'm sorry. It still doesn't scream foul play to me."

"Then how about this? We have friends named Bill and Wendy. They have a young daughter. We made plans to meet with them, but when we got to their house, no one was there."

Ray shrugged.

Trevor leaned forward as he spoke. His words were clear. "Their front door was wide open, their television was still playing, and there was blood on the floor. How do you es-plain that, Lucy?"

Krista popped him on the arm, and he leaned back.

Ray shifted in his seat. "Was it a lot of blood?"

Trevor shrugged. "Not Texas Chainsaw Massacre volume, but there was a bit."

"What did the cops say about that?"

Trevor sat back. "They investigated, but they didn't see any sign of struggle. They determined something happened to cause them to leave in a hurry, but they wouldn't go as far as to say there was any foul play. They told us to wait until the family contacted us again, since they had only been gone overnight."

"Possibly, overnight." Krista's voice told Ray she was mocking what the police had said to them. "Since we have no proof of when they actually disappeared. But it definitely had to be between six p.m. last night, when we made plans to see them, and eight a.m. this morning when we showed up at their door."

The coffee came, and they stopped long enough to fix their cups the way they liked them. Ray sipped his straight away, preferring it black. Krista added sugar and cream to hers, and Trevor just added cream.

As Trevor stirred his coffee, he looked up at Ray. "There's something else you need to understand about Ethan."

"He's the friend who's been missing the longest?"

Trevor nodded. "Yes. Ethan and my son have a very close bond. He wouldn't stay away from us this long without telling us where he is, because he wouldn't want Demy to worry."

"Demy is your son."

Trevor nodded again.

"Okay, I understand that you feel there is something sinister going on. And you know your friends better than I do, so I'm not going to presume to know what the situation is. If you believe your friends may be in trouble, then so do I. But how do we get the rest of the world to believe? That's the million-dollar question."

Krista looked at Trevor, and back at Ray. "You told us you had something to share with us if we talked with you. Now it's your turn."

"You're right. I told you I would share what I have. I'll tell you that your stories, alone, mean very little. But I know that in the past couple of months, murders and disappearances have been rocking this little town. There was a mass disappearance that occurred back in June. An entire field of onion workers vanished in a matter of minutes. The boss left the site and returned fifteen minutes later, and every single worker was gone."

Ray paused briefly, then resumed. "The people who ran the ice cream shop on Lakeport Road—vanished. Suddenly, people's houses were found abandoned, and their owners were nowhere to be seen.

"Then the murders started. There was the old couple on Fyler Road. The main suspect was a guy named Brody. He had a checkered past, but he was nowhere to be seen. The following day, his sister, and his sister's family, all vanished. The police think they all went into hiding, but I don't think so. There was a woman named Linda Reed, presumably murdered by her husband, but he is missing as well.

"Suddenly, there is case after case of people just walking out of their homes, never to be seen again."

Krista placed her cup on the table. "Have you gone to the police with what you know? I mean, sure, all these individual cases can be explained away, but when you put them all together, they must see a pattern, right?"

When Ray didn't answer, Trevor spoke up. "We thought we were crazy when we went to the police after Ethan disappeared—because he went away voluntarily—but I think now we were right to be worried about him. Now that Bill and Wendy have vanished, well, we know for sure something is wrong." He turned to Krista, and she nodded agreement.

Ray went on. "But a list of disappearances isn't where my research ends. I see a distinct pattern in the location of the disappearances." He pulled a map out of his briefcase and spread it out on the table in front of them. Krista and Trevor leaned forward and studied the map of the town.

"It all starts around here." Ray pointed to a cluster of trees on the border of Lakeport Road. "See, here is where the onion field is. The following night, the first individual disappearances started here."

He pointed to the first two houses on Tag Road. "In the following few nights a couple of houses on Chestnut Ridge Road fell prey to the phenomena. Then Dad's Ice Cream was hit. It slowly spread this way, and this way, and then finally toward town last night. My prediction is the disappearances will continue to spread out this way—" He indicated out of town to the east. "And this way." He indicated toward the west.

Krista stifled a cry. She looked up at Ray. "We live here." She pointed to the spot on the map. "How long before it reaches us?"

"I don't know. A few days, maybe? A week? Maybe you should get out of town until this is sorted out."

Krista shook her head. "We can't do that. We have friends, neighbors. We can't leave them to this. We have to warn them, or something. What can we do to stop this?"

"I don't know yet. I plan to do some more investigating tonight. I'll let you know what I find out tomorrow. Where can I meet you?"

Trevor and Krista looked at each other. Trevor turned back to Ray. "We can meet you at the police station tomorrow, say, around nine? We aren't giving up until they agree to investigate this properly."

"Okay then," Ray said. "Go home, lock your doors, and arm yourselves. We won't know how this is happening until it happens to us."

Ray paid the tab, and they walked out of the restaurant together. He walked them to their car, exchanging pleasantries. He watched them drive away. He then headed to his own car, tossed his briefcase onto his passenger seat, and climbed in behind the wheel. He sat for a moment, running the details of the story through his mind. When he could no longer think about the case, he started the car and drove back to his motel room. He entered the room, flicked off the lights, and closed the curtains. He stripped down to his underwear, splashed water on his face in the dingy little bathroom, then dropped face down on the lumpy bed.

He was asleep in seconds.

-:-:-:-:-

Ray woke with a start, sat up and scratched his groin. Squinting into the darkness, he read the digital clock next to the bed: 6:08 pm. *Good, I haven't slept through the night.* He stood and stretched, pulled the curtains open, but closed them again, shunning the light like a vampire. He found a half-full bottle of warm coke and downed it. Belched. He tossed the empty bottle into the corner, and pulled a clean set of clothes out of his suitcase. The Burnettes were on his mind as he regulated the water in the shower. They had been the most forthcoming with the information they knew about the events happening in town, and were the most open to the possibility that something sinister was happening. He planned to keep them in the loop with anything he learned, and hoped they would do the same for him.

After showering and dressing, Ray walked to Darlene's for a bite to eat. He sat in the same booth as he had with the Burnettes.

"Hi again, Mr. Sullivan," the waitress said. "What can I get for you?"

"Patty, I thought we were on a first-name basis here. Call me Ray."

"Ray, of course. I'm sorry. What can I get for you?"

"I'll get the steak and eggs special."

Patty scribbled on her pad, poured him a cup of coffee, and scurried off. He watched her go, smiling. *What a cute little behind she has.*

Not wanting to be *that guy,* Ray averted his gaze before anyone saw him looking. He sorted through his notes instead, and waited for his food. When the plate arrived, he thanked Patty and dug into the food as if he hadn't eaten in days—which was a possibility. He didn't remember when his last full meal had been. For the past few days he had been eating stale candy bars and chips from the vending machine next to his motel room.

Ray pulled a pen out of his briefcase and scribbled notes on the papers he had collected regarding the recent upward arc in the number of disappearances.

—*Where are these people going*?

Then he thought of something else and wrote.

– *When are they going?*

He stopped writing and thought about this one. He wondered if there was a certain time of day . . . or night . . . when the disappearances tended to occur.

"Is it not to your liking?"

Ray looked up, startled out of his thoughts. "Huh?"

Patty pointed at his half-eaten plate of food. "You're downing the coffee, cup after cup, but you've barely touched the meal."

"Oh, Patricia, my dear. The food is top-notch stuff. I'm just so preoccupied, I can't stay focused long enough to finish before it gets cold."

Patty refilled his coffee cup and sat down. "I demand that you put that work aside for now and finish eating. I'm not leaving until you do. Now eat up, or you'll get me fired."

Ray did as he was told, laughing. *She's flirting with me.* The thought made him divert his eyes from her face. *Is she flirting with me?* He crammed food into his mouth. *No, she's just being friendly. She's probably got a—* Ray chanced a quick glance at her hands . . . no ring. *She's probably got a boyfriend.*

When he finished the meal, she stood and took his plate. "Good man." She walked away with the dirty plate. Ray returned to his notes.

He set his pen down, looked up.

I'm going to ask her out. What can it hurt? The worst thing that can happen is she'll say no. I can handle that. Can't I?

He shook his head to clear his thoughts of Patty. There was a time for fraternizing with the waitress, and it was after this story was done. For now, he had to focus on the story.

When he had done what he could with writing down the details, Ray paid his tab and exited the diner. Though there was still light in the sky, the sun had set beyond the horizon in the west. Orange and red hues stained the clouds above. That means it's going to be a nice day tomorrow, wasn't that the saying? If the sky is red at sunset, the next day would be sunny. He would go with that thought, even if it wasn't true. *Tomorrow is going to be a beautiful day.*

He walked to the police department, but the place was still the madhouse it had been for the past several days. He tried to interview more people, but those he managed to single out were either too distraught to talk, or too angry. He listened to the stories being told to the cops, but there was nothing new being added to the mix; they were all so similar.

For the next hour, Ray wandered around town trying to understand what was happening in the town. He was baffled at the lack of response from the police, but he was also grappling with the perplexity of it all. Was there a cult taking over the town? Were people leaving of their own free will—as the police seemed to believe—or were they being abducted?

In an attempt to clear his mind, Ray thought about Patty at the restaurant. He should have asked her out before he left the diner. Now he would have to wait until he saw her again to ask her.

His thoughts circled back to Trevor and his wife, Krista (the name came to him after a moment). They had mentioned a son. Denny? No, it was stranger than that. *Demy*. Short for something, no doubt. He hoped they would keep themselves safe if whatever was happening to this town found its way to their doorstep. He would make another plea to them to leave town when he saw them at 9:00. He understood their reasons for staying, but there was very little they could do at this point. They could tell the neighbors of the danger, and encourage them to leave, but ultimately, it was up to the individual to get out or not. Staying wasn't doing their neighbors any good either, after all. Yes, for the sake of Demy—and any other children or loved ones they might have—they should leave.

He wrote his thoughts down. Those were damn good arguments to make. He wanted to remember them.

The darkness fell quickly after the disappearance of the sun. The streetlights clicked on, one after another as if someone was running by them and flicking a switch.

As he walked along the streets, he glanced into the houses. He saw many homes that remained dark after night fell. If he hadn't been hyperaware of the danger the town was in, he wouldn't have given those empty homes a second thought, but now he couldn't stop wondering if the people from those darkened homes would ever return.

After passing seven houses with opaque windows, and no movement at all inside, he came to a house with its lights on.

Someone is home there. How did they manage to escape the same fate as their neighbors? And are they truly safe, or will something be coming for them as well?

He reached the end of town, where the five-corner intersection brought Lakeport Road into town. There was a partition in the road, and then another street that ran adjacent to Lakeport Road called Oneida Street. This road had empty, lifeless houses on it as well. They would have been hit before any of the others, having been located so close to ground zero, which Ray believed to be somewhere in the forested area along Lakeport Road.

Ray found a wall that stood up to about three feet from the ground and sat on it. He waited for any sign of movement coming from the direction of Lakeport Road. He wasn't sure what he was looking for, but if anything out of the ordinary happened, he wanted to be there to see it.

After fifteen minutes, he wished he had brought something to drink. A combination gas-station-slash-convenience-store beckoned across the street, but he didn't dare leave his post and risk missing something.

To keep himself occupied while he waited, Ray counted cars that passed through the intersection. He kept his eyes on the people in the vehicles as well. Any cars, or trucks, that came up from Lakeport Road, he checked to see if there was something odd about them. He was looking for cars with too many people in them, maybe. Or cars that drove erratically. He was thinking whoever was causing the disappearance was most likely getting around by using some kind of vehicle. It was the most obvious conclusion, after all.

He saw nothing out of the ordinary, or strange in any way. Each vehicle that passed under the streetlight at the corner held a typical number of passengers, and all the drivers seemed bored, or tired. None looked crazed, or somehow suspicious.

Nearly an hour had passed since he had perched himself on the wall, and every moment that passed he thought: *See, I could have gone into the store and bought a drink without missing anything*. Still, he did not leave his station to get a drink.

He sang songs (or, at least hummed them) from his favorite 1970s artists to pass the time. He hated modern music. Nothing was as good as the rock and roll that came out of the seventies. And he only considered the mid-seventies—none of that disco shit. The rock in the eighties wasn't much better, except for the groups that came out of the seventies, and continued to have hits in the eighties. Of his favs, there was the Rolling Stones, and Heart. He'd been a baby when that music came out, but he remembered his first time hearing

"Sympathy for the Devil." He was hooked on that sound forever.

The cement under his butt began to cut off the circulation to his legs, so he stood and stretched. Activity at the convenience store caught his ear, and he glanced over. People in the parking lot were shouting and cursing one another. *Oh, look, the locals are providing entertainment.* He laughed. The commotion died down, and he returned to his seat on the cement wall.

Another half hour passed with nothing happening. He nearly fell asleep, but a horn honked and it woke him up.

He glanced around. A car passed, but nothing else of note happened. *This isn't going to be my night, I guess.* He resigned himself to going back to the motel and working on the story notes. Sure, there was something to tell, but it wouldn't get told until he put the words in some kind of order. *I probably have all the information I'm going to get to write this article.* He slid off the wall again and dusted off his butt. *I'm sure there will be follow-up stories.*

But, no. This story wasn't done, damn it. There was nothing in the article that would give him a gold star, let alone a Pulitzer Prize-winning story. He had to keep going. The story would break wide open. He was sure of it. He just had to keep looking. He couldn't give up yet.

The stone wall had grown too uncomfortable, and he couldn't consider sitting on it a second longer. He'd go to the store and get that drink he wanted so bad. He'd earned it.

He took one step when he saw the crowd of people walking toward town, coming from Lakeport Road.

He stood frozen in place, watching. When his paralysis broke, he hopped behind the wall and peered over it at the people. There were two aspects about this group that caught his attention and made him think it odd. The first thing was the size. This was a parade of people. At least a hundred, if not more. The second was how they were dressed.

There were people in street clothes, or work clothes. Nothing odd about that. But there were also people dressed in nightclothes. Pajama-clad men, women, and children. Little girls in nightgowns. One man wore a T-shirt, but was naked from the waist down.

He saw policemen—or, at least, people he assumed were policemen—still in uniform, and people wearing grease-stained overalls, the kind worn by men who work at garages. It was like a scene out of the movie *Night of the Living Dead,* though these people didn't move like zombies. Although they didn't speak a word, they walked with purpose. They were heading *somewhere.* And as he had his next thought, a chill travelled up his back, turning his spine into a taut guitar string that had been plucked.

These are the missing people.

He watched as they broke into smaller groups. Some headed into town, some came in his direction and were heading to the convenience store. Some started up Tuscarora Road. He watched the group walking to the store. Something so bizarre it defied understanding started happening. The people in the parking lot were approached by the travelling horde, and then they, too, joined in the march. These people entered the store, and as they came out, the shoppers—

and even the clerk—walked out and joined the march out of town.

When there was no one left in sight, Ray walked across the road to the store. He entered.

"Hello?" He waited for a reply. Nothing.

He looked in the back of the store. No one. Even the back rooms were empty.

He exited the store and headed up Tuscarora. The road was a hill that curved, much of it hidden by trees. He managed to catch up to the group that had walked in this direction. Larger groups broke off into smaller groups as they reached side roads. Cautiously, Ray followed the group that continued down the other side of the road, to the intersection. To the left, people headed down Lake Street. The others turned right, onto Bolivar Road. Still more continued further onto Tuscarora. Ray carefully followed the people on Bolivar Road.

It occurred to him that about a mile up this road was where Krista and Trevor lived.

Oh, God. They are even closer to invading their street than any of us had predicted. Ray's mind felt scrambled. He was torn. He wanted to find a way to get to the Burnettes, but he didn't want to take his eyes off this group. He watched as two members walked up to a house. The lights were on, and silhouetted people moved around behind the curtains. The invaders didn't hesitate. They didn't knock. They simply broke the door in and entered the house.

Ray heard screams. He quickly sidled up to the house and peered in the side window. The man who had entered the house grabbed a woman—maybe the screamer—and did the most peculiar thing.

He touched her ear. The woman stopped struggling, and assisted the man and the second woman, another invader, to catch other household members. When a little girl screamed and tried to run away, the woman that Ray believed to be the girl's mother grabbed the child and touched her ear.

The little girl calmed immediately and followed the adults out of the house. Ray ducked out of sight when the horde moved onto the road and headed to the next house. Ray tried to follow, but could only make it to the hedgerow that lined the property. If he moved any further, he would be in the open and visible. When the group disappeared into the house, Ray raced to the side.

Panting and exhausted, he peered into the window.

He clapped a hand over his mouth to keep from screaming. The woman in this house had been touched on the ear, and she instantly fell into step with the invaders. Instead of touching the ear of her husband, she picked up a knife from the kitchen counter, and stabbed him in the chest. He dropped to his knees, and she plunged the knife into his back. When he dropped to the floor, and stopped moving, the man that had begun the attack at the first house picked the dead body off the floor and flung it over his shoulder.

As the others continued on, the man carrying the corpse walked around the house. Ray barely made it to the back yard without being seen. The man seemed to be heading back the way they had come. Ray followed him.

The man carrying the dead body didn't take the road. He headed through the trees and over fields. Ray stayed as close as he could to keep the man in his sight, but without getting so close he'd be spotted if the man turned around. But the man didn't turn around. In fact, despite the dead weight, the man moved swiftly and deftly toward town. Ray did all he could to simply keep up.

When they reached Lakeport Road, the man holding the corpse followed the road for about a mile, and then headed into the trees. Ray steeled himself against his fears and followed. Ray moved step for step with the man in order to mask his own footsteps. When the man stopped to shift his weight, Ray stopped, too. He tried not to breathe until the man continued on again.

The man traveled through the trees until he reached a clearing. He hefted the corpse off his shoulder and dropped it on the ground.

Ray moved to the edge of the clearing. He watched from a crouched position as the people milling around a campfire interacted with each other. He was too far away to hear them clearly, but individual words reached him on occasion.

As the people moved closer to the fire, Ray was able to get a better view. He noticed that everyone around the fire had gray, mottled skin, and there were dark veins stretching across their faces. He saw these veins on their arms and hands, as well. The vine-like blotches, stretched across their skin, reminded Ray of varicose veins. His aunt's calves had been covered in them. He never thought he would see that kind of damage on someone's arms, though. Nor on their faces.

What is wrong with these people? Is this some kind of disease?

Ray had seen proof that the people being abducted from town were coming to this place in the woods, and they were coming—as far as Ray could tell—of their own free will. He didn't understand why, but that was what he had witnessed. What was going on in this clearing?

He moved slowly, quietly, to another spot in order to get a different view of what was going on past the bonfire. He also tried to get his bearings, so he could see where he was, and where he needed to go to get back to the road. Ray was no Boy Scout, and getting lost in the woods was not something he desired. And although he was no nautical navigator, if he could see the sky, he might be able to get some sense of direction. The problem was, the sky was not visible because of the tree cover, and because of the smoke from the fire.

When he had moved around the fire enough to see the activity happening on the other side, he strained his eyes to understand what he was seeing. He watched as the corpse was carried to a grassy spot away from the fire. Ray found it harder to see what was happening, the farther from the fire the people moved. There was a smoky area that Ray understood to be some kind of cooking rack. He could just barely make out the cuts of meat hanging over a slow-burning fire that caused heavy smoke to permeate the meat hanging there. He wasn't sure what kind of meat they were cooking at first. But that became evident.

The silhouetted figure standing over the corpse lifted a long, curved blade—a machete—into the air, and brought it down, severing the corpse's arm. The cutter lifted the arm by the fingers and handed it to someone else. This second person secured the arm to the rack over the smoky fire.

Ray turned away, nauseated. He felt gorge rise in his throat, but he swallowed it back down, for fear that the retching sound would draw their attention to him. He tasted regurgitated egg and medium rare steak in the back of his throat and almost retched again. After an epic battle with his stomach, and a lot of will power, Ray managed to get his sickness under control. He worked on slowing his breathing, fearing he might pass out from hyperventilating.

When he thought he could handle the sight, Ray looked back through squinted eyes. The corpse was nearly completely prepped, and all the appendages had been hung up to be cooked. In order to keep from running away, screaming, Ray thought of the corpse as a cow or a pig. This helped a little, but not much. He turned away again when they started hacking off the head.

Ray had learned his lesson about seeing too much and moved slowly back to his original position. He noticed that the crowd had grown bigger. *They are returning from their nightly excursion.* Making no sound, Ray started backing out of the clearing. He was sure the road wasn't far.

He turned to head in the direction he was sure the road would be, but bumped into a thick, wide chest. A tall, burly man lifted Ray off his feet. Ray squirmed against his captor, but he couldn't break free.

The man carried him like a fussy baby into the clearing. "I found someone lurking about the campsite."

The captor's voice was surprisingly feminine for such a large man, and it almost made Ray laugh. His laugh was stifled, however, because to release it would have driven Ray over the edge.

The giant man dropped Ray onto the ground. Ray tried to run, but the man grabbed his arm as if it were a twig and twisted it easily behind his back.

Ray cried out from the pain. His eyes welled. He watched through the blur of tears as a crowd of varicose-veined monstrosities swarmed around him, like hyenas to a fallen antelope. He stopped struggling when the pain grew too severe.

"I know him!" someone from the crowd said. "He's the reporter. Been nosing around, asking questions about the disappearances."

A small, wiry man, stepped up and stared Ray in the eyes. "You here looking for the next big scoop?" The man looked around. "Looks like you found it." He laughed from deep in his scrawny belly, bending over to slap his knee.

Ray struggled not to pass out.

"Too bad you're not going to get a chance to write your story, Scoop."

"Let him go."

The voice came from behind, and almost immediately, the burly man holding Ray's arm released him like a bug pinched between two fingers being dropped. Ray fell to the dirt. He sat on the cold ground cradling his injured arm. The man who had spoken stepped up and stood in front of Ray. Moving his head slowly, Ray lifted his gaze and looked at the man dressed in white. He wanted to run, but knew he had very little chance of getting away. He waited, and hoped against all odds that this stranger would allow him to go.

The man in white gave a nod to the burly man, and Ray was hefted to his feet like a puppet. The puppet master then brushed the dirt off Ray's clothes.

"I'm so sorry about the way you were treated. I assure you, it's not how we intended to treat the press."

The man in white had no blotchy marks on his face. He had creamy, tanned skin that contrasted nicely with his snowy white goatee and hair. He was, by all modern standards, a handsome man. Ray had once heard Anderson Cooper referred to as a silver fox. A white fox is how Ray would describe this man.

"I didn't come here to spy on you, I promise. It wasn't my intention. I stumbled onto your group by accident. Please believe me." Ray tried to keep the fear out of his voice, but it was there just the same.

"I believe you," the white fox said. "But it doesn't matter. We aren't afraid of you running a story on us."

"You're not?" Ray felt the first stirrings of hope rise in his chest. He smiled. "I'm free to go, then?"

The man in white smiled.

"Jennifer, come help us with our friend, here."

A woman stepped out of the crowd and took Ray by the hand. He looked at her shyly. He smiled at her. She smiled back. Ray took his first step toward the trees, but when Jennifer didn't follow, he stopped and turned back, confused.

She brought up the serrated hunting knife in her other hand, and gouged out a chunk of flesh from the forearm of his hand that she was holding so tenderly.

Ray screamed.

She popped a lump from the flesh she took from him into her mouth, chewed. She stepped back.

Ray moaned and clapped a hand over the wound. He turned to run, but someone was standing there. He, too, held a hunting knife. Before Ray could register what was happening, another bit of flesh was removed from his body. More people stepped up to him, cut into him. Ray staggered as if drunk, as one after another stepped up and removed bits of his flesh.

A knife tore into his cheek, removing half his face.

Ray dropped to his knees as more pieces of him were removed. He dropped into the dirt and rolled onto his back. He looked up and watched as the people around him ate his flesh. As the next knife plunged into his abdomen, Ray turned his gaze beyond the swarm of feasting heads around him, to a patch of sky miraculously clear through the swirling haze of smoke, and he marveled at the stars above him as he bled into the dirt.

Chapter Nineteen: Trevor

Trevor had moved back into his house with Krista. They were a happy little family again. Trevor and his wife were even making love nightly. He thought it may have more to do with Krista's fear of being alone, and her need for feeling safe, but that was fine with him. He didn't like staying at Ethan's place without him there. It made him feel like a squatter. For now, Trevor was fine staying with Krista. He needed to protect his family, anyway.

Trevor drove to the police station and parked. Krista stayed home with Demy. At nine o'clock in the morning it was already sweltering outside, and the walk to the building from the car left him sweaty and hot. He looked around but saw no sign of Ray. As he passed through the front door of the police station, a sheen of moisture on his forehead dried instantly in the cool air, causing a slight shiver.

He glanced around, but Ray was nowhere to be seen.

Trevor looked over the crowd inside the station. The number of people looking for their missing loved ones had dropped substantially. Either people were giving up or . . .

Or many of the people who had been coming here are now also missing.

The blood drained from his face. He shuddered. Suddenly, the air-conditioning inside the building was too cold.

As a cop walked by, Trevor stopped him. "Excuse me, but there was a reporter in here lately. Have you seen him this morning?"

The cop sighed, clearly annoyed. "No, I haven't."

Trevor watched the cop walk away. *Why aren't they more concerned about all this? Do they not see that this town is in crisis?*

He answered his own question. *They're afraid. They don't know what to do. They can't admit that, because we look to them for safety and authority. If they are powerless to help us, what does that mean?*

Trevor took a seat. He waited another half hour, but when Ray still didn't show up, Trevor sought out another officer.

"Sir, excuse me. I planned to meet up with that reporter who has been coming in here for the last couple of weeks."

The cop nodded. "Ray, yeah. I know him."

"Have you seen him this morning? I was expecting him to be here."

The cop gave a knowing smile and looked away. He turned back to Trevor. "Ray is a sensationalist. He comes here, works people up and makes our job harder, and leaves a mess in his wake. Don't waste your time on him. He probably found another big story and skipped out."

As the cop walked away, Trevor considered his words.

He shook his head. No, Ray wouldn't do that. He genuinely cared about this town, and whatever was happening to it. He wouldn't have just gone away without a word. Even if he thought this story was going nowhere, surely Ray would have kept his word and met them here. It's only good business for a reporter to keep open communication with potential sources.

Right?

Trevor waited another half hour. When Ray still didn't show, he returned home. Krista met him at the door. She looked for Ray. When she didn't see the reporter, she gave Trevor a questioning glance.

"He didn't show. The cops think he moved on to another place. Another sensational story."

"He wouldn't do that, would he?"

Trevor shrugged. "We don't really know him. I didn't peg him as the type to do that, but we just don't know. Maybe he is."

Krista spun around like a person half drunk and dropped heavily into a chair. "What are we going to do? We have to leave. We can't stay any longer. We're going to be in danger if we stay. We should leave."

Trevor dropped onto the sofa with a sigh. "Yeah, I think we should. When this blows over, we can come back and pick up the pieces. But right now, I think we should go."

"The question is *where* do we go?"

Trevor thought about it. He remembered something and turned to her. "Don't your parents have a cabin on Oneida Lake?"

Krista scowled. "Yes. It's on the other side of the lake, in Bernhard Bay. But is that far enough?"

"For now, it is. It'll have to be, I guess. I can't imagine whatever is happening here would reach across the lake. I think we'll be safe there until the cops get a handle on this."

"But what if it's not? What if it follows us there?"

"We'll go farther away."

"What about your job?"

"I have time saved up. I'll take a leave of absence."

Either she ran out of questions, or she finally felt secure enough to relax. Her shoulders sagged, and she let out a long, shuddering breath. She closed her eyes. When she opened them again, she turned to face him.

"We need to pack. We need to get supplies. It's a long drive around the lake. We should get going as soon as possible."

Trevor nodded. "We do. But I have another plan." He smiled.

Krista pressed her lips together, waiting to hear the plan.

"We go to the Whittlespoons, and take the boat over the lake. We have to warn them of the danger, anyway."

Krista nodded, enthusiastic. "That's good. I like that."

She went to Demy's room. Trevor headed to their room and packed a bag. When Krista finished getting Demy ready, she joined Trevor in their bedroom.

"Krista, I need to show you something." Trevor watched her walk over to him. She shot him a questioning look, but said nothing.

Trevor lifted the gun from the suitcase on the bed. She gaped at the weapon. After a moment, she pulled her eyes away from the gun and glared at Trevor.

"Why do you have that?" Her voice was a frightened whisper.

"For our protection."

"When did you get it?"

"Recently, from somewhere I'd rather not disclose at the moment...if you can understand, I mean."

"How? I mean, isn't it hard to buy a gun? The laws in place, the paperwork . . .?"

"I didn't get it through altogether legal means, if you understand what I'm saying."

Trevor watched her eyes. He could visibly see her mind turn from confusion and fear, to understanding and acceptance.

"Do not let Demy see it, or go near it."

He nodded and put the gun in the waistband of his pants and covered it with his shirt. He then snapped his suitcase closed.

"Pack light. This isn't a vacation. Pack just what you need to get by. Mementos, make-up, it all stays. Light, comfortable clothing only."

Krista smirked. "You think this is my first time packing for an evacuation?"

Trevor laughed, but there was no humor in the sound. He appreciated her trying to lighten the mood. Loved her more for it. He left her to pack and carried his suitcase out to the car. He returned and collected the bag Krista had packed for Demy. She carried her suitcase out. They returned and headed for Demy's room together.

She stopped him before he entered.

"We should bring Mrs. Kennedy with us."

Trevor nodded.

They entered the room.

Demy looked up at his parents. He must have sensed their distress. He furrowed his brow and with splayed fingers, middle finger bent in, he brought his hands out from his chest. *What's happening?*

Krista responded in sign language. *We're going on vacation.* She smiled. She indicated for him to take her hand. He stood and wrapped his small hand around hers. She led him out to the living room, and to the front yard. She bent down so he could see her. *We're going to leave you with Mrs. Kennedy for the moment. When we finish running errands, we'll come back for you. We'll get Mrs. Kennedy to join us for our vacation, okay?*

Demy nodded.

They walked him over and knocked on Mrs. Kennedy's screen door. She came out to greet them, smiling and wiping her hands on the flowered apron she wore. "To what do I owe this pleasure?"

Trevor bade Demy to go and play. As the boy headed into the house, Trevor turned to Mrs. Kennedy. Her mouth curled in a confused frown. She looked to Krista, but found no answer there.

"Should I be worried?"

They didn't respond to her question.

"Can you keep an eye on Demy while we run out and take care of some things?" Krista asked.

"Yes, of course. You don't even have to ask. But what's going on?"

"When we come back, we're going away for a little while." Krista touched the old woman's arm, looking into her eyes. "We want you to come with us, do you understand?"

"What? Go? Go where? And for how long?"

"Something's happening in our town. Something bad, and it's coming this way. We need to get out until it's over."

Mrs. Kennedy shook her head. "I don't understand. What kind of danger? If I leave, there is no one to take care of my plants. I can't just leave them—"

"You have to." Trevor's voice was forceful, authoritative. "You have no choice. This is serious. We're all in danger if we stay. You will be in danger if you stay."

"But..." The woman looked around at her plants.

"Promise you'll agree to go with us." Large, wet tears filled Krista's eyes. "Please."

The old woman's hand fluttered to her mouth. "Okay, I'll go. But what's all this about?"

"We'll explain everything later," Trevor said. "Right now, though, we need to go. We'll be right back, but while we're gone you'll need to pack a bag. Only take what you need, okay? The essentials."

She nodded, reluctantly.

He turned and headed back to their car.

Krista followed him out to the car, and climbed into the passenger side. They drove away.

"I hope the Whittlespoons are as easy to convince. We're about to invade their home. They might not agree to this."

Trevor squeezed her hand. "They'll come around. If not, we did what we could to help. We'll just go without them, and pray they survive what's coming."

As they reached the yacht, they parked and jogged up to the dock. Tessa met them at the top of the ramp. "Did we have plans? I must have forgotten."

Krista took Tessa by the hand and led her to the chairs. She sat the older woman down. "This is an unplanned visit."

Trevor sat down next to Krista. "We're going to ask something of you. We need you to take us seriously. It isn't a joke. Do you understand?" Trevor leaned forward and looked deeply into the woman's eyes.

Gavin approached, and Trevor gravely asked him to sit.

"This affects you, too," Trevor said.

Gavin sat down. "What's going on?"

"Have you heard about the rash of disappearances happening in town?"

Gavin nodded slowly. "We've heard talk. When we go into town, we hear people gossiping."

"It's no longer gossip. Something's happening to the people around town. There's disappearances, yes. But there have been murders, as well. Whatever is happening, it's spreading. And we believe it will spread this way as well. We want to know if you will ferry us over to the other side of the lake."

"Yes, of course." Tessa's eyes were stern, trusting. "Whatever you like. But tell us what's happening. What is spreading? I don't understand. How much danger are we in?"

Krista and Trevor shared a glance. Trevor responded. "It's life and death. We don't understand all of it either, but we've been talking to a reporter, and he has detailed notes that something has been happening to people, and the pattern shows that it's spreading. We don't know how long before it reaches you, but we know we are no longer safe here. We have a cabin on the other side of the lake. We plan to go there until this is sorted out. We can drive there, but—"

"No, no." Tessa placed a hand on Krista's. "Don't worry about all that. We'll take you by boat. It's much faster. But does this have anything to do with that man and his preposterous plan to open that business? I must say, I did not like him. That whole affair seemed like bad business. You'll be sorry if you go in on that plan with him."

Krista waved an impatient hand at her. "This has nothing to do with him or with that business. This is something totally different. None of that matters anymore. The only thing that matters now is staying alive."

"Is it really that bad?"

Krista nodded. "It really is."

Tessa looked around. "Where is Demy? Didn't he come with you?"

Trevor drew the old woman's eyes to him. "No, he's with our neighbor. Her name is Diane Kennedy. She'll be coming with us, if that's okay."

"It's fine. Will that man be coming? Ethan?"

Trevor didn't understand her dislike of him. He'd never done anything to offend her, as far as he knew, and he was a likeable guy, so why did she dislike him so much?

Krista responded. "No, he's . . . no."

"Okay, well, I won't say no if you ask if he can come. But I wouldn't be doing him any favors. It would only be because you are asking."

We don't have time for all this. Trevor nodded. "We understand, and we thank you. We're going to the store for some supplies. We'll pick up Demy and Mrs. Kennedy and return. We want to be underway by . . ." He looked at his watch: one thirty. "Three. How does that sound?"

"We'll be here."

Gavin added his say to the matter. "Yeah. Sounds good."

Trevor and Krista stood. The older couple followed suit and walked them to the dock. As they walked back to the car, Krista turned and waved. She climbed into the car, and Trevor drove them back to town.

He pulled up in front of the grocery store. "Buy as much food as you can, but only canned goods and bottled water. We're going to barricade ourselves in the cabin, and we're not coming out until it's safe again. I'm going to head back to the police station and see if Ray showed up. If he's there, I'll have him come with us. I'll meet you back here in a half hour at the latest."

She nodded and climbed out of the car. Trevor watched her walk into the store before driving away. As he drove into town, taking the curve in the road by the mortuary, his breath caught in his throat.

There were people everywhere, hundreds of people. They walked on the sidewalks, and in the road. As he passed through the crowd, the people looked into his car at him. He saw their faces, and his heart skipped a beat. His skin turned cold. He rolled slowly through the masses, and the people moved to allow him through. When he reached the end of the crowds, he saw no one. The crowd continued on in the opposite direction.

Trevor stopped the car and looked back.

It's happening.

He drove to the police station and climbed out of the car. He saw no one around the building. Every time he had come here, he saw people milling about, smoking and talking. He opened the door and walked inside.

The building was empty. There was no one, not a single police officer. He called out through the small opening in the bulletproof window leading to the back of the station. "Hello? Hello, is anyone here?"

He checked the door leading to the back. The door always remained locked. It was open. He entered the back of the station, but there was no one to be seen. He looked in the bathrooms. The building was completely devoid of any living beings. *Why would the police abandon their station?*

Trevor returned to the street. The mass of people was no longer visible. In fact, he saw no one. He walked to the next business, a hardware store. The door was open, but just like the police station, the place was abandoned. Looking into the shops and stores all along the main street showed the same thing.

The town had been completely abandoned.

Trevor looked back the way he had seen the crowd heading. They were going toward the west end of town. Toward . . .

The grocery store.

Toward Krista.

Trevor raced back to his car and climbed behind the wheel. He didn't want to take a chance driving through the crowd again, so he headed the opposite way. He could drive up Tuscarora Road and come out on the other side of the plaza where Krista was shopping.

Trevor drove as fast as he could up Tuscarora to Tom-Tom Street. He turned into the plaza's parking lot, and drove slowly past the Yellow Brick Road

Casino. There were no people in the parking area, or in the building. The place was as dead as the town. He moved on to the grocery store at the end of the strip.

There were no people here, either. When he looked up the street, he saw the masses heading back, toward town again. They had come, wreaked their havoc, and now were heading back the way they had come.

Panicked, Trevor jumped out of the car and ran into the store. He raced down every aisle, panting. The store was empty.

"Krista!" He called out again, louder. "Krista!"

He dropped to his knees.

Chapter Twenty: Diane

Demy sat on the floor playing with the Lego bricks he brought with him. Diane watched him, smiling pleasantly. Her mind was aflutter with all kinds of wild scenarios. She didn't want him to feel her distress, so she smiled and kept him occupied. After she got him to relax, she went to the kitchen where, if she looked upset, he wouldn't see it. She couldn't stop thinking about his parents. They looked . . . not scared . . . they looked *terrified.* They had scared her. She had no doubt something serious was going on.

Then they were talking about leaving. It all sounded so absurd. Leave her house, her plants? She couldn't do that. They would die without her constant care and attention. She talked to her plants. They were her best friends. She needed them as much as they needed her. She couldn't abandon her friends. The Burnettes didn't know what they were asking of her.

She filled her watering can and walked out to her porch. As she sprinkled water on the ferns, she spoke softly to her Nephrolepis, or her macho fern. "They won't take me away from you, no. So, don't you worry. I see you shivering. I will never abandon my babies."

She turned her attention to the array of spider plants hanging along the windows facing west. She stroked them individually, lovingly. She stopped at one with small, spindly offshoots. "Oh, you have babies, I see. I'm so happy for you. We'll have to take care of them for you." She picked up her gardening shears and snipped off the little appendages. The small plants went into a jar of water. "When you get your roots, we'll find a small patch of soil for you to live in. How does that sound?" She kissed the plants, and placed them on the sill. "You'll love it over here. You'll only see the fading light of the day."

She moved on to the next plant. And the next. No plant escaped her attention, and none saw more attention than the next. She treated each plant with individual care. This was her passion, where she felt most at ease and alive. She spent as much time with her plants as she could stand on a daily basis. She spent a minimum of three waking hours with her plants, and some days, even more.

She laughed aloud. "They can't take me away from my babies."

When all the plants had received her proper care, she checked in on Demy. The sweet boy could entertain himself for hours with the simplest toys. She leaned down and kissed his forehead. He glanced up at her, smiling.

"Are you hungry? Do you want some lunch?"

He nodded.

"Ham sandwich with mac and cheese?"

He considered it, nodded again.

She rose and headed to the kitchen. She scooped out a bowl of the leftover macaroni and cheese she made for her dinner the previous night, and popped it into the microwave. As that cooked, she pulled out the fixings for a ham sandwich. She knew his preferences, and put extra ham on white bread, with yellow mustard—not hot. Hot mustard shoots up his nose. American cheese.

The microwave chimed, and she retrieved the bowl of mac and cheese. She stirred it, making sure it wasn't too hot. She poured him a glass of milk, and carried the tray into the living room. She placed the tray on the floor next to him. He dropped his toys and commenced eating. Diane watched him bite into the sandwich, chew. He bopped his head back and forth, and his jutting elbows lifted on one side, and then the other as he twisted his body playfully from side to side. She giggled at his antics. It filled her heart with joy to watch him. His interest in being with her defied all logic, but she was happy to have him.

She could never understand why he liked to spend time with her. The house could hardly be described as kid-friendly. There were knickknacks and bric-a-brac everywhere—fragile pieces that should not have survived sharing space with a child. But after spending all this time with Demy, he had never once broken any of her things. She didn't know what toys kids liked, and had none in her home. She often encouraged Demy to bring some of his toys to her house to keep him occupied, but he brought very little with him. Demy was a self-contained kid. He could enjoy himself no matter where he was. He found pleasure, contentment, and joy in any place, at any moment. A gift, really. Even now, she could see his wonderful imagination at work. She could watch him play for hours, wishing she could hear his thoughts.

When he finished eating, and drained his glass of milk, Demy returned to the dragon he had been building out of Legos. She picked up his empty dishes and carried them to the sink.

She washed the dishes and placed them in the strainer.

She returned to the living room, drying her hands on a towel. She folded the towel and placed it on the lamp stand between the living room and the kitchen, then sat down on the overstuffed, cream linen sofa.

After a little while, Demy lifted himself off the floor and approached her. She motioned for him to join her.

"Moofie," he said.

"Sounds good. What movie were you thinking of?" She twisted to the side so she could see him better.

His eyes turned away as he thought about it. When he had a movie in mind, he pointed to her shelf of DVDs. She thought she knew what he was pointing to, and she stood. She picked up *Planet of the Apes*—the original—with Charlton Heston and Roddy McDowall. Demy nodded.

His interest in this movie confounded her. He typically liked movies with a lot of color and action, and this movie had that, but he also depended on being able to read the actors' lips to get the dialogue. There was no way to read the lips of those prosthetically altered simian faces.

But it was one of his favorites.

She tried not to be obvious, but she liked to watch him as he watched the movies. His lips moved with the actors' lips. His favorite line in the movie was when Mr. Heston gets caught up in the net and growls the line, "Get your stinking paws off me, you damned dirty ape."

Demy mimicked the line every time, and laughed. She had never been a fan of the movie herself. The

DVD had been a gift for her husband. But she got loads of joy watching Demy watch the movie.

During the final scene, she wondered if the ending escaped Demy's full comprehension. *How much does he understand that this planet is Earth, and that we humans had destroyed it?* The fact hardly mattered, however, since he enjoyed watching it, regardless of what he understood.

She put the movie away, returning the DVD to its case on the bookshelf, and then looked at Demy, feigning a calm she was trying hard to sustain. "Would you like to watch another?"

He shook his head. He yawned and drew the sign for sleepy across his face. Diane nodded. It was one of the signs she understood. She led him to the spare bedroom and pulled back the sheets. He climbed into bed, and she tucked him in. She kissed his forehead and exited the room, closing the door behind her.

She returned to the living room and picked up his Legos. She had stepped on enough of them to know they did not belong on the floor. She was careful not to destroy his creation, though. She placed the Lego dragon on her mantel, giving it pride of place.

She tidied up, first by taking the folded towel back to the kitchen. She cleaned the bathroom, scrubbing the floor around the toilet. Little boys were notorious for missing the bowl. She filled a spray bottle with fresh water from the sink and spritzed some of her plants with a fine mist, talking softly to them all the while.

When the place was clean and the plants attended to, she sat down and turned on her favorite shows. Her mind turned back to the time. She expected Demy's parents to return soon. She would have to deal with that. She tried to concentrate on her shows, but her hands fluttered and fretted with the lace antimacassar on the arm of the sofa.

During commercials, her eyes darted to the front door.

Something happened. She could no longer concentrate on the show at all. *Something happened, and they are in trouble. They should have returned by now.*

She looked toward the door where Demy slept. She forced the anxious thoughts from her head. It would do the boy no good if she showed worry on her face when he awoke, especially if his parents were not back by then.

With much effort, she was able to draw her focus back on the TV show she had been watching. Her attention was so absorbed in the show that she was startled when Krista entered her home.

She stood.

"Oh, Krista! You startled me." Diane placed a hand to her racing heart. As her hand dropped back to her side, it occurred to her that she could never remember a time when Demy's parents had ever entered her home without knocking. "Where is Trevor?"

Krista stepped forward. The younger woman seemed annoyed. Her head was down, and her eyes glared up at Diane. As Krista approached, she knocked furniture out of her way. Diane backed up.

"Krista, you're scaring me. What's happened? Why isn't Trevor with you?"

Krista stopped her approach and looked over her shoulder at the open front door. "I'm sure he will be here momentarily. He just has to be . . . initiated first."

"What? What are you talking about?"

Krista's head snapped back around to stare at Diane. The older woman stumbled backward, and she landed on the arm of the sofa. She tumbled over the side and landed on the floor. She scrambled backward on her hands. When she reached the wall, she used it to stand back up. She stood with her back to the wall and waited for Krista to come at her.

"If you don't struggle, old woman, this will go much more smoothly. That is, if you can accept the gift."

Keep her talking. "Gift? What gift?"

Krista mumbled—an annoyed sound—and stepped forward. "The gift is the spark of life. I'll pass it on to you, and your fear will be at an end."

"What about Demy? Will you give him . . . the gift as well?"

Krista stopped and looked around, searching for the boy. When she didn't see him, she turned back to Diane.

"He can't hear the call. We have other uses for him."

"What kind of uses? You . . . you're not seriously talking about harming your own child, are you?" Diane noticed the dark raised veins running up Krista's arms, and spreading across her neck. *She's sick or something. This must be the mysterious thing they were trying to avoid. But where is Trevor? Is he . . . sick . . . as well?*

Diane inched her way toward the door to the room where Demy slept. If she could get in there and lock the door, she could protect them both until help arrived. She just prayed Demy wouldn't pick this time to come out of the room and see his mother. He would run to her, unaware of the danger. Diane shuddered at the thought. Moisture covered her vision, and she wiped it away furiously, forcing her emotions to bend to her will. *I will not survive this by becoming a weeping basket case.*

She took another step toward the door.

Krista matched her step.

Diane's hand pressed against the wall as she worked her way to the right. There was a stand nearby with ceramic bunnies on it. On the other side of that was the door. Her hand touched the stand. Diane picked up the first ceramic piece that she touched and threw it at Krista with all her might. She ran for the door.

Krista batted the rabbit away and lunged. She caught the old woman by the bun in her hair and yanked her backward.

Diane cried out and brought her hands up, trying to release Krista's hold on her hair.

Krista spun the older woman around forcefully, and shoved her onto the sofa. Diane flew over the sofa's arm, and landed on the cushions in a prone position, face down. She struggled to upturn herself so she could face the attack when it came. Krista approached, her index finger pointed up. She looked like someone saying, "Wait a minute."

But then Diane focused on the finger, and she saw the blue spark humming at the end of the finger. Krista pointed the sparking finger at Diane. The older woman put her hands out in an attempt to prevent Krista from getting any closer, but she slapped her hands away easily and landed on the old woman. Pinned, Diane could do nothing to stop what Krista was about to do.

The finger came down, and touched the old woman on the ear. Krista stood up.

Diane scrambled into a sitting position. Then she stood as well.

"Now tell me where the boy is."

The old woman turned to Krista. She tried to feel something different, but she was still the same person she had always been.

"Why would I tell you?"

Krista stopped searching for the boy and looked back at the old woman. "You didn't hear the sound?"

"I don't know what you're talking about. I didn't hear anything."

The pale-faced and veiny woman rolled her eyes. "It doesn't work for everyone. You're one of the unlucky ones. You won't be getting the gift, after all."

"What's going to happen to me then?"

Krista's hands balled into fists. "You're going to die, just like the boy."

The affected woman charged at Diane whose hands flew up protectively. When the attack came, it landed on her arms instead of her face. The force knocked Diane to the floor.

Krista stood over the woman, looking down at her. Diane hugged her arms to her chest and waited for the fatal blow. Her only regret was that she would not be able to protect the boy from his mother's maniacal attack.

As the attacking woman lifted her foot, aiming it at Diane's head, the old woman closed her eyes. She didn't want to see what was coming. Her mind raced for something to say that would stop Krista from doing this. But this wasn't the Krista who had left her son in the old woman's care only a few short hours ago. This woman meant to kill her, and when finished with Diane, she would kill her own son.

She wondered if having her skull crushed would hurt. She had resigned herself to death when she heard the screen door screech open and slam closed again. Irrationally, her next thought was, *doesn't anyone knock anymore?*

No blow came. Diane dared to open her eyes. Krista's attention was turned toward the front door.

The door leading to the patio, to her precious plants, was open. Trevor. She had just enough time to wonder if he had been affected as well before this question was answered.

Trevor lifted the gun in his hand and aimed. He pulled the trigger, and the gun boomed. Diane screamed as the bullet took Krista in the eye, and the back of her head exploded. Blood splashed across Diane's face. The body dropped to the floor, draping over Diane's legs.

The old woman scrambled out from under the corpse.

"She was affected," Trevor said. His voice quivered. "I didn't have a choice. She really would have killed you."

"I believe you."

"I had to shoot a couple of others to get here. The entire town is gone."

Gone.

The word echoed in Diane's head, and she shivered.

Trevor entered the room and looked around. "Where is Demy? Where is my son?"

"He's in the back room, sleeping." She pointed to the door. It was still closed.

She started toward the door.

"Wait." Trevor dragged the body of his son's mother into the kitchen. There was a smear of blood and brains across the floor. "It'll have to be good enough. At least he won't see the body."

They walked to the room together. Diane opened the door and flicked on the light. Slowly, Demy opened his eyes. He glanced around. When he saw his father, he leapt into Trevor's arms. Trevor hugged his son. It was the hug from a man who thought he would never see his son again. Diane's heart fluttered with the love she felt toward them.

Trevor found Demy's shoes and dressed his feet. The boy was looking around, and when he used his sign language, Diane didn't need to know the signs to know what he was saying.

Where's Mommy?

Trevor didn't respond. He lifted the boy into his arms and carried him out to the living room. He pressed the boy's face into his shoulder to prevent him from seeing the blood stains and spatter. He carried Demy onto the patio and stopped. He turned back to Diane. She had been following him, but stopped at the door.

"Did you pack a bag?"

She didn't respond.

"Never mind. There's no time now. We'll have to figure something out later. We must go now."

Trevor turned and pushed through the screen door. He was halfway to the car when he realized Diane hadn't followed him. He turned and saw her on the porch, watering her plants, stroking them, and talking to them. He returned to the door and peered through the screen.

"Diane, please. We don't have time for this. We have to go."

Demy lifted his head from his father's shoulder and looked from the woman to his father, confused.

She caressed a leafy plant and turned to Trevor. "I can't leave my babies. They need me."

"Diane, do I have to remind you there is a corpse inside your house? This isn't the time to choose your plants over your life. If you don't come with us, you'll die. We have to get to the people I have waiting for us. Come with me now."

She acted as though she hadn't heard a word.

She watched from the corner of her eye as Trevor placed Demy on the floor, and opened the screen door. He took her hand and dragged her toward the opening. She resisted, but he was too strong for her. When she gripped the door frame, he pulled her out to the yard. She fell back, landing on him. She rolled onto her knees. After a moment, she stood. Now Trevor led her toward the car without resistance. He opened the passenger door and she dropped into the seat. He slammed the door to close her in.

She watched from the mirror as Trevor picked Demy up and opened the back door. As he attempted to put Demy on the backseat, a pair of hands reached around and pulled Demy out of the car. She looked back at the group of monstrosities taking Demy away. Trevor searched his pockets, but seemed unable to find what he was looking for.

The Gun.

Diane glanced back at the place in the yard where they had fallen. Even in the fading light, she could see the gun.

Diane climbed out of the car and ran for the gun, but she was grabbed around the waist and held in place.

She screamed.

Diane managed to witness Trevor being knocked out with a fist to the face before she, too, was punched in the head and rendered unconscious.

Chapter Twenty-One: Trevor

When Trevor revived, he felt the hard ground beneath his back. It was dark. He was unaware how long he had been unconscious since the attack at the car. He struggled to get his vision to return, shaking his head and rubbing his eyes. Eventually, he was able to see around him.

A large bonfire gave off enough light to illuminate the clearing around him. Trees stood in the distance. He was in the woods somewhere, he understood. He struggled to stand, as he searched his immediate surroundings for Demy.

He was not alone. Several monstrosities that had invaded his town milled about.

These monsters were not strangers. He recognized many of them. These *were* the townspeople. He saw Bill, and Wendy. He took a step toward them, but a strong hand stopped him. He looked to see who owned the veiny arm that held him back.

He recognized the police officer from his visit to the station. The officer's face was covered in dark blotches.

Trevor turned back to his old friends. "Bill, it's me. Trevor. Do you understand who I am?"

Bill turned to him with a disinterested glance, then looked away.

They're all *changed*. Trevor looked at more faces. He saw Patty from the restaurant, and Dan Reed. He saw other people that had been missing for weeks. They were all here.

Well, not all. Some were missing. People he knew to be dead. He searched the crowd for the reporter, Ray. Though the crowd of people was too large to see everyone, Trevor could not spot the reporter.

Trevor turned to the cop guarding him. "Can you please tell me where my son is? Is he still alive?"

The cop looked at him. "For now." He pointed back, over Trevor's right shoulder.

Trevor turned where the cop had pointed. Demy was there, as was Mrs. Kennedy. Both were alive and awake. Diane was on the ground, and Demy sat in her lap. Her arms were wrapped protectively around the boy, but her mouth was gagged. Demy's head leaned against her chest. She moaned against the rag in her mouth when her eyes met his. The fear he saw on her face caused his heart to race. He tried to go to them, but, again, the cop stopped him.

"Let me go to them. They're terrified."

The cop showed no emotion. He shrugged.

Trevor headed toward them again, but this time the cop did not stop him. Trevor dropped down beside them. Demy quickly wrapped his small arms around his father's neck. The boy was shivering. Trevor removed the gag from Diane's mouth. She took a big gasping breath. After a moment, her breathing returned to normal.

"Trevor, I'm sorry. If I hadn't been such a fool—"

"It's not your fault," he said. "Did you see where they brought us? Do you know where we are?"

She shook her head. "I was unconscious. I woke up on the ground. Demy was with me the whole time.

They gagged me when I wouldn't stop screaming. They covered my mouth, but my hands were free. I could have taken off the gag, but I didn't dare. I can't contradict their wishes."

Trevor only half listened to the old woman's ramblings. He was looking around for an escape route. There seemed to be no way out without being chased down and recaptured. Also, Trevor now knew the police officers had guns. Nothing would stop them from being shot in the back as they ran. However, Trevor didn't give up hope.

As Trevor's eyes scanned his surroundings for a weak spot, something happening near the fire drew his attention. He gaped in horror as someone carried his wife's dead body to the bonfire and threw it into the flames. He turned away as the corpse sizzled and popped.

His eyes caught sight of Demy. He stared with wide, traumatized eyes as his mother's body burned. When Mrs. Kennedy realized the boy was watching, she covered his eyes. The boy struggled to remove her hand so he could see. She forced his head into her shoulder, and the boy stopped fighting. The sound of Demy's sobs broke Trevor's heart. He dropped down and covered his son with his body. The three of them cried together.

It took only a few minutes for the body to burn down to an unrecognizable husk. Trevor dragged himself off his son, and Demy pulled himself onto his father's lap. The boy curled up there and passed out. He didn't wake up when Trevor returned him to Diane's lap. He kissed his son on the forehead, and stood.

He stood protectively over his family—yes, Mrs. Kennedy was his family now, too. He waited for someone to come and pull him away again, but no one did. He watched as more of the bodies of the people he had killed while he had made his way from town to save Demy were heaped onto the bonfire. The air was soon filled with the acrid smell of burning flesh. He gagged.

What are they waiting for? The large mass of people was clustered around in smaller groups. *Apparently, even monsters have their cliques.* The thought caused a small chuckle to escape him. He glanced around to see if anyone had noticed. No one seemed to care that he was there. He felt as though he could pick up Demy and run and no one would notice. Something told him, though, that if he were to attempt to escape, these people would suddenly show interest and hunt them down. He would bide his time and wait for his chance.

More of these people entered the clearing, coming out of the trees like wraiths. They ignored him, just as the ones already there had been doing. Within minutes the group had multiplied from about one hundred or so, to over five hundred. The smaller groupings were obscured as the masses packed into the clearing elbow to elbow. He wondered how many more were apt to come.

Trevor tried to inch his way around the bonfire. The conflagration was so wide, and so tall, that there was an entire section of the clearing that wasn't visible to him. No one stopped him. As he reached the edge of the trees on the opposite side of the fire, he was able to see what was happening there. The affected near him glanced at him, maybe debating if he was thinking of bolting, but no one seemed interested in stopping him. Perhaps they knew he would never leave without his son, or perhaps they simply didn't care.

Trevor stopped moving when he spotted the makeshift smokehouse. He saw a rack beneath a tarp, and there were cuts of meat hanging from it. It took him a few moments to recognize what he was looking at.

Arms, legs. Human body parts.

He retched into the dirt at his feet.

He wiped his mouth and looked back at the rack of human limbs. He shifted his eyes to the left and spotted a post driven into the ground. At the top of the post he saw a human head.

It was Ray. His eyes were missing.

Trevor scrambled away. He pushed through the crowd. They showed no resistance, nor did they attempt to get out of his way. He didn't stop until he was back standing next to Demy and Diane.

She looked up at him. His own fear was mirrored back at him from her face. Her lip trembled. "What's happened?"

He shook his head. "Nothing. We're okay for now. We just need to get out of here as soon as we safely can."

Demy stirred on her lap, but the boy didn't wake.

"I don't think we're going to get the chance." Diane's voice shook with emotion. She started to hyperventilate.

Trevor dropped down beside her, stroking her hair. "Don't talk like that. I don't want to lose you to that kind of talk. There is always hope."

She laughed at him through her tears. "That's corny."

He laughed, too. It may have been corny, but it did the trick. Diane had calmed down.

He sat down next to her and put an arm around her. She leaned in and kissed his cheek. "Thank you."

He looked at her. "For what?"

"For not giving up on me. If we have to die, I'm glad we're together."

He hugged her tighter. "Me too."

Trevor leaned back on his hands.

"Why are they waiting?" Diane motioned toward the crowd.

"I was wondering the same thing. I guess we shouldn't be in too much of a hurry to find out what they plan on doing to us."

Diane shrugged. "Better to know than to not know, I always say."

They laughed again, louder this time. Someone kicked Trevor in the ribs, but that only made him laugh louder. He stopped laughing when someone pulled him to his feet. Trevor looked over at the cop who had been guarding him earlier.

Look, I've made a new friend. He stifled the urge to laugh again.

When the cop pushed him forward, Diane reached out for his leg in an attempt to stop him from going, but she missed. The cop shoved Trevor out of her reach, and led him to the front of the crowd.

"Trevor." There was desperation in her voice.

"Take care of Demy. Don't let him see this."

The cop's rough shoves kept him moving. The crowd separated, and Trevor walked through the rows on his own free will. The cop only needed to walk behind him. The cop reached out and gripped his shoulder when it was time to stop. Trevor turned and waited for his fate.

The cop just stood there.

When something moved to his right, he turned to see what was going on. He stared in awe as a man in white emerged from the tree line and stood in front of him. The man smiled at him pleasantly.

This is him. This is the man Krista had been so afraid of. He is the start of all this.

"I'm sure you're wondering why you've been brought here." The man waited for Trevor to respond.

He said nothing.

The man continued anyway. "I guess I wanted to see the man who was able to resist the calling for so long. And I want to explain why I'm here." He gestured to the crowd around him. "Why we are all here. Wouldn't you like to know what all this is about?"

Still, Trevor said nothing.

The man seemed disappointed by Trevor's silence. "Well, I'll tell you anyway." The man lifted his head as if thinking, then looked back at Trevor. "I'll start by telling you my name. I am Azazel." When Trevor still didn't respond, the man continued. "And I will tell you where I came from.

"Before you can understand what I am going to tell you, I should first explain *what* I am."

Azazel stepped back. He leaned forward and shook his head. The movement was so rapid, Trevor could see only a blur. When his head stopped moving, Trevor felt his knees threaten to buckle. The cop grabbed him and held him up until his strength returned.

Gone was the old man's charming, handsome face. It was replaced with a face that was half-human, half-goat. Ram's horns had sprouted from his forehead, thick and ribbed, curling around the sides of his head, tapering to points near his ears. His mouth was full of sharp, needle-like teeth.

The lips curled deftly around the teeth as he formed his words. "Does this get your attention?"

The creature shook out his hands. The fingers elongated, grew spindly, and ended with long, black nails.

He stomped one foot. The knee buckled inward, and the bend inverted. The patent leather shoe tore away, and the foot beneath became a black hoof. He stomped the second foot, and this leg also changed.

Azazel stood before Trevor with his hands out at his sides, as if showing off a new suit. The thing turned, and a long, hairy tail ripped through the seat of the white pants. It turned around again to face Trevor.

"This," Azazel said, "is what I truly am. I come from a time before humans walked this earth. I come from a time when demons ruled. Millions of years ago, this was what God intended to be the dominant species. We were powerful, and we were immortal. We existed here on earth for millions of years before the dinosaurs came. We were unstoppable.

"But Jehovah, in his infinite wisdom, decided it was time for us to come to an end. But how do you destroy a being that is immortal? Not to mention the thousands more just like me?

"For His first attempt, Jehovah sent his angels down to slay us. But that proved to be a monumental task. For every demon that was slain, seven hundred angels had to die. The angels that couldn't beat us, chose to join us. They became the Fallen. When it became clear that the first attempt had failed, the Master recalled his remaining angels back to heaven.

"The second attempt came a thousand years later. It took that long, because that was how long it took him to form our prison. Jehovah created an alternate dimension that could contain us. You call this place Hell. There was a fiery pit that could burn us, hurt us, but not kill us. We lived in this torment for millions of years.

"Our first glimpse of freedom came when Adam and Eve were in the garden. One of my brethren escaped. He was eventually banished back to the nether, but he performed two vital tasks: He led Adam and Eve to turn away from Jehovah, and we learned how to escape.

"You see, the key to unlock our prison was the human race. When they walk through the world, generation after generation, they cover every inch of the world with their impact. When an entire area of the earth has been touched by humans, our door opens, and we are able to walk through.

"You see, God did not expect the human race to multiply like it did, as fast as it did. The world is so overly populated that soon there will be no place on earth that has not been touched by the human race.

"Now this brings me to my tale. I was banished under this part of the world. Almost every inch of my prison was touched by humanity. I say almost, because there was one small, barely detectable section of the earth that had not been tainted by human interference. One day, a worker from the onion field walked into the woods to relieve himself, and in doing so, he stepped on that one section of the planet, untouched by humans, that was keeping me in the nether. He opened the doorway to my prison, and I was freed.

"I had learned many tricks over the millennia of my exile. One of which was how to disguise myself as anything, including a human. This helped me walk among you without being detected." The thing chuckled. "Could you imagine if I walked around like this? I wouldn't have stood a chance. But you humans love a handsome face." He laughed again.

Trevor did not respond.

It continued. "Another of my tricks was to bring the spark of life through the nether with me. This allowed me to pull the countless lesser demons through with me. The sound that the spark emits is how the demon finds its host. Being locked away for so long, you can imagine how ravenous that could make you. My demons, as it turns out, have a taste for human flesh. Those who cannot hear the call, like your son, and the dear Mrs. Kennedy, become food for my demons. They prefer fresh, raw meat, but the flesh they do not consume has to be smoked, preserved, so it does not rot. Your son, I believe, will be eaten raw, but the old lady will probably be preserved for later."

Trevor's lip quivered. His hands clenched into fists. Tears blurred his vision. "Over my dead body."

The thing laughed again, a sound of pure evil.

"I think you're missing the point. You see, it will be you who will eat him, and very happily, I might add."

"I'll resist. I won't allow myself to be affected."

"You'll try, maybe. But you'll fail. You can't resist. Your wife couldn't resist. She was very excited by the prospect of eating your son."

Trevor wanted to scream. He wanted to shout that they were evil. He wanted to kill them all. But this thing knew what is was. Relished the knowledge, in fact. And he couldn't kill it.

But he had killed others.

"Your minions aren't immortal. I've already killed several, including my wife. You can be beaten."

The thing nodded its monstrous head. "Yes, the creatures you see before you are vulnerable. They have heard the call, but have not completely come through the portal. We are about to solve that problem now, however. We will complete the transmogrification process, and then we will be unstoppable. I know of all the places on earth where humans still have not travelled, and once these places are passed over—with the human slaves I plan on acquiring—the world will once again belong to us. Play your cards right, and you can be a part of this. Resist, and you will die. Has this been made clear enough to you?"

Trevor heard every word. He also was able to read between the lines. The thing that called itself Azazel had said it needed to hide itself among the human race, or be banished back to the world from which it came.

It could be pushed back. But how? How could it be sent back?

Maybe it would tell him. It seemed confident in its rule, clearly not afraid of him. He would at least try.

"You've made your position abundantly clear. I'm soon to become part of your fold. But before that, I'm curious about one thing. Can you tell me this one thing before you change me?"

Azazel blinked its goat eyes at him. "I'll indulge your curiosity. What do you want to know?"

"How can you be returned to hell? You mentioned being banished before your work was done. How?"

It chuckled again. "You think you can stop me, even now. That's precious. You amuse me to no end. I'll tell you, because even if you know how to do it, you can't. I'll tell you because humans do love a juicy piece of knowledge, and for that weakness I will be forever grateful." He laughed heartily.

"You don't possess the necessary tools to banish me, anyway. Here is the secret to my banishment: excise me into a smoke form, and then send that smoke back to the nether with a very complex ritual."

"You're describing an exorcism."

"Yes, exactly. But there is an even easier way."

Trevor waited.

Azazel raised his voice to an unnatural volume. "Get God to do it, Himself. He can banish me any time He chooses."

He returned his voice to a normal level. "But here's the kicker. He's given up on the human race. Really, He's finished with you. It's probably the only thing the Bible got right. You see, when God destroyed Sodom and Gomorrah, it caused Him to rethink his position. He decided that he must leave humans to their own devices. He would never again interfere with their lives. And ever since, He has held true to his word. Bottom line: He's not going to help you in this. You're on your own. It's the price you have to pay for being spoiled little brats, and wanting your own free will."

The monstrosity stopped talking and smacked its lips. It ran its black tongue out from between its razor teeth. It leaned down, and its foul breath hissed into Trevor's face. Trevor closed his eyes and forced the gorge rising in his throat to go back. He shivered, but otherwise tried to hide his fear and repulsion.

Azazel stepped back, its hooves leaving divots in the earth.

Several of the creatures walked by Trevor, studying him. Perhaps they were wondering how he would taste.

Trevor met each of their gazes without turning away. His throat threatened to close up and choke him as he noted that some of these things had pulsing sores on their foreheads. On one female, the sores had torn open, and the nubs of horns were protruding from the cracks. Pus oozed from the base of the appendages. The stench was stifling.

I feel like an exhibit in a zoo.

Azazel drew Trevor's attention with a wave of its gnarled hand. "I can imagine what you're thinking, but you'll soon understand our position once you have been brought into the fold. You just have to be patient. I can see the repulsion, the disgust you feel, on your face. You hate us."

"Yes, I hate you. I would banish you back to hell myself if I could. You forced me to kill my wife. You want me to kill my son—to eat him for God's sake. This is evil. You all are evil. You do not have the right to even exist. Just kill me, why don't you. I want no part of this world."

"You think we have no right to exist, but where do you get off thinking you are a better species to exist? Do you not do all that I have described to creatures you consider to be lesser beings? You eat animals you think to be lesser creatures. You force them to your will, just because you can. We see the human race as lesser beings. You are our cattle. How is what you do any different than what I described? We do not war with one another, as you humans do. Why should your species be considered better than mine? It isn't, except in your own eyes.

"And, think about this, if you will. The human race was meant to be immortal, as well. But God, in his infinite wisdom, saw the error of his ways, and revoked the status of immortality when he learned of your propensity for evil. He was proved right, too. The minute he cursed the human race with mortality, Cain slew his only brother."

Trevor wasn't big on religion, never had much use for it, but wouldn't dignify this creature with a rebuttal. Instead, he provided one of his own. "Your race couldn't have been much better, if you were banished to a world of torture and pain. Seems to me, that's a fate worse than death. God was being merciful when he gave us death instead of doing to us what He had done to you."

Azazel's lips peeled back, and Trevor couldn't tell if it was a smile, or a snarl. Then the thing shrugged. "None of that matters, because the human race has no defense against what is coming—what we are going to bring upon you."

"We'll try, anyway. Someone will rise up against you."

Azazel laughed. "Let them try. Now, we are finished with this discussion. It is time for the transmogrification. Someone give this human the spark."

The beast waved a dismissive hand and walked away.

One of the veiny-faced things approached Trevor. He waited for it to do its thing; he thought that if he fought, they would kill him and spare him from this fate worse than death.

But he couldn't do that. He couldn't take the easy way out, and leave Diane and his son at the mercy of these monsters.

Trevor closed his eyes as the thing reached out with a finger.

"I have this one, Jeffrey."

He opened his eyes. The creature, Jeffrey, dropped his hand and walked away. Trevor's eyes focused on the being standing behind Jeffrey.

Trevor locked eyes with Ethan. His friend's face had less veins than the others, but he was clearly affected. Trevor's chest grew heavy, and it felt as if his heart detached from the other organs and floated away. His eyes filled with tears. *No, Ethan. Not you. Please, not you, too.*

Ethan stepped up and stood directly in front of Trevor, standing so close, in fact, their chests were almost touching. Ethan's hand came up. A single finger pointed toward Trevor's ear. Ethan touched him . . .

The touch was on the neck, below the ear. Nothing happened. Ethan leaned in and whispered.

"Stay with me and do as I tell you."

Ethan walked past Trevor.

Trevor fought through his shock and confusion. He turned and followed Ethan back to where Diane and Demy still sat on the ground. Ethan stood behind them, and Trevor stood next to him. They both turned and looked toward Azazel.

Azazel had taken up a position on a fallen log, and was raised high enough to be seen over the heads of the others standing around. He lifted his hands and spoke. "My devoted followers. The time has come to complete our journey. I applaud you for your patience, and now your persistence is about to be rewarded. Come through the gateway and join me. Come to me, my loyal friends."

In the next few seconds, many of the affected townspeople dropped to the ground and writhed around. They moaned, some in pain, but most in the throes of ecstasy.

"Don't fight. The transfer will be much more pleasurable if you don't fight it. Let the change happen." Azazel studied the progress of his minions.

Trevor noticed that a few of the affected were not feeling the effects. He risked a glance over at Ethan. His friend did not look back at him. Trevor returned his gaze to the scene unfolding in front of him.

He looked over the select few who stood near Azazel, unaffected by the change happening to the others. Trevor decided they must be guards. They aren't changing because they are protecting their leader.

After another minute, Ethan touched Trevor's arm. He whispered, his lips barely moving, and speaking low but loud enough for Trevor to hear. "When I say to, pick up Demy and follow my lead."

Trevor looked over at him.

"Now."

Trevor bent down and snatched up Demy. He pulled his son into a tight embrace.

Ethan lifted Diane and held her draped over his arms. He ran toward a line of trees to their left. Trevor didn't hesitate. He followed Ethan, deftly jumping over writhing bodies.

Behind him, Trevor heard Azazel's booming voice. "Stop them."

As Trevor reached the tree line, a gunshot echoed through the trees. The bark on a tree exploded near Trevor's head. The chunks blew off and ripped into his cheek. Blood drizzled down his face, but he didn't stop.

Azazel bellowed again. "Kill them. Kill them all."

Trevor pushed on.

Although Ethan's weight was substantially heavier than Trevor's, the other man ran quickly. Trevor could barely keep up.

Trevor heard the rustle of pursuers approaching from behind. He ran faster than he thought was possible. By the time he made it out of the trees, he saw that Ethan was already several yards ahead of him.

"Keep up, slowpoke."

Ethan had led them out of the woods, and into the plot of a trailer park. Ethan ran between the mobile homes, and continued on to the road beyond. Trevor felt a burst of speed when he realized they had made it to the end of Lakeport Road. He dared not look back, but Trevor heard the sound of someone running over gravel.

Running on the blacktop was much easier, and Trevor somehow managed to catch up to Ethan. Sweat ran down his brow and dripped into his eyes, but he ignored it. After safely reaching Highway 31, they ran to the right, and then left down the road leading to the Whittlespoons' dock. As the yacht came into view, Trevor could see the couple on the deck. The pursuers must have been close behind, because Gavin waved them on, encouraging them to run faster. The old fellow dropped down, out of sight.

When the old man came back into view, he was holding a spear gun. Gavin took aim.

Trevor felt the fingers of one of his pursuers grazing the back of his shirt. The sweat running down his back turned cold as Trevor realized he was out of time. In another second, the thing chasing him would overcome him.

There was a sound like two sticks hitting together, and then a whump as the spear grazed past Trevor's ear. The thick spear thudded into the face of Trevor's pursuer, and the presence disappeared from behind him. Trevor made it to the dock and crossed to the ramp unimpeded.

"Manny, get this thing moving," Tessa said. She took the spear gun from Gavin, and the old man headed to the controls. Tessa turned to Trevor. "Where's Krista?"

Trevor's voice trembled. "She didn't make it."

Tessa reached out and hugged him with one arm, the gun pointing at the deck. "I'm sorry. We knew when you didn't show something was wrong."

Ethan placed Diane on her feet, and she collapsed, exhausted, onto the deck. The boat jerked and began moving away from the dock.

Tessa spotted one of the things that had made it to the deck and took it out with a spear in the throat, then reloaded.

She pointed the gun at Ethan's chest.

Chapter Twenty-Two: Ethan

Ethan watched as the woman raised the weapon and pointed it at him. He put his hands out in front of him, defensively. To his right, Trevor nearly dropped Demy, and shouted.

"Tessa, no!"

"He looks like one of those things that was chasing you. He can't be trusted."

Trevor stepped closer. "Tessa, please listen to me. Ethan saved us. If it hadn't been for him, we'd all be dead right now. We owe him our lives."

"I owe him nothing." Tessa stepped closer to Ethan.

"But I do. Demy does, too. You don't understand what's happening."

"Enlighten me, then."

"I'm not sure—"

"Not you." Tessa's eyes flicked to Trevor and quickly back at Ethan. "You. Explain yourself."

Ethan's hands stayed up where she could see them. He was about to speak, but Diane woke with a gasp. The startled woman glanced up at Ethan and cried out. When she saw Tessa holding the gun, she crawled behind the armed woman.

"Go on," Tessa said to Ethan.

Ethan spoke softly. "I was affected. It happened the night I left your yacht after being unable to make that deal with you. They came upon me on the road as

I walked home. The leader touched my ear, and I heard the call.

"But right away I knew something was *wrong*. I didn't feel any different. I was still who I had always been. I played along with them. I watched and listened. I learned their secrets. And I promise you this; I never used the spark to turn anyone. I never killed anyone."

"The spark. It's what they use to make people like them?"

"Yes."

"You have it? You could use it if you wished?"

He knew this was a dangerous path, but he was determined to tell the truth. "Yes, I have it. But I would never use it."

"Kay, fine. But why weren't you affected like the others? What made you different?" Tessa seemed less threatening now.

Ethan continued. "I think it's because of my birth defect. My hearing works differently than everyone else's. There is one of those things banging on the door, but I refuse to let it in. My mind is my own."

Tessa had let the spear gun drop by about an inch, but now she raised it again. "And what if one day it finds a way in?"

"It can't. It doesn't work that way. I am in control, and nothing that thing can do can change that. My wiring won't allow it." Ethan kept his hands up for Tessa to see, but turned his gaze to Trevor. "I was thinking about what Azazel said about God not interfering in the world of man. What if that's not true? What if I was given this extraordinary gift to resist so that I could stop them from taking over?" Ethan turned back to Tessa. "If you kill me, you might be dooming the human race to extinction. What if I'm the key to stopping this?"

Tessa froze. Ethan watched her face for any sign of agreement, or dismissal. If she shot him, he wanted to see it coming. Her face was unreadable, however, and that scared him. He realized he had been holding his breath, and he sighed.

The woman lifted the gun suddenly and pulled the trigger. Ethan's blood turned cold in his veins as he waited for the spear to rip through his flesh. But the spear moved past him. He turned in time to see that one of those things had been climbing over the railing. It took the spear in its chest, arched its back, and fell away from the boat, splashing into the murky water of Oneida Lake.

When Ethan turned back around, he expected to see Tessa reloading the weapon. Instead, she stood with the unloaded gun pointing down at the deck. Ethan dropped his hands.

She turned to Trevor. "So how bad is it?"

"The entire town is gone, taken over by those things. Those monsters. They got Krista. She was trying to kill Diane and Demy when I found them. I . . . I had to kill her. But it wasn't her, not anymore. The demon had taken possession of her. She would have killed all of us."

Tessa lowered her eyes and shook her head. "Just awful." She flicked her gaze up at Ethan again. "I want to know everything you know . . . what they are, who you are. . . If I'm ever going to trust you, I need to know how you came to be the savior of the human race." The word *savior* dripped with venomous sarcasm.

He soberly nodded agreement to her request.

Tessa lifted the spear gun by the stock and handed it to Trevor. As he took the gun, Tessa took Demy from him. He set the gun down and shook out his arms. When Gavin returned, Trevor handed the weapon to him.

"I'm going to take the little one downstairs." Tessa turned to Diane. "Follow me, Sweetie. I'll find somewhere for you to rest. We're out of danger for now. It sounds like you survived quite the ordeal."

Diane showed her appreciation by touching Tessa's arm. Before they walked away, Diane stepped over to Ethan. "You carried me out of that horrible place, didn't you?"

Ethan nodded.

She leaned in and hugged him. She whispered into his ear. "Thank you. I'm sorry for . . . you know. She had the gun on you. I was confused."

As she backed away, Ethan took one of her hands. "It's all right." He lifted the hand and kissed it. When he let go, she reached up and gently stroked his cheek. She used the sign language for thank you, then turned away and followed Tessa into the lower decks.

Gavin set the gun on the hooks where it was intended to be stored when not in use. He walked slowly around Ethan, studying him. He whistled. "They did a number on you, didn't they?"

Ethan made a soundless, tired laugh. "That they did."

"So, what, you were . . . what do they call it . . . affected? But you don't have the urge to kill?"

"I don't. I may look different, but I'm still the same person I was when you last met me."

"Yeah," Gavin said. "Sorry about my wife. She's a handful."

"It's quite all right. I understand her trepidation."

"And I'm sorry she turned you down for that loan. Didn't see that one coming."

Ethan took the old man's hand and shook it. "No need for apologies. None of that matters now."

Gavin turned to Trevor. "I have us headed toward Bernhard Bay. That's still our destination, isn't it?"

Trevor looked around. "I guess it is."

As Gavin walked away, Trevor turned to Ethan. It was the first chance the two friends had to get reacquainted with each other. Trevor rushed forward and threw his arms around his friend. Ethan hugged him back.

"We looked for you, Krista and I," Trevor said after they separated. "We never gave up on you."

"I appreciate that."

Trevor's eyes filled with tears.

Ethan led him to a chair and helped him sit. Ethan sat beside him. "I'm so sorry for your loss, Trev. I don't know where to begin to console you."

Trevor closed his eyes, and the tears moved down his cheeks. He touched Ethan's hand. "Knowing you are okay helps. I was so worried about you. And Demy . . . Demy's okay."

"I have to ask you, though..."

Trevor wiped his eyes and looked at Ethan. "What is it?"

"Do you . . . do you trust me? I mean, Tessa . . . she—"

Trevor tapped Ethan's leg. "Look at me." Ethan did. "You saved me. You saved Demy. What you said about this master plan where you were blessed by God with the ability to resist . . . it makes sense. I never believed in God, not really, but this ability you have? I think I have to believe now. I trust you completely."

When Trevor smiled, so did Ethan.

"You don't know how happy that makes me to hear you say this. I won't let you down."

"I should think not." Trevor laughed.

Ethan looked down at his hands. "You know something? I haven't looked at myself in the mirror since…" He indicated his hands, which carried the mark of the affected.

"Your face is actually not that bad." Trevor leaned in and studied Ethan's face. "You're still as ugly as you've always been."

Ethan laughed, and Trevor joined in.

They stopped laughing and let the quiet of the night fill the void. A long time passed, and the two friends simply let the sounds of the boat, the water, and the quiet night wash over them, easing their weary minds. Everything seemed so peaceful and perfect. Yet a dangerous world awaited them.

"We have to stop him," Ethan said, and Trevor didn't need to ask who he was referring to. "We have to destroy him, or send him back, or whatever it takes to end this threat."

"We will." Trevor leaned back. "He was even nice enough to tell us how to do it." He chuckled.

Ethan didn't laugh. He stared out at the night sky and wondered if there would be any more help coming from the Great Beyond. Ethan didn't know what more he could do to help prevent the future Azazel planned to inflict on the world. He shuddered at the thought of the human race being turned into monsters, or used as slaves. He felt nothing but anger when he thought of what they had planned to do to Demy. He would protect that boy with his life.

"Ethan?" Trevor said.

They were both leaning back in their chairs and looking up at the stars.

"Yeah?"

"You don't have the urge to eat human flesh, do you?"

Ethan sat up and scowled at Trevor.

Trevor laughed.

Ethan understood that the question was a joke, but he didn't want any uncertainty on the subject. "No, of course not."

Trevor stopped laughing. "Don't sound so hurt. I didn't mean to offend you. I know you wouldn't do that. It was a joke."

"Not funny."

"It was a little funny," Trevor pinched his fingers together. He spoke again, this time in a high-pitched voice. "A little?"

Ethan didn't respond, but he gave Trevor a small smile of camaraderie. He stood. "I'm going to see if Tessa's ready to talk to me yet."

"Okay, can you check on Demy for me, please? Let me know if he's okay. I think I might fall asleep here. I can't seem to move."

"Sure."

Ethan walked across the deck and headed down the steps to the lower deck. He looked in on Demy and Diane. They were both sound asleep and snoring. He walked to the kitchen.

"Tessa, do you want to talk?"

As Ethan entered the kitchen, he froze.

"Brody."

The thing that had pinned Tessa in the corner turned and looked at him.

"A friend of yours?" Tessa didn't take her eyes off her oppressor. "He was hiding. He trapped me in here."

"Brody, get out of here."

"Not until I kill you, traitor, and give the spark to all the others."

Ethan searched the room for a weapon. He spotted a cutting board near the sink covered in blood, two fish heads stared at the ceiling with milky, dead eyes. Next to the severed heads was a boning knife. Ethan inched his way toward the sink, and the knife.

"It's all over. You know this, Brody." Ethan took another step. "Azazel is going to be returned to the nether."

"The transmogrification is complete. The lesser demons have been pulled through."

"It doesn't matter. When Azazel gets sent back, you all go back with him. The plan he threatened to unleash on the world will never come to fruition."

"Says the traitor." Brody took a step toward Tessa.

"You will forever be trapped in the transitional phase. You will never become a true lesser demon. You will be their whipping boy. You will be just as enslaved as the humans they plan to use."

"I have a purpose. I'm essential to the Master."

"You are fodder that he will trample into the dirt with his cloven hooves. You are nothing."

"Liar." Brody lunged at Tessa, and she screeched.

Ethan picked up the knife and flew at Brody. The thing sensed the attack and turned. Ethan brought the knife down in an arc and drove it through the monster's throat. The Brody thing gasped and gurgled, choking on its own blood. It dropped to its knees, then collapsed onto its face, dead.

Tessa kicked it, and when it didn't move, she exhaled heavily, but still was shaking.

Ethan tossed the knife into the sink. He turned to Tessa. "Are you okay?"

"Don't touch me." Tessa jerked away from him when he reached out to her. She cowered from him.

Ethan took a step back. "You know, I came down here to try and plead with you to accept me. I've done nothing to you, but still you hate me. Even when I came to see you for the loan, you hated me. I am not someone you are ever going to like, am I? Especially now. But do you realize that if you hadn't turned me down that night, I wouldn't have been so distraught that I wandered off? Because of you I was put in the path of those things. I'm what I am because of your intolerance."

"I'm not intolerant. I just have morals. I don't see the nobility in being a homosexual. You ruined your own life when you chose that path. That has nothing to do with me." She looked at him blinking hard, and too often.

She was afraid of him, he realized. He took a step toward her.

"Gavin." Her voice cracked. She shouted louder this time. "Gavin." She screamed. "Manny."

They heard the sound of rushing footsteps on the deck above. She tried to rush past him, but he grabbed her. He turned her to face him. She was looking into his eyes when he touched her ear and passed on the spark.

He stepped back and leaned against the counter.

Trevor and Gavin rushed into the kitchen. They looked at Tessa, saw the veins that had begun to spread over her fish-belly-white skin. Trevor looked at Ethan with a question shining in his eyes.

Ethan pointed at Brody's corpse. "He had been hiding. He jumped out. . . I killed him, but . . ." Ethan looked at Tessa. "She's affected."

Tessa flicked her wild eyes at Ethan. She seethed. She snarled, saliva dripping from her lips. She turned on Gavin and Trevor, and charged. Gavin lifted the spear gun in his hand and pulled the trigger. The spear took her in the eye, driving her back with its force. The tip of the spear embedded in the wall, pinning her in place. Tessa's body twitched and writhed as she dangled there.

Gavin screamed and dropped the gun. He panted and shook. "Tess!" His voice left him. He ran to his wife and pulled her off the wall. She dropped into his arms, and he carried her to the floor. He sat there cradling his wife, sobbing.

"Is there any more on board?" Trevor asked Ethan.

"I don't think so."

Trevor raced to where his son lay sleeping. Ethan followed him. They searched the room, but found nothing unexpected. Just a boy succumbed to the healing power of sleep. They searched the room where Diane slept. She woke when the light came on. She curled into a ball against the wall.

"What's happened?"

One of those things snuck on board, but we killed it. I'm checking to make sure there are no more." Trevor looked under the bed as Ethan looked in the closet.

"Oh, God." Diane's words came out in a breathy whisper.

"It's okay. We're safe. There are no more." Ethan stroked her hair.

Well, there's me.

Ethan was ashamed of himself for what he had done, but Tessa had given him no choice.

"Are you sure?" she asked.

"Yes, we're sure." Trevor headed for the door then turned to face her. "But we'll keep searching."

Ethan followed Trevor out of the room. They searched every inch of the lower decks, and then searched the deck above. They found nothing, and the rest of the trip to the cabin was uneventful.

Brody's body was tossed overboard. Tessa was buried in the backyard at the cabin. Gavin was inconsolable, but Ethan didn't dare go near the man, for fear the old man would see the truth of what happened on his face.

Ethan studied Trevor closely. Did he know what had happened? Did he suspect? If he did, he showed no sign. Ethan would do anything he could to keep Trevor from knowing the truth. Except one thing—he could not lie. He managed to skirt the truth of that night on the boat, letting Trevor and the others believe it had been Brody that turned Tessa, but if Trevor ever asked for the truth, Ethan would admit to what he did.

Trevor never asked.

Epilogue: Trevor

Gavin eventually overcame Tessa's death. It took more than a year for him to come around to his old self again, and he thought Demy had a lot to do with that. But it was good to see the old man laugh again.

They couldn't return to their homes. As far as the world was concerned, the survivors of the town were just as missing as the rest of the town. Gavin had stashes of cash that he could access without drawing attention to his bank accounts. They used this money to rebuild their lives. They took on new identities, and found a new place to live. Their new home was big enough for all of them to live there. A large greenhouse in the back burst with plants for Diane to fuss over. She was content. And this place was so far away from the general public, that if they never left, a nuclear bomb could drop and they wouldn't know about it.

The FBI investigated the disappearances of the entire population of the town, but they had no answers. The papers did stories on the phenomenon, calling it a modern-day ghost town. If Ray's notes had ever been found, no one took up where he left off. Trevor thought that was probably a good thing. He didn't know how the world would handle learning the truth.

Ethan seemed unaffected by the demon that wanted access to his body. He had been true to his word, and proved time and again to be faithful. On the rare occasion that they came across one of the other affected that hadn't been changed completely, it was always Ethan who dispatched them.

Ethan remained tight lipped about what happened in the kitchen of the yacht that night, and would only say that he killed Brody, but was unable to prevent Tessa's transformation. He didn't want to push Ethan too far. He supposed his friend harbored some guilt over her loss. Ethan had many regrets that he had confided to Trevor. He understood his friend's pain.

"If I hadn't run off that night," Ethan had said one night to Trevor when they were alone. "Maybe I wouldn't have been captured. Maybe I could have helped you all get away before the danger got too bad."

Trevor said, "There's a lot of maybe's and what if's in your scenario. It is also possible that if you hadn't been caught when you were, you wouldn't have been in a position to help us escape when the time came. There is no point in dwelling on how things might have turned out. Sure, they could have turned out better, but they also could have been much worse."

That had been the last time they discussed that topic. Trevor needed Ethan to concentrate on the future.

Ethan, for obvious reasons, avoided going out in public. Even if they didn't suspect him of being half demon, they surely would run away screaming at the sight of him. When he did go out into public, he wore makeup, and only went out at night. Mostly, he avoided being seen.

Trevor and Ethan finally returned to the clearing where the transmogrification took place, but they found nothing. The bonfire showed no signs of the bodies that had been burned there. They couldn't even find evidence that there had been a slaughterhouse. The big question that had been on their minds—one that didn't need to be voiced—was, where did they go? Where did the lesser demons that had completed the change go? And, more importantly, where did Azazel go? The group would continue to look for him. They searched the papers for any sign that what had happened to their town, was happening again somewhere else. If that goat-headed demon showed its ugly face, they would be there to drive it back into the shadows. They refused to let it return to power.

Trevor had taken up learning all he could about exorcisms. He prepared to turn that horny bastard into smoke, and drive him back to the nether. He traveled to nations that still believed in demons, and knew how to perform exorcisms. He became an unofficial expert, and scholars wrote papers on the information he shared. He tried to subtly warn people of the impending invasion, but avoided any statements that would leave people thinking he was a raving lunatic. He hoped to someday come across another person who shared the same knowledge he had about Azazel, or any of the other demons out there.

To date, that person escaped him.

As Trevor exited the plane, he collected his bag from the conveyor, and swung the strap over his shoulder. He had ordered an Uber driver to take him back to the town nearest where he lived. From there Ethan would pick him up and take him home. He'd been away for three weeks, and he was excited to see Demy again.

The drive from the airport was peaceful. The driver spoke very little, and he was glad for the peace. When he was dropped off in front of the train station, Trevor took a seat on a nearby bench, and waited for Ethan to arrive. While he waited, Trevor logged onto the Uber site and gave his driver a favorable rating. He turned his phone off and shoved it into his pocket.

Trevor glanced across the street to the supermarket. As he watched, a man emerged from the darkness of the store's interior. The man was dressed in white. Trevor's blood chilled in his veins. As the man came closer, Trevor could see that it was the same handsome face, and maniacal smile, of the one he knew as Azazel. The demon in its human form waved at Trevor.

Ethan pulled up. Trevor climbed into the car. When he looked back over to the sidewalk in front of the supermarket, he saw no one standing there. When Ethan asked him what was wrong, Trevor waved a weary hand.

"Nothing," he said. "I'm just tired. Take me home."

The End

An Afterword

People reading the preceding story may notice the name of the town is missing. This was intentional. But anyone who grew up in my hometown of Chittenango, New York, will undoubtedly recognize the landmarks and locations mentioned in this novel. In my previous novels—namely *Keepers of the Forest* and *Immortal Coil*—I have mentioned the town where each story took place (Tupper Lake in *Keepers* and Philadelphia in *Immortal*), but the locations were so drastically changed they were nearly unrecognizable. This was not intentional, but it was necessary to the plot. There is no pool in Tupper Lake but I needed one, so I stole it from the town of Oneida, New York. Conversely, there is no spooky hill with a mansion at the top on Lansdowne Drive in Philadelphia.

With *The Affected,* I made very little changes to Chittenango. Well, there is the little issue of the funeral home mentioned in the story no longer being where I placed it, and Deb's Hardware is really a Napa automotive store. But everything else is pretty much where it is today. I kept the town as close to modern-day Chittenango as I could. It was least the I could do, considering I wiped out all of the town's inhabitants. I'm sorry about that, but it was all in good fun.

Thanks for reading, and I do hope you enjoyed my book.

A few words of thanks

I would like to take this time to thank a few people who helped with the production of this book. First off, I wanted to thank BookBaby.com for the professional editing. I also want to thank my proofreaders, Lisa Streeter, Jennifer Francisco, and Millie Gawarecki.

A special thank you goes out to Jennifer Gwilt, who allowed me to "borrow" her persona, and turn her into a flesh-eating monster, if only in an alternate universe.

Last, but not least, I want to thank the early readers who provided their input and critiques in their reviews of The Affected.

www.ingramcontent.com/pod-product-compliance
Lightning Source LLC
Chambersburg PA
CBHW030353310726
48979CB00001B/291

9781732827714